CONNIE BRUMMEL CROOK

Connie B. Crook was born near Belleville, Ontario, during the Depression. As a child she had to walk more than a mile no matter the weather to her one-room primary school, and later three miles to her high school. When she grew up she taught English in several secondary schools across the province.

Although Ms. Crook has always loved writing, she didn't get a chance to pursue it until her retirement. Now living in Peterborough, Ontario, she spends her time writing, visiting schools, walking, swimming, reading, and being with her grandchildren. She is currently finishing another novel, the third in the Nellie McClung trilogy.

OTHER BOOKS BY CONNIE BRUMMEL CROOK

MAPLE MOON
(picture book)

FLIGHT

MEYERS' CREEK

NELLIE L.

NELLIE'S QUEST

FLIGHT

CONNIE BRUMMEL CROOK

Stoddart Kids
TORONTO • NEW YORK

*We acknowledge the Canada Council for the Arts and the Ontario Arts
Council for their support of our publishing program.*

First published as an Irwin Young Adult Fiction in 1991 by Stoddart
Publishing Co. Limited

Published in 1994 by Stoddart Publishing Co. Limited

Published in Canada in 1999 by Stoddart Kids,
a division of Stoddart Publishing Co. Limited
34 Lesmill Road
Toronto, Ontario M3B 2T6
Tel (416) 445-3333   Fax (416) 445-5967
E-mail Customer.Service@ccmailgw.genpub.com

Distributed in Canada by
General Distribution Services
325 Humber College Blvd.
Etobicoke, Ontario M9W 7C3
Tel (416) 213-1919   Fax (416) 213-1917
E-mail Customer.Service@ccmailgw.genpub.com

Canadian Cataloguing in Publication Data
Crook, Connie Brummel
Flight

ISBN 0-7736-7412-8

1. United Empire Loyalists — Juvenile fiction.
2. New York (State) — History — Revolution,
1775–1783 — Juvenile fiction.
I. Title.
PS8555.R6113F55 1994   jC813'.54   C93-095301-0
PZ7.C76F1 1994

Cover Design: Brant Cowie/ArtPlus Limited
Cover Illustration and Inside Map: David Craig
Typesetting: Tony Gordon Ltd.

Printed and bound in Canada

To my mother
Pearl Carr Brummel,
who still toils for her family
from dawn to midnight,
and to
the memory of my grandmother
Ada Stapley Carr,
the granddaughter of
Sarah Ann Bleecker Stapley,
whose grandmother was
Mary Meyers

Contents

GEORGE WALTERMYER'S JOURNEY TO NEW YORK CITY

ADIRONDACK MOUNTAINS

TO MACHICHE

LAKE CHAMPLAIN

FORT TICONDEROGA

LAKE GEORGE

SKENESBOROUGH

HUDSON RIVER

MOHAWK RIVER

BEMIS HEIGHTS
BALLSTOWN

BENNINGTON

ALBANY
SCHUYLER'S HOUSE

COOEYMAN'S LANDING

GRANDFATHER'S FARM
WALTERMYER'S FARM

CATSKILL MOUNTAINS   ATHENS

HUDSON

KINGSTON

WALLKILL   POUGHKEEPSIE

NEWBURGH

WALLKILL RIVER

WEST POINT

WESTCHESTER COUNTY

HUDSON RIVER

YONKERS

MANHATTAN ISLAND
NEW YORK CITY

LONG ISLAND

GEORGE'S ROUTE ------

Part One
Dangerous Journeys

One

George jumped up on the fence and looked his father straight in the eye. "We have to talk."

"Well, what is it?" said Hans Waltermyer, who put down his scythe to walk to the edge of the field when he saw his son running towards him.

"Rebel troops have moved into Albany. And there are rumours the British are coming to attack. When are you going to pledge allegiance to the cause?"

"Pledge allegiance to the cause? Which cause are you talking about?"

"The Rebel cause, of course. You surely don't think I'd take the side of the British Redcoats. All the boys at school are cheering for the Rebels."

"Well, it's not my battle, George. The best I can do for the cause is grow food because people on both sides need to eat. And I can't see either side attacking us on the farm."

"Both sides! Both sides! That's the problem. We can't be on both sides!" George flushed almost as red as his hair, which was only a shade lighter than his father's.

"You can't believe rumours, George. The war isn't here yet. It's far away in Boston and other cities. The people there, the Whigs and the Tories, are fighting each other. And I don't intend to leave your mother and the rest of you and go off to battle."

"Uncle Jacob is!"

"What my brother does is his business."

"All my friends' fathers have sworn allegiance," said George more quietly. "Why don't you?"

Waltermyer leaned against the fence and looked away across the hay field to the woodlot that separated them from the Sagers' farm before he answered. "I'll make my own decision, George. I've been thinking about it. But I really don't have any quarrel with the British. My father used to tell me how it was in the old country, and our lot in life is much better here. We work hard but eat well, and I pay a very reasonable fee for our leased land. Life has been good for us under British rule."

"That won't last if the taxes keep on." George repeated what his friends were all saying.

"I'll deal with that then," Waltermyer replied. He turned to his son and studied him closely. He hadn't realized his son was so concerned.

George was staring straight at his father. "Don't you understand anything? That'll be too late! The Revolutionary War's been going on for two years now — since 1775! You can't just sit on the fence forever like an old man."

Waltermyer's face flushed as red as his son's and he shouted, "That's enough, George!"

But George wasn't finished. His red hair flying out in the breeze, he shouted, "No, it's *not* enough. The war's not that far away. There are British troops under a leader called Burgoyne coming from Quebec. They could be in Albany now. The Redcoats and Rebels might even fight on our farm. We have to get ready. Why can't you face it? Are you afraid?"

George was silent then, for he had not intended to

accuse his father of being a coward, even though he had thought it for some time now. The words had just slipped out.

Waltermyer stared at his son in disbelief. Then he grabbed George by the shirt collar and pulled him off the fence. George struggled to get free, but he was no match for his father. Tightening his hold, Waltermyer threw his son to the ground.

"That's no way to speak to me, George," he said in a quiet voice that was more frightening than if he had shouted. Then he turned and hurried back to his work.

Humiliated and furious, George stood up and brushed the hay and dust off his clothes. Then he ran for the barn. Father would pay for this. He would see that he did. He would run away and join the Rebel army. So what if he was small for his almost twelve years! A drummer boy didn't need to be big.

George slowed his pace as he began to make plans. He'd finish the day as usual and then after his brothers and the rest of the family were fast asleep, he'd sneak down to the kitchen and pack a lunch and be on his way. He'd travel south to Athens to join up where he wasn't known so well. Father was bound to go to Albany first to look for him. By the time he came to Athens, it would be too late. He'd be enlisted in the Rebel army.

Then Father would be sorry! And anyway, someone had to defend the family's honour by fighting for the cause. As first-born it was his duty!

***

George woke up with a start. He had intended to stay awake and hoped he had not slept too long. He could smell a sharp odour like burning biscuits. Why would Mother be cooking at this hour? Then he heard a shrill sound coming along the night air through the open window.

He climbed out of bed without disturbing his eleven-year-old brother Tobias, whose dark head dug deeply into his feather pillow. Eight-year-old Leonard rolled over in his sleep on his cot across the room.

George grabbed his twill trousers and baggy shirt from the bedpost and pulled them on. He took one look at Leonard, who had settled into a deeper sleep, and stepped lightly towards the door.

He crept along the hallway. As he passed his sisters' bedroom, he noticed that their door was wide open. An unusual light shone from the room. Looking in, he saw the same eerie brightness filling the whole room and falling across the faces of his sleeping sisters.

George walked softly past little Anna in her trundle bed and Mary and Catharine in their big feather bed, to the open window. The muslin curtains were billowing towards him in the night breeze. As he pushed them away from his face, he saw what had been causing the weird light. Bright flames leapt in the distance. His startled gasp woke ten-year-old Mary.

"What are you doing here?" she grumbled. Then she saw the light and scrambled out of bed and over to the window.

"Go back to bed. Father and I will see about this," he said, stepping back into the dark hallway.

Forgetting their differences, he rushed to his parents' room and was surprised to find the door open. The empty bed was neatly made up.

Stumbling through the dark, down the back stairs, he

burst into the kitchen. There, by the light of a candle on the table, he could see Father standing by the back door. He stood a full six feet four inches tall, a handsome man with slightly messy auburn hair that curled around his ears and hung in a ponytail over his collar. He was in his work clothes, a leather bag over one shoulder, his musket resting against the other. His mother's brother, John Kruger, was standing beside him.

"Father, there's a fire! Look outside. You'll see it!" George exclaimed.

Hans stared at his son. Then his eyes softened and he said, "It's just a bonfire. Now, I have to go south to buy a horse to replace old Duke. I'll be away a few days or maybe weeks."

"A bonfire! It sure looked worse than that," George blurted out. "What's wrong? You don't just take off in the middle of the night to buy a horse . . . . And why do you need Uncle John?"

"We're just getting a head start," Father said.

"Why?" George asked.

"It's better you don't know any more than that. Just remember you're the oldest, and I'm leaving you in charge."

Father looked at George for a few moments, then shot a worried glance at his wife, who was standing at the work table across the room. "Goodbye, Polly," he said softly. "May God protect you until we see each other again."

"Wait!" Mother said, as she scooped some bread and cheese from the table into a basket. "You'll need this." She handed the basket to Father. Then he and Uncle John went out the back door into the night.

George looked around the kitchen. It was clean and

everything was in its place — except for the large bread board. Mother was brushing crumbs from it. Then George noticed that the kitchen shutters had been tightly closed. Perhaps Mother had not noticed the fire outside.

"Why are the shutters closed, Mother?" he asked.

Mother turned then and looked at George as though she had forgotten he was still there. "Go to bed, George," she said sternly.

Seeing the worried look in his mother's eyes, George realized that this was definitely not the time to ask questions. He left the kitchen and started feeling his way up the steep back stairs. When he reached the upper hall, he hurried past the girls' room and walked into his own.

Tobias was leaning out the open window. He turned at the sound of George's footsteps and said, "Quick! Get Father. There's a fire near the Vandervoots."

"He's gone," George replied.

"Already?" Tobias gasped. Then he added more quietly, "I might have known. But he could have taken us to help." He sounded disappointed.

"He didn't go to the fire. He went to buy a horse."

"C'mon, George, be serious," said Tobias.

"There's more to it than that, but Father and Mother wouldn't tell me what it is. Uncle John was here and left with Father."

They were silent for a minute. Then Tobias said, "Maybe it's the British troops. They'll be firing our house next . . . Father didn't really leave us, did he, George?"

"He said he was going for a horse, but I don't know . . . Something strange is going on."

"What?"

"I don't know, Tobias, but I intend to find out. I'm

going over there right now." George started for the door. Why *had* Father left? he wondered. And how could he desert the family? So Father was a coward. I was right, George thought, but he couldn't tell Tobias that.

"Well, you're not going alone," Tobias said as he grabbed his trousers and pulled them on over his night-shirt.

As they passed the girls' room, Mary appeared at the door and asked, "Where are you two going?"

"Nowhere that you need to know about," George said sharply, then added more kindly, "You go back to bed, Mary. We'll take care of things."

George led the way down the front stairs. He didn't want to run into Mother in the kitchen if she was still there.

In an instant they were out the front door and running around to the back. Past the short stretch of grass beyond the back stoop, it was only about two hundred feet to the apple orchard and the short-cut to their neighbours' farm.

They had just reached the cover of trees when they heard a sound behind them. They ducked behind a tree trunk and waited. The sound got closer. Then, through the darkness, a white form came into view. George rolled his eyes. It was Mary. Even in the shadows, he could see that she had borrowed Leonard's twill trousers and was wearing them over the white shift she'd been sleeping in.

"George! Toby!" she shouted.

George reached out and grabbed her and clamped a hand over her mouth. "Mary, be quiet. Why didn't you stay in the house? There may be trouble here."

"I've come to see what's happening! You've got to tell me. I'm not a baby, you know."

George looked away for a moment. "You've heard them talking at school about the fighting up north of

Albany. Well, I think maybe Burgoyne and the British have come. Maybe it's the Rebels. Maybe it's both. But whoever it is, you won't be safe here. You'd better go back."

The silence was broken by the hooting of an owl. There were two more hoots, then dark silence again. It was Tobias's signal. He must have gone on ahead. Before George could move, Mary gave him a hard push and ran ahead through the orchard and up a hill to where Tobias was crouching. George followed. The three crawled along the rail fence to get a closer look at the fire. The Vandervoots' barn was burning.

A crowd of men came into sight; their voices were drowned out by the sounds of the screaming farm animals running loose in the yard. Many of the men still held torches. A few were holding up clenched fists and shaking them at the Vandervoots' house. As they drew closer, George could clearly make out some of the faces. They were people he knew. The father and brother of his school-friend Reuben were there, and so were the Sagers, Junior and Senior. They looked as angry as the others and they too were carrying torches. Flames were now leaping through the gaping holes in the sides and roof of the barn.

The three inched their way farther along the fence and took shelter under the gnarled apple tree that stood not far from the house at the edge of the Vandervoots' dooryard. George looked at Mary and Tobias. A shadow had fallen over them.

Then he looked up into the apple tree and squinted. Something was swaying on the largest branch. Suddenly he realized it was a man hanging lifelessly by his wrists. His body was smeared with stinking tar. The feathers sticking to the tar rustled stiffly in the breeze.

Two

"urly's gone!" George shouted as he stepped into the kitchen with a partly filled pail of fresh milk. Mother took the milk and poured it into a clean pitcher. She was a short woman with a rosy complexion and light blonde hair inherited from her Dutch ancestors.

"The dog'll be back," she said. "Now have your breakfast, George. The others are finished and will be leaving for school soon. I'm sorry you'll have to stay home until your father comes back."

George brightened a bit. "Well, *I'm* not sorry," he said. "Anyway, it's almost summer and school will be closed." He was still worried about last night, and it didn't help that Curly had disappeared, but this was one good thing — he probably wouldn't have to go back to school until after the fall harvest.

He ate his oatmeal silently by himself. His brothers and sisters were dressing for school, and five-year-old Anna was playing with the cat on the back stoop.

"Will you have another glass of milk, George?" Mother asked.

She was waiting on him almost the way she served Father. Then George remembered that Father had put him in charge until his return. Well, he couldn't be in charge if he didn't know what was going on.

As he was finishing his fried potatoes and ham and

eggs, he looked up at Mother. She was rocking Baby Jacob, who was only four months old. He didn't like to bring up the subject, but he felt he must.

"Mother, there was a fire at our neighbours' last night." He watched her closely.

"I know, George," she said quietly.

"And there was a man hanging from a tree. He'd been tarred and feathered. It was horrible."

"Yes," she said very quietly. She did not look surprised.

Suddenly George realized that she knew already. "Did father know too?" he asked.

"Yes. It was Mr. Vandervoot," she said, and looked up then with anguished eyes.

George could not believe this. Father had known about Mr. Vandervoot, and he had not helped him. The silence hung heavy between them.

Then Mother continued, "Those men who . . . who took Mr. Vandervoot's life, they've sworn allegiance to the Rebel cause and they call themselves the Sons of Liberty. When they came for Mr. Vandervoot's sons to go to war, Mr. Vandervoot wouldn't let his sons go. He shot at the men to make them leave. Then they . . . they . . . there were just too many of them."

"And didn't Father even *try* to help Mr. Vandervoot?" George asked.

Mother looked angry then. "George, be reasonable," she said. "There were over twenty armed men. What could one man do?"

"And he's left us too."

Polly noticed her son's shaking voice. "We are in no danger. The Sons of Liberty have never harmed women and children. We are safe."

Suddenly George understood the truth. These men would be looking for Father. "Has he gone to Albany to swear allegiance to the cause?" he asked.

"Your father has been neutral, but he thinks differently now. Last night he said that whatever side he was on, it was not on the side of those torturers."

George gagged on his last bite. Suddenly he didn't feel so well. "I'm gonna get to work," he said. He rushed out the back door. He would be able to think things through better outside. He grabbed a hoe from the back toolshed and headed towards the pear orchard.

It was a perfect June day. The grass tickled his bare feet as he walked through it. The fragrance of mock-orange blossoms was sweet in the air. He heard Anna giggling as Catharine, who was standing in the swing, pumped them both towards the top of the maple tree. Anna's plump little legs were tucked up under the wooden seat, and she held tightly onto the ropes that Father had tied to one of the maple's lower branches.

George marched over and grabbed the swing rope. "You'd better be on your way to school, Catharine," he said sternly. "Anna, you run along to the house."

"Who said you could boss us around, George?" Catharine shouted. Although she was nine — just a year younger than Mary — she was much shorter and slighter. But her curly, light blonde hair and large blue eyes had already marked her as a beauty.

George stared sternly at her as he held the swing, and said nothing. Anna hopped off the wooden swing seat and kicked him in the shin with her bare foot.

"Get in the house!" George yelled at her. She started running to the house as fast as her short chubby legs would take her.

Just then Mary came out the front door. "We're gonna be late, Catharine," she called. "Toby and Leonard left ten minutes ago."

Catharine glared at George for a moment before she turned and joined Mary. George watched them walking down the lane together. Perhaps he could have handled that better. Still, they would have to learn that he was in charge now.

It was then that he heard a low bark in the distance and thought of Curly. He followed the sound, and before he realized it, he was emerging from the far side of the pear orchard into a tangle of raspberry bushes and wild grapes growing along the edge of the path that led towards the Sagers' farm — their neighbours to the south. To his surprise, he saw a group of men marching along the path towards him, heading for the main road. They were dressed like ordinary farmers, but most of them carried muskets and powder horns. One of them had a pitchfork.

George stepped quickly behind the raspberry bushes and huddled into a little hollow in the ground. The men stopped nearly opposite the place where George was crouched.

"You go right up to the house now, and we'll wait for you in front, on the main road." The man's hoarse voice was stern and abrupt.

"All right." George recognized the voice of Mr. Sager.

"Just ask fer Waltermyer. The Missus trusts you, you bein' a good frien' an' neighbour an' all. That way we'll know what's goin' on. She'll not be tellin' us where he's hidden but she'll tell you. Maybe ask you fer help."

There was a short silence. Then Mr. Sager replied, "All right, all right . . . but stay back a piece. Don't let her see you even after I leave the house. You might want information later. No need to let them know today which side I'm on!"

"What we need to know is which side Waltermyer is on, and we need to know now," the hoarse voice answered impatiently.

"All right, all right . . . I'm going!"

"We'll all go a bit farther, and then you go on alone. We'll stay just out of sight . . . for now."

George felt his heart racing. Then before he knew what he was doing, he had turned and started to run back through the orchard. When he reached the yard, he didn't look in either direction, but ran straight for the back kitchen door.

"Mother!" George gasped. "Mr. Sager is coming. He's with some other men. They're waiting for him on the main road at the end of our lane. They all want to get Father."

Just as he finished blurting out the words, a gentle knock came at the back door.

Polly laid Jacob in his cradle. "I'll answer that," she said firmly to George as she headed for the door.

"Good morning, Peter," Polly greeted Mr. Sager as she opened the door for him to enter. "What can I do for you?" George could not understand how she could be so nice to him.

"I can't stay, Polly," Peter replied. "I've come to see Hans. It's important."

"You've just missed him, Peter. He left early this morning to buy a new horse to replace old Duke. Perhaps I can help you."

"Well, really, I've come to help you folks."

"Oh? Why?"

"Have you heard about the Vandervoots?"

"What about the Vandervoots?"

"The Rebels strung him up in a tar and feather suit last night!"

"Why?"

"I heard he shot at them when they came to call."

"How is he now?"

"Dead. I met the Committee of Safety returning from the farm this morning. They told me they buried him there on his farm. So it's important I see Hans. You know how stubborn he can be. He must be persuaded at least to swear allegiance to the Rebel cause."

"It's kind of you to be on the lookout for your neighbours. Did you bring anyone with you?"

"No, I'm alone. Who did you think was with me?" asked Mr. Sager suspiciously.

"Sally and Tim, of course. How is Tim coming along? Did he get over that bad bout of croup?"

"Yes, he's fine now. Polly, give Hans the word I'd like to see him as soon as he gets back. When was it you said he'd be back?"

"I'm not sure. He may find a horse as near as Claverack or he may have to travel on to Poughkeepsie or farther. And he's going to pick up a few other supplies we need."

"Haying time's always busy. Guess he'll be back soon. It's a wonder he'd even leave just now . . . it being such a busy time."

"I'll tell him you were asking for him. Give my love to Sally and Tim."

"Sure will. See you folks later."

Polly slowly closed the door and walked to the parlour window, from which she could see her neighbour striding briskly down the lane. When he turned onto the main road, he doubled his speed to join the others, still hidden from view.

Polly stood quite still for a few minutes as she stared at the now-empty road. Then she wiped away the silent tears from her eyes and with a sigh started back towards the kitchen.

George was standing just inside the dining-room door and had heard every word. He was glad Mr. Sager was gone. He wondered what he would be telling those other men.

"Well, they're gone for now," said Mother. She bent over to lift Jacob from his wooden cradle.

Thump! Thump! Thump!

This time, sounds were coming from the direction of the front door. It sounded as if someone was going to break right in.

"Let me go," George said and started for the front hall.

With one hand, Mother grabbed him and said, "No, George!" She handed Jacob to him.

George watched Mother take a deep breath and walk slowly out of the kitchen through the dining room to the parlour and into the front hall, where the banging had not stopped. He put Jacob into the cradle and walked into the dining room.

George heard a man say harshly, "We want to see Hans Waltermyer."

"My husband has gone for a few days to buy a horse," Polly said simply and directly.

George walked on into the parlour. He could see the man at the door and more beyond in the yard.

"When did he leave?" he heard the same voice say in a louder, more threatening tone.

"This morning," Mother answered without hesitation.

"This morning, eh . . . ?" the man repeated. "Well, we'll be back in one week and he'd better be here then to answer for himself. Those who are not faithful to our cause have met with strange accidents lately. Hear about the Vandervoots?" He did not wait for an answer but turned and went down the steps.

George saw the leader walk over to the others, and they all mumbled together for a few minutes. One of them took a step towards the house, but the leader motioned him back, and they started down the lane to the road. George went into the hall and, stopping beside his mother, put his arm around her shoulders. They stood there together in silence and watched the men march away.

George did not need to ask now which side his father was on. Those neighbour men who were once their friends were now their enemies.

Three

George's father and John Kruger had been travelling steadily for over a week now, going through farmers' woodlots to avoid the open fields. One time they looked out onto a road below them and saw half a dozen Rebel soldiers headed south. After that, they stayed well back in the woods. They kept cool enough in their beige cotton twill overalls, loose-fitting shirts, and linen waistcoats, but they were constantly swatting at mosquitoes. Occasionally they stopped to grab a few wild strawberries and scoop up fresh water from a running stream. Finally, they reached the wilderness trail that led north to Lake George. They hoped to meet General John Burgoyne and his troops coming down from Canada.

Late one afternoon as they were tramping up a long slope, Curly fell over panting beside Waltermyer. Kruger stepped around him, but Waltermyer squatted beside the worn-out dog to encourage him. "Come on, Curly." He ruffled the sheepdog's thick mop of tangled hair. The dog did not move.

Reluctantly, Waltermyer followed his brother-in-law, who was now climbing several feet ahead. He looked back and called Curly again, but the dog did not move. When Waltermyer rounded the bend in the trail, Curly was no longer in sight.

"Come on, Hans," Kruger urged.

Waltermyer paid no attention. He headed back down the trail to Curly. The dog lay still on the rocky path. He bent down, scooped him up, flung him over his shoulder, and rushed up the incline to catch up with his brother-in-law.

When Kruger saw what he was carrying, he looked at him in disbelief and said, "Hans, you'll wear yourself out carrying that miserable animal!"

Waltermyer strode steadily forward. "We may have to eat him yet," he replied.

Hunters often took an animal with them on expeditions as a safeguard against starvation, but Waltermyer had never meant Curly to come. He had awakened the third morning of their journey to find the dog asleep beside him, still wet from swimming across the Mohawk River. By then they were too far from home to send him back.

The first night of their flight under cover of darkness, they had reached Albany and the home of Dr. Smyth, who was said to be a British sympathizer. Since he was the only doctor in town, the local Rebel authorities had chosen to overlook the rumours and let him carry on his practice undisturbed.

The weary fugitives had been thankful to find that the rumours were true. Dr. Smyth, known to his spy network by the secret code-name "Hudibras," explained to them that they could hope to find the British troops stationed along Lake George. According to Hudibras' informers, Burgoyne was heading south from his great victory at Fort Ticonderoga, which he had recently captured, and would welcome new recruits. Dr. Smyth told them that if a man could recruit sixty men for a company, he would be commissioned as their Captain, but first, they would have to obtain Ebenezer Jessup's permission. Jessup, from Albany, was now Commander of a battalion of Loyalists, the King's Loyal Americans, who were fighting as part of Burgoyne's forces.

When the war began two years ago, Waltermyer never imagined that he would one day be joining up with the British army to fight against his neighbours, and even members of his own family — his only brother, Jacob, and his father. He had tried to stay neutral, but that was impossible. Poor Vandervoot! He'd been neutral too — until the Rebels came to take his boys — and now where was he? Buried in his own yard, powerless to protect anyone.

Waltermyer had suffered nothing under the British — in fact, he had prospered. Yes, the merchants in the cities, especially Boston and New York and Philadelphia, had complained bitterly about taxes put on imported goods. But these merchants had conveniently forgotten about all the money Britain had spent to protect them from the French. Up in Boston, they had managed to incite the unemployed youths who, for want of anything better to do, had joined the cause. But the siege of Boston had not affected the people around Albany. Most farmers had believed it would soon be over. They had no complaint and no time to start trouble like people in the cities.

Waltermyer hadn't even paid much attention last July when a Declaration of Independence was posted outside the Town Hall in Albany. But in the fall, things had begun to change, and his neighbours had grown a little uneasy when it was rumoured that the British, who had taken over New York City and Long Island, were building up a large army to march north and stop the Rebels. During the winter, Waltermyer saw tensions build as neighbours began to take sides, and in the spring, people started saying that roaming mobs were forcing neutrals into the Rebel army. But he hadn't really thought his neighbours would get involved in a press gang.

So now he was on his way to join the British, sick at heart for leaving his family and hoping against hope that it would all be over soon. When the British and Loyalist troops coming south with Burgoyne joined those going north from New York with General Howe, they would snuff out this rebellion, and life would return to normal.

But now there was this journey to complete. Kruger and Waltermyer hurried through the hills, still heading for Lake George, hoping to meet Burgoyne and Jessup. Waltermyer shifted Curly to his other shoulder. The animal was heavy. He certainly didn't want to eat his children's pet. In fact, he almost gagged at the thought. Yet their food had run out a couple of days ago, and this trail was barren. A few berries from time to time were not enough to keep a man going at this strenuous pace.

Kruger stopped suddenly in front of Waltermyer. "The trail seems to end here," he said, taking off his straw hat and mopping the sweat off his forehead with his handkerchief.

"I'll lead if you like," Waltermyer replied. He stepped around Kruger and out into the bush. He had hunted in these mountains since he was a boy, so there was little chance of getting lost here. He would have liked to stop and hunt for food too, but he kept pushing ahead. A stray band of Rebels might be cutting through these trails or even retreating from the British troops. He didn't want to alert anyone with a gunshot.

It was sundown before the two starved men slackened

their pace and began looking for a spot where they could sleep. Kruger collapsed onto a bed of maple leaves left from the previous fall, and Waltermyer stretched out on a long, flat rock. Curly lay where he had dropped him, a few feet away, in a grove of young ash trees. Waltermyer said a short, silent prayer, asking God to keep his family safe and to bring peace back to his country soon. Then he dropped immediately into a deep sleep.

***

Waltermyer woke up abruptly. Someone or something was nearby. He reached for his musket and aimed it towards the sound. In the misty morning light, he could see an elderly man ambling into the clearing. He put down his pack and started to prepare a site for a campfire.

Waltermyer jumped to his feet and crept forward with his gun ready. He saw that the man was a Mohawk, and he knew they were friendly to the British. Still he didn't want to take any chances, for the elderly man might mistake him for a Rebel. Waltermyer came even closer to the man, who was now kneeling over his pack.

Without turning, the man said, "I am going to roast bear meat. Will you and your friend join me?"

"We certainly will," said Waltermyer as he leaned his musket against a tree. Kruger and the dog were awake now too. Waltermyer had to restrain Curly, who had smelled the strong odour of the meat.

As they sat eating the first filling meal they had had in days, Waltermyer said, "Thank you. You came just in time."

The elderly man nodded. He had even given the dog a big chunk, and Curly was busy now with the bones.

"Have you seen any soldiers to the north?" Waltermyer asked.

"The Redcoats are far north," replied the man.

"How far?"

"Three days north as we Mohawk travel, but eight days as the Redcoats travel."

Kruger looked across at Waltermyer, amused by the answer, for the trip was straight along Lake Champlain and there were no short-cuts. Waltermyer did not smile back. He respected the Mohawk and knew there would be a reason for his remark.

"May we buy some of your bear meat to take with us?" Waltermyer asked.

Waltermyer took two shillings from his pocket and held it in his hand. The Mohawk shook his head. Waltermyer reluctantly emptied his leather money pouch into his palm. He had only three shillings and sixpence. He held out the money.

The elderly Mohawk looked at the empty pouch and nodded. Relieved, Waltermyer picked up the bear meat and grease and packed them into his leather bag. He rubbed a generous amount of bear grease on himself. He did not like its sharp, strong smell, but neither did the insects.

Now that they had their provisions, they would move faster. But they had far to go if the British were eight days away. They set off again under the warm June sun, heading northwest.

Four

I'm harnessing the team, Toby," George shouted as he stepped into the horse stable. It was two weeks now since their father had gone, and George was enjoying being in charge.

Tobias already had the collars buckled around the horses' necks. George grabbed a harness from the horizontal post on the barn wall and pulled it over his right arm. In each hand, he grasped a hame, the foremost part of the harness, and strode over to Duke. Throwing the harness over the horse's neck, he went around to the front of the animal and strapped the hames to the collar.

"Can't I help?" Tobias asked. He stood waiting.

"I can manage fine. You better get busy with your own chores, Toby." George went over to the other horse, Bonnie, and started harnessing her.

"There are always plenty of chores, but I could help you first."

"I know how to harness these horses and I don't need help. Mother has asked me to drive her to town today." George could not hide the pride in his voice. Tobias turned away silently and headed for the hay mow.

"Thanks anyhow," George shouted after him.

He fastened the gird strap on the harness, placed the bits in the horses' mouths, and slid the bridles over their heads. Then he fastened the snap end of the reins to the bits. Attaching the horses together with the reins, he removed the other end of the reins from the hames and then drove the team to the wagon. He strapped the neck yoke to the bottom of the hames and inserted the wagon pole through a ring in the middle of the neck yoke. Then he removed the traces from the horses' backs and fastened them to the whippletrees at the base of the wagon pole. George remembered that his father counted the links at the end of the traces to make sure the correct link on each of the traces was fastened to each of the four whippletree hooks. Finally, he gathered up the reins and stepped into the wagon.

George trotted the horses a hundred yards to the house, where Mother and Mary were waiting with thirteen baskets of strawberries to load onto the wagon. They were partway through the loading when Leonard came to help.

"What's that piece of harness doing down there?" Leonard asked George, pointing to Duke.

George looked at Duke and, sure enough, there was a very important piece of harness dangling in the air. He rushed around to the front of the horse, grabbed the martingale, ran it between Duke's front legs, and attached it to the gird strap. He went back to the wagon feeling a bit less confident.

"It's really nothing," he said. "Bonnie is fine. I just forgot that one strap on Duke."

"Isn't that the strap that keeps the horses from rearing and helps them hold the wagon back from going too fast down hill? I don't call that nothing." Leonard's smirk irritated George.

"I'm sure George has it correct now," Mother interrupted. "Catharine, take good care of Jacob and Anna this afternoon. I've told Tobias to work near the house."

She was still giving instructions as Mary and Leonard were climbing into the wagon. It was their turn to go to town.

George was glad to be going to Albany — he hadn't been there since Father had left. He was looking forward to visiting his friend John Bleecker, whose father ran the store. People were always going in and out of the General Store, and John was sure to have lots of news. He might even have heard about Father.

Mother sat beside George on the front seat. Leonard and Mary rode with their backs against the front bench and watched the berries, which had been carefully shaded with thick, dark cloths. This was the first of many summer trips to Albany when they would be taking produce in to Mr. Bleecker to trade for supplies like salt and flour.

Because of the load of berries, they could not drive quickly, and it was over an hour later when they arrived at the edge of Albany. George turned the team of horses onto one of the town's three wide streets. The rest of the streets were narrow and twisting. They passed high, narrow houses built right against each other. One house was so high it had four rows of windows and a line of crow gables at the top. Their own frame house on the farm had just two storeys and an attic for storing things.

When they came to the Bleeckers' store on Main Street, George drove the horses into the yard and fastened them firmly to the hitching-post before going to the back of the cart to help the others unload the berries.

"Good day to you, Polly," Janse Bleecker called out cheerfully as he came forward to hold the door open for them. He was a rather heavy-set man with plump, red cheeks and eyes that twinkled with good humour. "What fine-looking berries! It looks as if you have a good crop this year."

"Yes, it's the best in years," Mother replied proudly. "We had to take Leonard off the harvesting this morning to help us pick them."

George walked right up to the counter with Mother while Mary and Leonard waited at the door as Mother had told them to do. On the left side of the store as you faced the counter were all the grocery supplies — rye and wheat flour, fine salt, coffee, molasses, and other fresh produce from nearby farms; on the other side were all kinds of interesting things. There were muskets, hunting knives, boots, and material for clothes. Much of the cloth had been made and traded by the local farm women. George knew that his mother made her own materials, but his sisters liked to look at the ones in the store too.

Mother had given Mr. Bleecker the list of items she needed, and he was putting them together. "Go on back," he said as he passed by the children. "John has something to show you."

"Thank you, Mr. Bleecker," George said as he led Mary and Leonard to the back storage room where he often visited with John, who was already twelve. They passed through a narrow passageway that had shelves along both sides filled with barrels, packages of varying sizes, and dozens of pairs of boots. Behind these, they found John kneeling beside a litter of golden and white collie puppies.

"Oh . . . ," exclaimed Mary. "Aren't they beautiful!"

John looked up at Mary. He was sturdily built like his father and had the same robust cheeks. His blond hair was so fair it was almost white — as his father's had been at his age.

Mary reached out to pick up a little pup at the side, but George cautioned, "Be careful, Mary. They're very young."

"I know how to handle pups," Mary shot back as she let the little dog snuggle into the crook of her arm.

"They're doing quite well," John said proudly. "That one with the white spot on his forehead that Mary is holding is the only one who isn't very energetic. He's the runt of the lot. We think we'll be able to sell them all, except maybe that one."

"I'll take him," Mary said eagerly, surprising George. Actually he wished *he'd* thought of asking.

"You may have him, Mary; I think he'll manage without his mother if you nurse him along. My sister has started him drinking from a dish because the other pups don't let him get much from his mother anyway."

John gave Mary a piece of thick broadcloth to wrap around her new pet. "We really don't have the time to bother with him. You'll be doing us a favour by taking him."

"You sure will," said a voice behind George. He looked around to see John's sister, Lucretia, whom all the kids called Lucy, standing there.

George had no intention of getting into an argument with John's skinny sister. What the eleven-year-old lacked in size, she always made up for in volume. He was annoyed she was there because he had hoped to talk with John alone for a few minutes.

So George said no more as he watched Mary cuddle the limp little body of the sickly pup. He was wondering what Mother would say. But he was more concerned about other things. He motioned John to the side of the room. "Any news?" he mumbled.

"Lots," Lucy said just behind him again. George was tempted to grab one of her long blonde braids and give it a great jerk, but he didn't. His friend John took care of the problem.

"I thought you were headed for your friend's birthday party," he said to Lucy.

"I am. I was just cutting through the store." Then she knelt over and patted the little pup that Mary was holding. "He likes his milk warmed a little," she said to Mary. "I'll be coming out to see him sometime. Bye, Mary."

Her blue linen gown and patterned petticoats swished against the wall as she passed the boys, her head held high. The boys paid no attention.

When she was gone, George asked again, "Any news, John?"

"Some say that Burgoyne is headed south with British troops. We don't know for sure. Dad never talks about it and most people in the store say it's just a rumour started by British sympathizers."

"Did you hear about Vandervoot?"

"Yes. There have been incidents in town too. The jail is filling fast."

"Jail is one thing. Stringing up and killing is another! I don't know which is the right side anymore."

"I'm sorry, George." Then John whispered, "Walls have ears. Be careful what you say. It could be misunderstood." George remembered he was responsible for the family now. He nodded in appreciation of his friend's warning.

"We'd better see if Mother's ready," he said. George and John headed out to the front of the store, with Mary and Leonard trailing along behind.

Back in the main room of the store, Mary picked up

one of Mother's empty strawberry baskets, tucked the pup into it, and pulled the cloth over him.

"That will be all, thank you, Janse. I plan to preserve the next strawberry picking, but I'll be back with more on Friday," Mother said.

"Good. I'll look forward to getting them. They go fast."

As Mother turned to the door, Mary went out ahead of her, hiding the puppy basket under her shawl. George walked out behind Mary, trying to think what Father would have said about the pup and wondering if *he* should say something. Actually, he knew what Father would say, but he didn't want to think too hard about that because he wanted Mary to keep the pup now that Curly was gone.

"What's that?" Mother said, looking sternly at the side of Mary's shawl, which was starting to move suspiciously. Mary pulled the cloth back. The furry animal blinked his eyes in the bright sunlight, and the white star on his forehead glistened.

"A pup!" Mother exclaimed in a tired voice. "Where did you find *that*?"

"In the rows of boots at the back of the store. John says he's the smallest and I may have him for free."

"I don't know, Mary. We already have Curly."

"Curly is gone, Mother. He's never been gone so long before, and we need a dog on the farm. Besides, I'll take care of him. I promise." Mary stood still and waited.

Mother got a heavy look in her eyes, then almost smiled. "Well, I suppose you're probably right about Curly . . . I guess we might as well take him home. But I think he should belong to all the children, so you can all care for him."

"Oh, thank you, thank you, Mother. We *will* take care of him!"

"Well, I'll see that you do," said Mother, gathering her shawl around her shoulders. "Now let's head back home. Catharine and Anna will be wondering where we've got to. Boys, help Mr. Bleecker and John carry out the supplies."

Mr. Bleecker, his red cheeks bulging, puffed a little as he loaded the wagon with the bags that the children handed to him. "The pup comes from a good mother," he said between puffs. "I think he'll become a good cow dog — not vicious, but mean enough to make a good watchdog too." As he lifted the last bag onto the wagon, he boomed out, "See you Friday," and turned back towards the store.

John stayed a moment to pat the little pup on the head. "What are you going to call him, Mary?"

"Boots."

"That's a good name. You noticed his four white feet."

"Yes, but I named him Boots for a different reason — because we found him with all the boots in your father's store."

"Oh, I see." John laughed heartily, just like his father, only at half the volume. He stood back as George swung himself into the driver's seat. George was proud to be the driver, especially since John was looking at him with such admiration. He turned to smile at his best friend. It was then that he noticed a group of men standing in front of the store. He thought at once of the mob at the Vandervoots. These men did not appear loud or violent, but they were starting to knock loudly on the front door.

"Where's your father?" one of the men snarled at John, who had run towards them to find out what they wanted.

"I'm here. What can I do for you?" Mr. Bleecker said in his usual cheerful tone. He was standing just inside the door.

"We want you out here now," barked one of the men in a hoarse voice as he stuck his pipe into the loops of his cocked hat. He waited with his thumbs hooked into his waistcoat pockets. George recognized him. He was the chief of the watchmen who kept order in the town.

Mr. Bleecker stepped out onto the front stoop, into the morning sunlight. The men were becoming more rowdy, and one burly man shoved Mr. Bleecker off the stoop. Then he and an older man in a powdered wig started to nail boards across the main door of the store.

Mr. Bleecker was no longer smiling. "What's going on here?" he shouted. John had raced over to his father and was now standing firmly beside him.

An officious man with a scroll came right up to Mr. Bleecker and read out loudly, "We are accusing you, Janse Bleecker, of treason. Questionable characters have been seen leaving your store at late hours."

"I've always opened the store late at night at this time of year to serve customers. All the farmers are busy with crops just now and some of them come in late at night for their supplies."

"That's why you sneak them in the back door?" asked the man, with a sly grin.

"Sometimes it's handier. I don't want to open the front and have the whole town shopping in the middle of the night." Mr. Bleecker was shouting as loudly as the other men. His face had turned very red and he took out a handkerchief to wipe his brow.

"Guilty as hell; he's starting to sweat," the hoarse voice said to a man beside him.

"Let's feather him right now," another added. "There'll be tar in the store and a goose behind."

Just then Mrs. Bleecker came around from the side of the building. She was fair haired and much younger than her husband. She said nothing, but stood on the other side of Mr. Bleecker.

The man with the scroll continued to read. "Bleecker, you are to accompany us to the jail, where you will stay until your case is heard by all Albany's commissioners. In the meantime, your store must remain closed."

"I am innocent of any wrongdoing. Take me if you must, but let my son and wife run the store," Mr. Bleecker said.

"No," the commissioner replied. The burly man and the watchman pushed John and his mother aside and grabbed Mr. Bleecker by the arms.

"Please let them keep the store open," Mr. Bleecker pleaded. Mrs. Bleecker ran towards her husband again, but the man who had gripped his left arm shoved her away. Mr. Bleecker swung out against the man with his free hand, but he did not hit him. He grabbed his own chest instead and sank to the ground, groaning. John, who had been pushed back by the crowd, fought his way through to where his father lay, and stood frozen at the sight of the pain twisting across his face. George, frozen in his driver's seat, was staring in disbelief too — first at his friend, then at John's father.

"Get the doctor," John shouted finally. "Somebody, get the doctor!"

The fear in John's voice jolted George into action. "I'll go for him, John," he shouted. "You stay here." He whipped the horses into a run and clattered towards Bridge Street, a short-cut to Dr. Smyth's.

Mother jumped down from her seat almost before they

were stopped and rushed to the doctor's door. She disappeared inside and a few minutes later returned with Dr. Smyth. Without a word, they jumped up to the front seat beside George.

George had the horses well in control. He had already turned them around and was ready to head them back by the short-cut.

"What were Janse's symptoms?" the doctor asked as they sped back up Bridge Street. He was a small man with thin strands of white hair. But behind his round spectacles, he had sharp, black eyes.

"He collapsed on the ground," George said. "It was those men who caused it. They closed his store and accused him of treason."

"I see. Are the men still there?"

"They were when we left." George slapped the horses' backs with the reins to force them up the hill more quickly. "The men were even talking about tarring and feathering, but the commissioner said he was taking Mr. Bleecker to jail."

George turned into Main Street, and steered the horses around another wagon and a line of horses tethered at the side of the street. Then he urged them ahead more quickly. He could see the General Store just ahead.

George pulled the horses to a sudden halt.

"Don't wait for me, Polly," the doctor advised. "I'll take care of everything, and you can do nothing more to help. Take your children home." Dr. Smyth could not tell Mrs. Waltermyer that he knew she and the children were alone now, for her husband had been at his house just two weeks before.

Dr. Smyth rushed over to Mr. Bleecker, who was still lying on the ground. Mrs. Bleecker had her arms around her husband. John was kneeling beside him. Mr. Bleecker was very quiet. The men had all left.

George turned the horses and whipped them to go, but Mother's voice rang out, "No, George!"

George pulled the reins tightly and yelled, "Whoa!" The horses stopped. Mother jumped out of the wagon and hurried across to where Mrs. Bleecker was kneeling over her husband. George tied the horses to the post and rushed over behind her.

Dr. Smyth was already examining Mr. Bleecker and shaking his head. Without looking up, he said to John and George, "Help me get Janse into the house, boys."

As they lifted Mr. Bleecker, George realized that he felt very heavy and still. He looked at the doctor, but the doctor was silent. Inside, Mrs. Bleecker motioned them to a horsehair-covered couch in the hallway.

George stood, expecting Dr. Smyth to continue examining Mr. Bleecker. Instead, he looked at Mrs. Bleecker and said very quietly, "I'm sorry . . . I believe it was his heart. He's gone."

For a moment, she stared back at the doctor without emotion. Then tears began to stream silently down her pale cheeks. Mother reached out to touch Mrs. Bleecker's shoulder, but John reached her first and wrapped his arms around her.

"George, check on the horses and children," Dr. Smyth said with a broken sharpness in his voice. Without a word, George turned and left.

As George went around past the front of the store, he saw the half-dozen boards the men had nailed across the front door. The word "CLOSED" had been scrawled across one of the boards in large letters. The men had not returned.

"How's Mr. Bleecker?" Leonard asked. Mary, still hugging her little pup, looked over the side of the wagon.

"Not the best." George would let Mother tell them. "Whoa," George said to the horses, who were becoming restless. Finally he quietened the team, and they all waited without even talking to each other.

It seemed like hours before Mother returned, and when she did, she looked pale and tired. George was relieved to hear her say, "Home now."

The team needed no urging. They were off in a hurry. "No, George!" Mother said. "Go slower until we reach the edge of town."

As the horses slackened their speed to a steady pace, George could see that up ahead there was a problem in the street. Another mob had gathered. He knew that if he turned back, people would notice and become suspicious, so he steered the horses ahead slowly.

In the middle of the crowd was a man imprisoned in a wooden box. Helpless, he faced the crowd with his head, arms, and feet sticking out through holes in the front of the box. The people standing around him were throwing eggs and even stones at the man. Others were insulting him.

"Traitor!"

"Skunk!"

"Tory!"

"Pig!"

The words rang loudly in George's ears. He guided the horses easily past the crowd, but even when they were out of earshot, George felt he could hear the names and the snarling voices.

"Go faster now, George." Mother's welcome voice came to him through the voices in his head. He gave the horses a sudden whip with the reins. They broke into a fast trot, for their load was light and they were headed home.

George was glad to leave Albany behind. At this speed, they would cover the eight miles to home in less than an hour. It was good to feel the breeze in his face again.

The little pup in Mary's arms whimpered. "Mother, how was Mr. Bleecker?" she finally asked.

Mother did not answer.

Five

George's father leaned back against a granite rock and gazed up at the cloudless blue of a mid-July sky. The forest was silent except for the sound of wild bees. His aching feet were resting in the patch of spindly green horsetail that covered the clearing where he and Kruger had stopped to rest. Curly was lying beside him, with his long, pink tongue hanging out the side of his mouth.

"Poor ol' Curly," Waltermyer said to Kruger, who was lying on his back with his arms and legs spread out flat and a piece of wild rye dangling from his mouth. "I'll bet he wishes he could take off that fur coat."

"Yeah, that's one thing we can be thankful for — we don't have to carry *that* excess baggage."

Kruger rolled over onto his side and gazed out of the clearing through a thin line of trees that edged the hill they were on.

"Well, I don't believe it. What's that coming over the horizon? Talk about coats. You'd think they'd have the sense to take them off in this heat. It must be ninety-five in the shade."

"What are you talking about?" Waltermyer mumbled. He had started to doze off after "coats." "Curly can't take his coat off, poor beast."

"Not *Curly*, my friend. German soldiers. Look!

They're tramping along the creek just below us." Walter-myer peered down from the top of the hill and saw on the road to Skenesborough a column of soldiers — almost two hundred — marching through the heat in long coats. They were wearing caps with heavy brass ornaments and carrying huge haversacks. Their extra-long swords hung from their sides and swung back and forth as they plodded along. If the soldiers had been going at a decent pace, the swords would probably have tripped them.

"Those are our troops, Kruger. They're hired soldiers fighting for the British. Let's go! We've got to catch them or we may be another three weeks in the bush before we find any more."

He and Kruger had not met the British troops headed for the Lake George trail as they had expected. A scout they had met along the trail reported that Burgoyne had chosen a route for his men along the east side of the Hudson River. So he and Kruger had turned about at Ticonderoga and headed south on the east side of the Hudson. Until now they had been searching for the troops in vain. Kruger and Waltermyer leapt to their feet and scrambled down the hill. Curly panted after them.

"Ho, there," Waltermyer shouted to the approaching soldiers. "We are friends who approach in the name of Hudibras."

A sergeant turned and shouted to his men in German, "Take these men. They may be Rebel spies."

As the soldiers lumbered towards them, Waltermyer, who had understood the command, shouted again, "We are not Rebels. We are Loyalists, who have come to join forces with the British. We need an escort to the Commander, Ebenezer Jessup, and his Loyalist battalion. He will know us."

The Sergeant looked at Waltermyer without blinking. There was nothing about them — their bearded, grimy faces, their scruffy overalls, their determined stares — that could give him any clue about their loyalties. Kruger and Waltermyer stood and waited. The air hung heavy and silent.

"Well, come with us, then. But mind you march brisk enough to keep up."

Waltermyer shot a glance of relief at Kruger and tried to suppress a smile. Tired as they were, they would have no difficulty keeping up with these cavalry men who were forced to march in their heavy boots.

After an hour's march over marshy fields, the German troops with their two strange-looking companions finally rounded a hill and came to a wide stretch of green pasture, where long, bright lines of British soldiers were standing for a firing and reloading drill. Waltermyer and Kruger had finally reached Burgoyne's forces.

It was a loud procedure, directed by the shouting of orders and the beating of drums. At least they were not firing real ammunition, Waltermyer noted. The Brown Bess muskets that they carried could not be aimed properly, for they did not have rear sight. But if these muskets were inaccurate and awkward for the British, who were trained soldiers, they would be even more so for the Rebels, who were amateurs. In open combat, the Rebels wouldn't stand a chance against the British with their disciplined use of the Bess and their skill in delivering a great volume of fire. Still, Waltermyer knew the Rebels' determination. Their supplies were also near at hand. Would the British keep *their* supply lines moving?

"Jessup's camp is a few hundred feet to the west of Burgoyne's men," the Sergeant explained as he led them past a grove of maple and oaks where a group of boys were chasing each other, waving their cricket bats. They were all younger than George. Nearby, under a big maple tree, a few girls about Mary's age were sitting on canvas stools in cool white dresses, playing with dolls. Their mothers, dressed in pastel pinks, blues and greens, sat on short wooden benches and fanned themselves.

"Who are these women?" asked Waltermyer.

"They're the wives and children of the officers," the Sergeant replied. "The wife and three small daughters of our Commander, Baron von Riedesel, just arrived yesterday from Fort St. John's. The ladies are having a party for them."

"I thought you were preparing for battle soon. Is it wise to have the women and children here?"

"No problem that I can see. But these are just the officers' wives. There are other women in the camp too. Many of the common soldiers have wives who follow the troops. But we see to it that they give us no trouble."

"How's that?"

"Well, when a woman's man falls in battle, we give her twenty-four hours to get herself another husband or leave the troops."

Waltermyer was shocked. "That's some choice," he said. "The woman is stranded far from home in hostile territory."

"It's no problem. Most women have at least a dozen proposals."

"What about the officers' wives?"

"They're sent back home with an escort."

Waltermyer walked on silently beside the Sergeant. He was worried about the British and their hired soldiers. They would have been impressive on a European battlefield, but in the forests of America, their rigid discipline and complex drill might fail them. More homegrown American Loyalist battalions were obviously needed. American Loyalists who knew the country and the ambush tactics of the Iroquois would stand a much better chance of winning a battle. Waltermyer decided that he would raise his own company. He knew men back home who would be eager to fight for the farms they had lost to the Rebels.

Six

George trudged along behind the cows on the path to the barn. It was dusk. He and Tobias had been stooking wheat all day. Every muscle in his body ached. Since Curly had disappeared a month before, he had to run all over the field to catch the cows, and he even had to push some of them to start them ambling back to the barn. His brothers and sisters weren't much help either. He had told Leonard to have the cows in the barn waiting to be milked when he and Tobias came from the field, but when they rode in on the wagon, there was no sign of the cows or Leonard. George knew he was stronger than Tobias, so he gave his brother the job of unhitching and feeding the horses. And he had set out for the cows. He would like to get his hands on that Leonard! Being in charge was starting to be a lot less fun than it was at first.

Something else was bothering him too. Today was his twelfth birthday and no one had even mentioned it. If Father had been home, there would have been a special celebration. But it didn't help to think about that because it made him miss his father even more. He had been away for a whole month and no one knew where he was or when he would be coming back.

Perhaps he had joined the British by now. Or maybe

he'd decided to join the Rebel cause after all. That was not very likely, George thought. If he had joined the Rebels, he would have sent word home. Anyway, it was a good sign that the Rebel soldiers had not come back to look for him.

Then George started to think that his father might not have gone to war at all. Maybe he was just having a great time hunting and fishing. He knew the Mohawk Valley and the area of the Adirondack Mountains like the back of his hand. He could hunt and stay in those mountains undetected for months, maybe even years. In the meantime, here was George working like a slave and nobody appreciating him. Even Mother didn't seem to notice lately. She just kept telling him to plan the work, and the rest of the family would help. They did sometimes, but he had to work the hardest. If Father had thought ahead, they wouldn't be in this mess now.

George thought about John's father, Mr. Bleecker. He had asked Mother why Mr. Bleecker died if God was really powerful and could save him as it said in the Psalms. Mother had answered that we don't always know why God lets some people die. But the important thing was that Mr. Bleecker was in heaven now. She had explained that we only see part of the picture, but God sees the whole picture. And we'll know his purpose some day when we're in heaven.

George wished he knew right now where John and his mother and sister were. The day after the funeral, he had gone into town to see John. The Rebels had taken over the Bleeckers' store, and it was up for sale. One friend told George that the family had sailed south on a Hudson River sloop to visit their cousins. He hoped that was true and that they were not in the Albany jail. George knew they had cousins at Bennington, which was northeast, not south. But he didn't mention that.

The sun was almost all the way down when he reached the barn with the cows. Tobias was waiting for him at the door and lazy Leonard was standing beside him.

"I can explain," said Leonard.

"I'll bet," George said and held up his switch, ready to strike his brother.

Leonard did not move. He really did look sorry. "I was picking wild raspberries," he said. "I lost track of the time."

George flung the switch to the ground and said in a tired voice, "I — I'm sorry, Leonard."

All three boys then fell to their work in silence, herding the eight cows through the cow-stable door. Each animal instinctively went to its own clean stall and waited there for the boys to close the wooden stanchion about its neck. Tobias had clean water ready, and he quickly washed the cows' bags. Then each boy grabbed a milk pail and a stool and sat down to milk. George took the harder cows, who did not let down their milk so easily. Bessie was the kicker, so he had tied her back legs together with a rope. He couldn't afford the time to be laid up with a broken leg. When the boys had finally stripped out the milk from the last cow, they filled the cows' mangers with fresh hay and hurried out of the barn.

As George headed back to the house, it was already getting dark. All he wanted now was to eat and then drop into bed. Sun-up came early these days, and there was still a lot of wheat to harvest. Then there were the vegetables, which would soon have to be taken to market twice a week. It was a bountiful year, but George knew they would need all their produce to get through the winter. There were seven hungry children to feed — and the animals too. They might not get anything from town if the war grew worse, and they had already received notice of the quota they were required to drop off in Albany to help feed Schuyler's Rebel troops stationed just north of Albany. None of the crops could go to waste.

George was last at the washbasin that Mother had set on the back stoop. He washed his hands and face on the towel that Tobias and Leonard had left all soggy and streaked, then dumped the water out onto the sunflowers beside the back door.

As he stepped inside the kitchen, he could smell freshly cooked chicken, and he wasn't sure, but he almost thought he could smell sage dressing too. That was strange. Mother was standing over the table, slicing large pieces of tender white and dark meat from the bone and placing them on the pale rose platter. Then George saw the dressing, two bowls of it — and a pitcher of giblets and gravy beside them. Mother smiled at George and said, "We're eating in the dining room tonight." Usually, for supper, they just ate warmed-up leftovers in the kitchen.

"Happy Birthday!" shouted the children as George walked into the dining room. Mother motioned him to sit at the end of the table, where Father usually sat. George began to feel a bit sorry for complaining to himself about the hard work. It looked as if everyone did appreciate him after all.

After Mother said grace, which was fortunately short, George filled his plate with huge mounds of chicken, dressing, mashed potatoes, and carrots. Then he covered the whole thing with steaming gravy. He piled big cobs of buttered corn on a smaller plate.

Half an hour later, when everyone was sitting around the table feeling full and happy, Mary reached down under the table and picked up a big parcel. She pushed it towards George.

George smiled and started to pull the strong broadcloth wrap off the parcel. The rest all crowded around to watch him. The next layer of wrap was a piece of his old overalls. Then he pulled another piece off the parcel. It was taken from Mother's rag bag. George was beginning to suspect something. Then he saw his old school reader through the corner of the last piece of cloth. They all laughed loudly.

"I thought you needed to catch up on your lessons," said Mary with a giggle. George couldn't help laughing. Reading was the last thing he had time for just now.

Then Leonard came in from the kitchen. A strong smell came with him — something was steaming out of the holes in the little wooden box he held. George was ready this time. He took the box very carefully, and pulling back a loose board on top, he peeked inside.

"Oinkkkkkkk," squealed the little pig, squirming out of the box. It rubbed its rough hide past George's nose and got loose. The piglet was darting all around the floor between the children's feet. Anna grabbed its short tail, but it was too strong for her. Leonard grabbed the squealing streak, but it slipped through his hands too, fast as lightning.

Finally Mary and Leonard got the pig in a corner. Panting, George scooped him into the box and asked, "Where'd you ever get him, Leonard?"

"From the Vandervoots. And he's no joke. His sire won prizes at all the country fairs last year. I've had to do chores for Mrs. Vandervoot for a month now to pay for him."

George swallowed. So that's where Leonard had been so many times when he'd tried to find him. "Thanks, Leonard," he said. "I'll put him out on the back stoop, in his box, until supper's over."

Stepping back into the kitchen, George could not believe what he saw. Little Boots was licking away at a pan of whipping cream that was resting in a pail on the cupboard countertop. The dog must have come in with Leonard and the pig.

"Boots!" he said in a nasty low tone. He didn't want Mother to know. He would have to train him better than that. Boots followed George around so much that the rest of the family were starting to call him George's dog.

"Mother's gone upstairs for your present," Tobias told George when he went back into the dining room.

"What do you think it'll be?" Anna asked.

"I thought she might get me a horse of my own, but I can't see her hiding it under her bed!" Catharine and Mary giggled. Just then Mother came down the stairs carrying a beautiful big musket. Over her shoulder hung a finely carved powder horn and a leather bag for carrying ammunition and small flints. Hanging down around the edges of the bag were "tinklers" made of glass beads, tin cones, and deer hair dyed flaming red. George could hardly believe his eyes.

"For you, George, with Father's blessing," Mother was saying. "You have become a fine hunter. Now mind your father's rules for its use."

So Father had remembered. George took the gift and looked it over closely as his sisters and brothers crowded around.

Mother went to the kitchen and brought back the raspberry pie topped with whipped cream.

"Now, George, look what *I* made you," said Catharine. She pointed to the large cake on the counter out in the kitchen.

From his chair in the dining room, George could see Boots through the open doorway. There he was, right up on the countertop again, and his nose was covered with maple-sugar icing. George had forgotten to hook the screen door and had been too busy eating to notice his dog sneaking back inside.

"Boots!" George shouted. But Mother was faster than George. She grabbed the dog roughly and headed for the door. Before she could open it, however, a loud noise came from outside, and three armed men burst into the room. Mother dropped the dog and stepped back.

"Where's the man of the house? We want Hans Walter-myer!" the first man said. Four more strangers pushed in behind the others. Then more came. There was a crowd of men now in the kitchen. A few of them were neighbours, but George hardly recognized their angry faces. They reminded him of the mob at the Vandervoots.

Mother stood firmly in the doorway between the kitchen and dining room. George was right behind her and Boots was huddling at his feet. The others sat frozen around the dining-room table. Anna spilled some pie into her lap, but she didn't pick it up. She was too afraid to move.

Mother faced the men and said quietly, "He went to buy a horse and supplies."

"You told us that a month ago. He's had plenty of time to return by now. Any decent, respectable man with seven children — and a wife — would have come back before now." A few of the men guffawed loudly.

"I know only what I have told you, but I do have fears."

"Fears, eh? You fear us? Why? You have reason to fear us?"

"No, I do not fear you," Mother continued in a quiet, steady voice. "But I do fear that my husband may have continued on to New York for his supplies, and that even now he may be held there by the British authorities against his will."

"We have fears too, Ma'am. We fear he may be spying for the British."

"I only know what I have told you."

"This man here has something to say to you."

George heard scuffling in the kitchen as someone was pushed forward. He finally appeared in the outer kitchen doorway holding a piece of parchment. The man was their elderly landlord. "Due to the fact that your husband's lease for this farm has not been signed, you and your family must leave. You may take your furniture and your personal belongings, but you must leave all your stock and produce. You have one day to pack and go."

Catharine covered her face with her apron and gave a muffled sob. George put his hand on her shoulder. "We'll be all right," he said. But he did not feel all right and his voice came out all soft and shaky.

"That's not fair! You can't do this!" Mother said angrily. "We did our part in cultivating the land and giving you a good return. You promised us the lease." She was looking only at the landlord now and seemed to have forgotten the other men.

"I am sorry, but you have one day to go," the landlord said. George thought he looked a bit like an old sheep.

"One day!" Mother almost screamed at him. "How can we possibly be ready in one day!" The landlord looked sadly away from Mother.

The first man pushed the landlord back and snarled, "We'll be back to help you out if you're not gone by this time tomorrow!" The angry faces around him laughed loudly, and George knew that their help was not the kind they needed.

Mother turned very pale but spoke more evenly when she said, "Is that all you have to say?" She was still standing in the doorway between the kitchen and the dining room.

"That's it, but mind you're out in a day," the leader said roughly. "We'll be back to see how you're doing with your preparations. It's lovely weather for travelling. Good day, Ma'am." He turned around abruptly and barked a command at his men, and they all walked heavily through the kitchen and out the back door.

"Mother, do we *have* to leave?" Mary burst out as soon as the kitchen door-latch clicked shut.

"Where will we go?" Catharine asked.

George looked up from his musket. "To Grandpa Waltermyer's, where else?"

Their grandparents lived five miles northwest of Father's farm beside Cooeyman's Landing on the Hudson River.

"At sun-up," Mother said quietly, "Tobias will drive to Grandpa Waltermyer's for help. Then they'll come back with your grandpa's wagon to help us take our things to his place."

"What if those men tell them to leave their home, too?" Catharine asked.

Jacob cried from his cradle on the other side of the room. Anna giggled, then fell suddenly silent.

Mother went to Jacob and picked up the baby. He, too, became quiet almost instantly. Still standing, she said, "They won't. Your grandpa has already signed his lease. Besides, he has sworn allegiance to the Rebel cause, and your Uncle Jacob is a soldier in the Rebel army."

Looks of relief came to the children's faces, and they turned to admire George's fine musket.

George was still rubbing his hand along the barrel when Mother said, "Put your musket away now, George, and come back to the table."

Still cradling Jacob on one arm, Mother reached over to the walnut mantel of the dining-room fireplace. With a trembling hand, she picked up the very old Bible with the worn leather cover that her parents had read from when they were still alive.

George returned to the table and all the children sat quietly. Even chubby Anna did not wiggle on her chair. Mother began reading from Psalm 121.

I will lift up mine eyes unto the hills, from whence cometh my help.
My help cometh from the Lord, which made heaven and earth.
He will not suffer thy foot to be moved: he that keepeth thee will not slumber.
Behold, He that keepeth Israel shall neither slumber nor sleep.

George wondered where his father was. He knew now that it would not be safe for him to come back home.

The Lord is thy keeper: the Lord is thy shade upon thy right hand.
The sun shall not smite thee by day, nor the moon by night.

The Lord shall preserve thee from all evil: he shall
preserve thy soul.
The Lord shall preserve thy going out and thy coming
in from this time forth, and even for evermore.

Mother closed the Bible and prayed a short, quiet
prayer. "Will the Lord really keep us?" George thought
to himself after she'd finished. How long would they be
safe at Grandpa's? And if they were driven away from
there, who would take them in? It looked as if all their
neighbours were their enemies now.

Seven

Waltermyer hoped he would be able to see Burgoyne's troops when he reached the top of the next hill. He was about twenty miles north of Albany. The yellow leaves of the elm and oak and the red of the maples fell down around him and covered the ground.

It was the middle of October, 1777. Four long months had passed since he had seen his wife and children, but he had heard from Dr. Smyth that they were living with his parents. He felt relieved, for he knew they would be safe there.

Back in June, Jessup had given him official permission to scout for his own Loyalist company. All summer, he had been scouting for recruits in the countryside on both sides of the Hudson. It had not been easy. He had travelled as a labourer looking for work and tried to decide which men to approach. He had to be very careful before he revealed his identity. And many men refused to take sides until they were forced. Then those who chose to be loyal to the Crown found themselves running for their lives to the Quebec border. Many just couldn't be convinced until the war came to their own doorstep.

His brother-in-law had stayed with Burgoyne's troops. John Kruger had no desire for the dangerous work of recruiting, back among the Rebels. One could never be sure of friend or enemy there. At least in battle you could be sure, he'd said. On his way back, Waltermyer left Curly with the Freemans — a Loyalist family who had a farm two miles west of the Hudson River. He couldn't risk taking the dog home just now.

He had eventually managed to round up thirty-five men. That was not enough to make up the sixty required for a company, but he hoped Ebenezer Jessup would commission him anyway. He and his recruits had been marching several days now, and he thought they were near Burgoyne's forces. The long-awaited battle would take place soon, and he wanted to be a commissioned captain, leading his own men. Just now he had left his men to wait while he scouted the area ahead.

He was almost at the top of the hill when he heard footsteps. He drew back behind a spruce tree to watch and listen. At first he thought they were the steps of Rebel soldiers but as they approached, he saw that the men were wearing red coats with green facings — one of the Loyalist uniforms.

Then, as they came even closer, he recognized one of them. "Thomas," he shouted.

Turning instantly, their weapons cocked and raised, the men stared at Waltermyer as he emerged from behind the spruce.

"He's ours," said young Thomas Sherwood, an ensign in the Queen's Loyal Rangers. The men lowered their muskets.

"Are you all Loyal Rangers?" Waltermyer asked Thomas.

"Yes," Thomas replied.

"Very good! We'll travel with you. I take it you're headed north to join forces with Burgoyne." Not noticing the grim expressions on the men's faces, he continued, "Why are you taking a detour back this way?"

"We're not taking a detour," Thomas said. "We're headed to Canada."

"*Canada*?" Waltermyer could not believe he had heard correctly.

"Burgoyne is going to surrender shortly. He gave us a head start."

"You're going away from the battle?" Waltermyer mumbled in disbelief.

"Burgoyne warned us that the Rebel forces would hang all American Loyalists for treason. He said he wouldn't be able to protect us like his regular soldiers. So he ordered us to leave."

The reality of the defeat was sinking in. But Waltermyer could still not grasp it fully. "How did it happen?"

"Stupidity from start to finish," said a dark-haired, middle-aged man standing just behind Thomas. The lines in his brow were deep. "The British took up their position at Freeman's farm, two miles from the Hudson, in a swampy area. It was a miserably poor position. A force of Rebels was waiting behind Bemis Heights. Then more Rebels poured in from all three sides. They cut us off from the supply lines at Ticonderoga and we couldn't fall back into the Hudson. The British forces came overland and were unprepared to sail back by the Hudson."

Waltermyer nodded sympathetically. He remembered the German force on the road to Skenesborough clumping and clanking along with their long swords at a mile an hour to the beat of thudding drums.

"*Gentleman Johnny*," one of the older men said with contempt, "doesn't know much about fighting the Rebels."

"He's talking about Burgoyne," Thomas explained.

His men call him that. He's kind to them, though. And he's fair to Loyalists too. Right now he's delaying the truce arrangement to give us time to escape. We must move on."

Still not satisfied with their report, Waltermyer asked, "Surely Freeman told the British that his low, marshy farm was a poor place to set up for battle?"

"When they positioned themselves there, Freeman had already fled with his family for the Quebec border. Bemis was just ready to escape too when the Rebels set up on his land. Anyway the British officers wouldn't have listened. They think the Loyalists are untrained country bumpkins who know nothing about warfare."

"Or much else," the older man added. "We're going now. And you'd best return or be hanged."

Thinking of his brother-in-law, Waltermyer asked, "Do you know a man called John Kruger?"

"Yes, he was with Jessup's men, but I didn't see him after the battle began," Thomas told him.

"There'll be more battles. They haven't seen the last of us Loyalists yet," Thomas said as the men left.

Waltermyer nodded. Still stunned by the news, he headed back to his men. How could he tell them to return home after he had brought them all this distance? Some of them lived south of Albany, far down the Hudson River — Caleb Seaman, for one. He'd left his blacksmith shop at Great Nine Partners to join up.

Then Waltermyer thought of his wife's brother. Was he returning home now or was he dead or wounded? If he *was* alive, Waltermyer knew he didn't need to worry much. John was strong and resourceful. And then there was Curly. What might have become of him? Had the Freemans taken the dog north with them? Or was he holed up in a barn somewhere or wounded and lying on the battlefield? He pushed the thought away and hurried between the thick growth of spruce and pine so he could get back to his men as quickly as possible. As prisoners of war, they would be no help to the cause. And perhaps Burgoyne was right. They might be hanged if they were caught. At thirty-three years of age, Waltermyer was older than most of his recruits. He would have to advise his men. Then he decided. Why couldn't they go on to Quebec and join a Loyalist force there? Maybe they could even go back to New York City. The British were in command there too now, and he had heard that a rich Loyalist, Oliver DeLancey, had formed three battalions and was paying his men out of his own pocket. All reports about DeLancey had been good.

He quietly came upon the man who was posted to look out.

"Any news?" Christopher Quin asked.

"Plenty, and not good."

They walked speedily to where the rest of the men were sitting and lying on the ground beside their muskets. "I've news," Waltermyer told them in a loud voice. They all looked up immediately.

"The British have been defeated at Bemis Heights near Saratoga and Burgoyne is preparing to surrender even now. He has ordered all Loyalists to travel to Canada in small groups. He says he cannot protect them under the treaty as he can his soldiers. The Rebels say the Loyalists are guilty of treason."

The men stared at Waltermyer. They had not expected this. They had come with high hopes of joining the battle. Now, after travelling all this distance, they were too late.

Waltermyer saw their disappointment and was quick to speak again, "As I see it, we do have alternatives. We can go out around the Rebel troops through the Adirondacks and then back again and north to Quebec and join forces with the British there. Or we can go south to New York and join one of Oliver DeLancey's battalions." The men would need a few minutes to think. Still he knew they must move soon.

"Do we travel together?" asked sixteen-year-old Henry Shufelt.

"Not all together. I'd say groups of three would be right for safety and to avoid suspicion. We could meet in New York or Quebec."

"I think I'd just like to go back home," the boy replied. With the talk of hanging, the adventure had lost its thrill.

"That's up to you, Hank," Waltermyer said. "You do what you think is best."

Christopher spoke out, "For now, I'm going back too, but I may still join you. It all depends on things back home." He knew his home might be a charred ruin by now.

It wasn't long before a number of others decided to go back and, deeply disappointed, Waltermyer helped them organize themselves into groups for the return trip. Those who lived near each other would travel together.

After they had divided their supplies, Waltermyer spoke briefly, "I'm sorry it didn't turn out as we expected. But remember, men, I'll welcome you into my company at any time. Inquire from Oliver DeLancey in New York. He'll know where I'm stationed."

Waltermyer then grouped them into threes, and they started moving out quietly, one group at a time.

Young Hank lingered behind and said in a half-whisper, "I'll find you, Waltermyer." Waltermyer smiled. Then he turned off the pathway. He travelled best by himself. Taking long, fast strides, he headed north.

Eight

George hurried out his grandma's kitchen door, swinging an empty bucket back and forth on his way to fetch water from the well. It was a balmy September day — almost as warm as summer. The dirt path was hard and warm under his bare feet. The family had been at his grandparents for a year and two months, and there was still no word from Father. Only Grandpa went to Albany now, and the news he brought back was never good. In spite of the reassurances of all the grown-ups, George wondered if trouble could come here to them on the farm. Adults weren't always right.

Today George was helping his grandma with chores. She believed the quotation about cleanliness being next to godliness, and she did not spare those who helped her. He had heard folks say that Grandma's kitchen floor was clean enough to eat off. Not that she would ever hear of such a thing. Every child sat in his own place and hardly spilled a crumb at the table. And she never allowed Boots in the house. A fine, healthy collie now, he still followed George almost everywhere he went. He was running along beside him now, rubbing against George's legs, and finally nearly tripped George as he nipped at his bare feet. George put down his bucket and rubbed the short hair on the dog's forehead. The white spot had kept its star shape as he grew.

"Mary should have called you Star," George said. He thought about Curly and wondered if he had gone with Father. And where was Father? Would he ever return? News of a great battle fought by the Albany Rebel troops last October had spread rapidly around the whole area. For a while, the great victory of Saratoga was all that visitors to the farm ever talked about. Everyone gave the credit to an officer named Benedict Arnold, who had led the men so bravely. It seems he'd had a quarrel with a general just before the battle and wasn't even supposed to lead anyone that day. He had rushed into the battle anyway, all the men had followed him, and they'd won. Of course, General Gates took all the credit for the Rebels' victory, but everyone knew that Arnold was behind it all.

Since then, there had been no more battles nearby, but some produce was required from each family for Schuyler's troops at Albany. The Waltermyer family had all worked very hard on the farm. The children had been kept busy in the fields alongside Grandpa and the few elderly slaves who had not gone to war, and they had also helped their grandma in the house.

George stopped patting Boots and looked back at the house. Good . . . Grandma wasn't looking out the window. He'd been sitting there with Boots longer than he'd meant to — mostly because he didn't really like doing all these house chores anyway. He liked the barn work much better. He set the bucket down beside the well. Maybe he could get Tobias to swap with him. Grandpa, Leonard, and the slaves had gone out to a barn raising at the neighbours, but Tobias was cleaning out the stables.

"Toby," George yelled, pushing the gate in the open doorway. He could hear the scrape of the shovel in the basement stables. He climbed down the ladder, walked along the cool corridor that ran past the rows of cow stalls, and opened a door into the large, square pigpen where Toby was shovelling out a big load of pig manure.

"What are you doing here? Aren't you supposed to be helping in the house?" Tobias sulked. He had wanted to help Grandma bake pies, but he'd been given this manure-shovelling job, which he hated.

"I've got an idea."

"Oh, oh. Last time you had an idea we all got in trouble for shooting that skunk — and *I* fell in the creek. Remember?"

"Well, I thought he was a squirrel — and how was I supposed to know you were going to wade through the creek to get to him? Anyway, I think you're going to like this idea: I'm going to shovel the rest of the pig manure and I'll finish your other chores too if you swap with me and do the house chores. I left a pail beside the well. Grandma needs more water."

Tobias stared at George in disbelief. "You mean it?" he said.

"Sure. I hate house chores. Here, hand me that shovel."

Tobias handed over the shovel and ran out the stable door before George could change his mind. George started cleaning out the pig stall. He couldn't honestly say he loved that job, but he thought he couldn't stand one more hour of his grandma's cleanliness. In fact, it felt good to get dirty — even if he could have done without the smell.

An hour later, he'd finished his work — and there was still some time to loaf in the hayloft before going up to the house for the noon meal.

He climbed up the ladder to the loft on the upper level. A rustling sound was coming from one corner.

"Perhaps it's the new kittens," he thought. He had seen them once, but the mother cat had kept them out of sight ever since. Mary and Catharine had been hunting all over for them.

He stepped lightly along the wide floor boards. The morning sun was glinting up through the knotholes and cracks. He could not hear anything, not even the faintest meow.

"I guess I was hearing things," he said to himself, and flopped down on a big pile of sweet, itchy hay. He was reaching out for a stem to chew on when he heard a rustling movement again, definitely from the far corner of the loft. George inched his way along towards the sound. A huge mound of hay suddenly started to move.

George froze where he stood. "That's no litter of kittens and it's not the mother cat," he thought to himself.

He waited, his heart thumping. Was it Grandpa's new mother pig? No, of course not. She couldn't get up the ladder. Grandpa had said she was acting ugly, but she wouldn't be way up here.

His eyes rivetted on the hay pile, George moved slowly step by step, towards the ladder. The hay did not move again. Still, George continued to creep ahead. With only three steps to go, the huge mound of hay rustled again. This time George heard someone whispering.

George got to the ladder, and nearly flew down, shouting, "Toby! Grandpa! Help!"

"Be quiet, George," someone said from under the hay.

"Father!" George scrambled back up the ladder. There was Father lying on his side, propped up on one elbow, with hay sticking out of his curly red hair — and out of his beard, which George had never seen before. That beard made Father look strange, but beard or no beard, it was Father's grin all right.

George ran and jumped right on him — the way he used to when he was much younger.

"Ouf," said Father. "You're not as light as you used to be. And you're stronger too." George pulled away. He was embarrassed that he'd acted like a small boy — but he had to admit he was happy that his father had noticed how strong he was now.

"Go tell your mother I'm here, George. I can't stay. I'm in danger. And don't tell anyone else, not Grandma or Grandpa or anyone. Go quickly but don't let the others suspect. Can you do that, George?"

"Of course I can, but I'd like to know what's going on with you first."

"Bring your mother and I'll explain to you both. Hurry."

***

George strode into the kitchen and found his grandma and Tobias taking pies out of the oven. "Where's Mother?" George asked.

"She's peeling apples outside the shed." Fortunately, it looked as if Grandma had decided not to say anything about George's job swapping right now.

George rushed out through the kitchen door and detoured around by the shed. He was about to beckon to his mother when he heard wheels grinding along the dirt path that led in from the road. In a few minutes, Mrs. Sager came into view, riding in a cart. She was the mother of the Mr. Sager who had been their neighbour to the south back on their farm, and she was also a friend of Grandma.

"Good day, Polly. Isn't this a right fine September day?" said Mrs. Sager, squeezing herself out of her cart and slowly reaching the ground.

"Yes, Mrs. Sager, it is," Polly answered from the doorway.

George stumbled into the shed to get a stump of wood. He brought it outside and sat on it, to make it look as if he'd come to help Mother peel apples.

"Well, I've come to fetch Addie to the barn-raisin'. We used to visit a lot before this past year. Seems like she's too busy now to see anyone, poor soul. Hard for a woman her age to have all these young-uns about."

"We all do our part, Lottie."

"Seems to me seven young-uns need more help than give it. Anyhow, that's Addie and Hans's business. Shame though that young Hans isn't man enough to come back for his family at least . . . even if he *is* too chicken to fight for the cause."

Polly refused to rise to the bait. "I fear Hans may have no choice."

"Seems to me Hans could've got word through somehow if there's nothin' to hide. There are rumours he may be workin' for the British. You know the sayin' 'Where there's smoke there's fire.'"

"You know that isn't . . ."

George sat very still as Mrs. Sager interrupted his mother again. He picked a piece of bark off the stump of wood and started to break it into smaller pieces.

"When you're raisin' 'em, you never know how they'll turn out," Mrs. Sager went on. "I was just sayin' to my other half, just yesterday, I was sayin', 'Now, look at those Waltermyer boys. There's Jacob, a fine lad, off to defend his land and home, but the older one, Hans, just went off, heaven knows where . . . and left a wife and seven young-uns!' Now, I must say we've been specially blessed with our family. We're proud of every one of them. All loyal to the cause, they are.

"Now, how is Addie bearin' up, poor dear?"

"She's in the main house and looking for you to come. She's baked a pile of fresh pies and tarts for the barn raising. Been up since dawn."

"Really! Well, I'll be gettin' myself right up there." At her greatest speed, puffing breathlessly, Lottie lumbered on up to the back door. Her slave, Joel, a large man with greying curly hair and a noticeable limp, had taken her cart and horses back to the hitching-post in the laneway, and stood waiting.

George watched his mother return to her pan of apples. Her cheeks flushed, she started peeling them rapidly. She had forgotten George was there. George leaned towards her and whispered, "Father's in the barn, in the hayloft."

Mother looked startled and then put a finger to her lips. "We must continue with the apples for now," she said, recovering herself, but George knew Mother was excited and a bit scared.

They heard Mrs. Sager's loud voice again, and it was coming closer. "Land sake's, you've got enough to feed an army, Addie. I'll send Joel back up for the rest. We'll just catch our breath in the wagon while he brings them. These sure are tasty tarts, Addie. I've missed them this summer and our visits together. We'll just wait for Joel in the wagon and catch up on things. I always say a body should rest oneself when one can, there bein' so much work to do always."

Five long minutes passed before Joel got all the baking packed into the cart and the horses began moving back down the lane, with Grandma and Mrs. Sager in behind. George and his mother watched the cart turn into the road and then hurried to the barn. George barely had time to say, "Father doesn't want anyone else to know he's here."

Father was lying in the hay where George had left him. Mother ran to embrace him. Father held her close. "Hans," Mother said, with tears rolling down her cheeks.

After a moment, Mother spoke again, "The men could come back at any time. You must hide in the woods until night. When the others are sleeping, I will go to the stream . . . our special place." Then Mother took two large apples out of her pockets and pressed them into her husband's hands.

Father hesitated. "Polly, you must tell me. What has happened?"

"We were put off the farm. The unsigned lease, they told us. They suspect that you are helping the British but have no proof. If they had proof, we would all be in jail by now. I told them I feared that the British had seized you in New York."

"Good, Polly, you handled it well. I knew my father would protect you all. I'll see you tonight." Father brushed the straw off his face and hair and clothes and headed down the ladder. "And George," he hesitated, as he turned to face his son's searching eyes.

"Father, I must know. What are you planning to do?" George asked.

"There isn't time now, George. Your mother will give you the details later. We'll all be together soon. I have a plan." He turned and slipped silently down the ladder and walked out the cow-stable door.

Mother stood staring down at the spot where Father had hidden in the hay. Above her, a spider slowly descended on its fine cord from the low roof beams. It seemed like minutes before she turned slowly around, ruffled the hay back into place, and said, "George, do not say one word of this to anyone. You must remember. Father's not safe here."

Nine

George pitched a huge forkful of hay from the main loft to the landing below. He could hear Tobias and Leonard talking to Grandpa just outside as they cleaned and repaired the farm implements for winter storage. George was beginning to regret his bargain with Tobias now that he'd been cleaning out the stable every morning for half a month. But it wouldn't be long now. Mother had gone to Albany today to apply for a pass for the family to travel to New York City. That was what Father had asked her to do when he met her by the stream that night two weeks ago. He was going to New York City, and if the family could get a pass, they would all be together there.

George sighed and said to himself, "Does Father really know how dangerous it is for Mother to appear before that Board of important men in Albany?" Realizing that he'd said the words out loud, he looked around quickly, hoping Grandpa had not heard him. Father's visit was still a secret between him and Mother.

One thing George still didn't know for certain was whether Father was working for the British — but he had to be. Otherwise, why would they have to keep Father's visit secret from Grandpa? He remembered those people in Albany yelling at the man caught in the frame, "Traitor! Skunk! Tory! Pig!" Was that what his father was?

Who were the real traitors? And which side was God on? Grandpa thought He was on the Rebels' side, and Mother thought He was on Father's side, but if Father was on the British side, then how could God be on both sides? It was mighty confusing.

Does Father know the danger he is putting us in? George thought silently this time, but with some irritation. He remembered that the men on the Board were the same ones who had visited Mr. Bleecker. No one knew what had happened to John and Lucy and Mrs. Bleecker. Folks said they packed up and left town the very next day after Mr. Bleecker's funeral. It almost seemed as if they'd disappeared. Now what would happen to Mother when she faced these same men? Maybe he wouldn't see her again either.

George climbed down the ladder to the cow stable below, pitched the hay from the lower mow into the mangers, and then walked outside. It was a brisk, sunny morning. He circled around behind the barn and took a route to the front laneway without going past his grandpa and brothers. He hoped Grandpa would think he was still doing chores in the barn. He felt too restless to work just now.

Reaching the end of the laneway, he sat down by the main road and leaned against the trunk of the apple tree that had been growing there as long as he could remember. All of a sudden, a sob seemed to go right through him, and he knew his shoulders were shaking. He gritted his teeth and tried to stop shaking. He couldn't cry like this. He was the oldest in the family — and he was still in charge, even if they were living at Grandpa's. He jumped up and turned around to make sure no one had seen him.

Only Boots stood there wagging his tail. George sat down again while the dog came over and pressed his body against George's leg. George gave Boots a big hug. That seemed to stop the shaking. Boots' soft thick coat of white and red-gold hair felt good against his bare arms. After a while George realized he'd have to go back and face the others. It would be many hours before Mother returned, and there was no sense waiting at the end of the road most of the day. George got up slowly and circled back to the barn the way he'd come. He hoped no one had missed him.

*****

George was the first to see the team trotting over the knoll and up the driveway. Even before Grandpa's slave, Levi, had reined in the horses, George ran out to meet them. He took Mother's hand to help her climb down from the buggy seat. She looked pale and sad.

"Is that our pass, Mother?" George asked anxiously as he looked at a scroll in her hand.

"Yes, George."

"Why are you sad, Mother? We're allowed to go now!"

Mother did not answer but put her arm on George's shoulder and leaned on him a little as she walked to the house. She dropped her shawl on the hall bench and walked straight through to the kitchen, where she collapsed into a chair beside the fireplace.

"I'll have a cup of tea right ready for you, Polly," Grandma said, bustling around the kitchen. Catharine, Mary, and Anna burst through the kitchen door.

"What happened, Mother? May we go?"

"Yes, yes, I'll tell you everything. But where's Jacob?"

"He's still sleeping," Catharine answered impatiently.

No Rebel would want to see Grandma making tea. British tea had been outlawed in the colonies some time ago. In fact, no tea was sold in stores anymore because it came from Britain, and people had all been told to throw their tea away. But Grandma and Mother never threw anything away if they could help it. So Grandma still had some left.

The colour seemed to come back to Mother's face as she sipped from the cup Grandma gave her.

"Tell us about it, Mother," George said anxiously.

"Well, I didn't know what to expect. I wondered what they would ask me, and how I could answer them. I was afraid I would say the wrong thing, and they would keep me there."

George remembered John and his father.

"When I was going into the town hall, I was barely up the steps and inside when the smell hit me. I could hear noise and moaning and I supposed it came from the prisoners in the basement below. I showed my letter to the soldier at the door, and he checked the appointment date, October 1, 1778. He read the letter through carefully and led me to another door. He told me to stay right there and he'd be back. Then he went into another room, but thank goodness, he came back almost right away. He asked me to follow him, and we went to the first door and into a large room. There was a long table in the centre, with a number of men sitting around it. They were smoking their pipes steadily, and the air was so dense I almost coughed. But at least the smoke killed the stench from below.

"The men looked me over while I stood there and waited. Finally, Mr. Stringer at the end of the table said

'We, The Board of Commissioners for Detecting and Defeating Conspiracies, wish to ask you, Mrs. Hans Waltermyer, about your husband's whereabouts. Have you had any communication with your husband since he left in June of '77?'

"'No,' I said. Then they asked me where he had gone. I told the man that he'd left to buy a horse and other necessary supplies and that I was afraid he had travelled on to New York to get them and was being held against his will behind the British lines. Then they asked how we could know that he wasn't *working for the British* behind those lines. I told them that he had no military training and was not used to city life. What could he do for them in New York?

"Then the man said, 'Well, what's your point? We aren't about to send out an expedition to rescue him.' All the men laughed uproariously at that and blew all the more smoke into the air. I just looked at them and said, 'I would like a pass for myself and my seven children to travel to New York City to find my husband.' Then they asked if our 'present accommodations' were not satisfactory, and I told them that Grandpa had welcomed us into his home and that he was a supporter of the Rebel cause, with a son already fighting in the Rebel army. My questioner did not seem impressed, so I just told him it was too much for an elderly couple to have seven children around all the time. 'Besides,' I said, 'the children are young and they miss their father. I must go to New York City to find my husband.'

"There was a big, long silence — all you could hear was the clock ticking on the mantlepiece and Mr. Stringer shuffling some papers. Finally the man on the far left whispered, 'Why not?' into the ear of my questioner.

'They may become an expense on the public purse if they stay here.' He needn't have whispered — I could hear every word he was saying. I was afraid of getting my hopes up, but finally Mr. Stringer nodded, then looked up at me and told me to retire to the hall while they made their decision."

"What did they say, Mother?" asked George, though he already knew his mother had the pass.

"They gave me a pass to take passage on a sloop down the Hudson River to New York City. They said that I could take my personal belongings and all my children . . . all my children except for you, George. I-I don't know why. They said you had to stay to help your grandpa on the farm."

George looked back at his mother in stunned silence.

Finally, Mother broke down and sobbed into her hands, "How can I leave you behind, George? How can I leave you?"

Ten

George sat glumly in the back of the wagon. He and his grandparents were leaving Cooeyman's Landing on the Hudson and heading back to the farm. Three days had passed since his mother had returned from Albany with the pass, and George had just said goodbye to his mother, sisters, and brothers. *They* were on their way to New York City in Captain Schoonhoven's sloop, but *he* was going back to be cooped up on the farm. It was cold sitting on top of the wagon. After all, it was October and the sun had been up only a few hours.

This whole war was spoiling his life. Here was a chance in a lifetime — a chance to go to New York City where important things were happening — and where did he end up? Stuck on the farm with the neatest, cleanest grandma in the world and a grandpa who was all right, he guessed, but it wasn't as if he was his father. Father used to take him hunting and show him how to handle a musket and all the farm tools. He also trained him to care for all the farm animals. And Father had promised him the pick of the colts this summer for his very own. His grandpa hardly talked to him and never did anything you could call fun. All he and Grandpa ever did together was work, and Grandpa didn't really need him, since he still had a few slaves to help. Well, maybe Grandpa had done some nice things — like giving Curly to the family — but that was before the war. Now everything was strictly business.

George hugged Boots close as they turned into the laneway to the house — the same old house.

"You help your grandma, George," his grandpa ordered as they stepped down from the wagon.

George's blue checked shirt was pulling out of his trousers. His grandma had often told him that he looked very much like his father at his age. Well, he bet Father didn't have to help in the house. Anyone should know that a boy who was thirteen would be much more useful in the barn or out in the fields. He trailed into the kitchen behind his grandma.

"Help yourself to the fritters in that crock, George," she said as she stepped into the sunny room. At least it felt good to be warm, but that was the only good thing about the day.

"Oh, no thank you," George replied, almost forgetting that Grandma had spoken to him. "I'm not hungry."

"Well, that's hard to believe, George. Here, I'll cut you a piece of apple pie. I baked fresh pies early this morning and I saved this one for you."

George had to admit that he was starting to feel a bit hungry. "Well, all right, I reckon I'll have a piece," he said, sitting down at the table where Grandma was dishing out the pie. Before long, he was gulping it down in huge mouthfuls.

"Do I really look like my father?" he asked abruptly, with his mouth full.

"You certainly do, George." His grandma ignored the bad manners for once.

"But he's tall and big and I'm not. All my friends are taller than I am, and even Toby is just as tall as me."

"Some boys grow faster than others, that's all," Grandma replied. "Why, I've seen boys your age jump in height every year for the next seven years."

"Really?"

"Oh, yes. It's different with girls. They reach their height at a much younger age. Don't worry, you're not going to be short. You'll grow up to be tall and big like your father."

"It doesn't really matter. Just thought I'd ask."

"Of course. You know, too, your father used to like to read and write after he finished school. He sure used to practise his handwriting. He could write very neatly."

Sounds like something Grandma would like — neat handwriting, George said to himself.

George finished eating, then stared at the pie left in the dish.

"Do you want some more pie, George?" Grandma asked with a little smile. She cut him another generous-sized piece. George continued to eat without talking. Maybe Grandma wasn't so bad after all. He guessed you'd have to be neat if you were baking pies like this all the time.

"How far down the Hudson do you think they've got, Grandma?" George asked. He wiped his mouth on his sleeve, got up, and walked over to the window. Jacob's little wagon was sitting empty on the pathway.

"Oh, not far, dear," Grandma answered. George thought she sounded tired. "They have a long way to go . . . Now isn't that Boots whining at the door? Maybe you could see to him. I don't really need you right now. After you've seen to the dog, you could ask your grandpa if he needs any help."

George trudged out through the kitchen door. Boots

jumped up at him before he'd even got off the stoop and nearly knocked him down. He was a full-grown collie now, not heavy, but strong and sinewy. The cows never lingered when Boots chased them.

"You silly dog. What do you want?" Boots jumped up and tried to lick George's face. "Hey . . . you haven't done that since you were a pup . . . I guess you miss them too. Here, why don't you come and help me and Grandpa with the chores?"

Grandpa was standing by the well in the barnyard. There was a pail of milk beside him, cooling in a bucket of water. "Here, take this fresh milk up to your grandma," he said gruffly before George had time to say a word. He lifted the pail out of the bucket and wiped very carefully around the outsides and bottom. The iron hoops on Grandma's buckets were always scoured bright.

George wasn't too happy about going back to the house again. At least in the barn you didn't notice how empty and still everything was. He grabbed the pail from Grandpa faster than he should have, whipped around, and started up the hill. Then Boots came bounding over and ran straight into his legs. George fell headlong onto the stony ground, but he somehow managed to hold the pail up so the milk didn't spill.

George sat up and pushed Boots away from the milk. His elbow was sore where it had hit a stone.

"What happened there?" he could hear his grandpa yelling from the other side of the well. "Did you spill that fresh milk?"

George felt like crying from the pain in his elbow. How could Grandpa be asking about the milk? Didn't he care about him? Well, he'd show Grandpa he didn't care about the dumb old milk. He got up and kicked the pail as hard as he could. A white puddle foamed out over the grassy slope around the well.

"I did now," he yelled and ran for the corn field. Boots took a few licks and then galloped after his master.

George raced through the field between the rows of dried-out cornstalks. They were soon going to be cut down, chopped up, and turned back into the soil, but for the moment they made an excellent hideout. Once he was out of sight of the house and barn, he looked around and saw that no one was following him but Boots.

"You stupid dog," George said. "It's all your fault." Boots whined and blinked at George with sorry eyes.

George didn't know what he felt like anymore. He'd lost his family, he was in trouble with Grandpa, and he was getting angry at his dog. He stopped at the end of the rows of corn and stared around at the stretch of grass where they'd had their farewell party the day before. Mother had packed chunks of cheese in a basket, along with Grandma's fresh bread and fruit cake. Just he and Mother with his brothers and sisters had come out here for supper. Now he was here alone. Perhaps they'd all be grown up before he saw them again.

He thought back to his twelfth birthday, his last birthday at home over a year ago. Things had gone wrong ever since Father had left, and the meeting in the barn had been all too brief. In spite of their differences, he longed to see Father now . . . to have a real talk about everything.

If only he were with his brothers and sisters! It had been bad enough here on the farm all the time when Mother, Toby, Leonard, and the girls were here, too. Now, it seemed unbearable.

He picked a piece of ribbon grass and tore it into shreds. He took another one and made a squeaking sound with it, against his teeth. Boots was sitting a few feet away with his head down on his front paws, but George didn't notice him.

"If only I were with them," he said out loud. Why couldn't he go with them anyway? He thought about the trip on the boat. He knew Tobias and Mary and Leonard would love that trip. They'd be up on deck with the captain all the time if he'd let them. They'd be leaning over the railing and watching the gentle, foaming waves washing against the sloop. Maybe they'd spot soldiers in the woods on the far shore. Maybe they'd forget all about him stuck on the farm. They might *never* come back. That would be terrible. He'd probably end up working for Grandpa until he was as old as Father. He shook his shoulders in disgust. Then he brightened. There was one simple solution to this whole problem. He'd have to run away and catch up with the sloop before it got too far.

But would he have the courage to do it? If Grandpa caught him, he would get a tanning to remember. And what if the soldiers from Albany came out to find him? He couldn't even imagine what they might do.

He would have to be very careful that no one knew his plans, but if he was going to go, it would have to be soon. He would need to catch up to the sloop and his family before they reached New York City, where they'd be next to impossible to find.

George leapt to his feet and started thinking about what he should take with him. He was even getting a bit excited. Then he remembered the milk pail. He'd have to go back to the barnyard and face his punishment. Then he would quietly start sneaking food and other supplies and stashing them away. He'd need to go equipped.

Grandpa was leaning over the well, pulling up the

bucket. George, just behind him, stood there until he set the pail down and looked up.

"Grandpa, I . . . ," George began and then stopped and stared at his grandpa, who was now lowering another bucket into the well.

"Yes, George," Grandpa said. He looked at George and waited.

George felt encouraged. Grandpa did not sound as angry as he had thought he would. "I'm sorry," he said directly.

"That's all right, George. It's not a good day for any of us." Grandpa continued to lower the empty bucket down into the well. George heard the splash when it hit the bottom. Then Grandpa turned the axle and started pulling up the full bucket.

George stared at the second pail of water, which was now at the top of the well. As Grandpa pulled this bucket off the hook and lifted it over the low stone wall around the well, he said sadly, "It's not so long ago another red-headed boy used to live here. I mind the temper he used to have. But like you, he used to come right back. I knew you'd be back soon."

George thought about his plans and swallowed. Then he asked, "Father . . . are you talking about Father?"

Grandpa smiled kindly now at George. "Yes, my boy, you're a lot like your father."

George couldn't agree that he was much like his father in either actions or looks, except for the red hair, of course. But he had no intention of arguing with Grandpa now.

"I'll take the water up to the house," George offered.

"That's a good idea. Here, take these two buckets. I'll do the rest."

The kitchen was empty when he got there. Grandma was probably upstairs doing the cleaning and making the beds — as she did every morning except Sunday. She'd be packing away the quilts that the family had been using.

It was then that George decided to go through with his plans for sure. There wasn't a moment to lose. He grabbed the big knife by the bread board and cut off a thick slab of bread, hoping Grandma wouldn't notice how much smaller the loaf was now. Then he opened the door of the cupboard beside the baking table and looked around inside. He yanked out a chunk of cheese and cut off a big piece.

"I knew your appetite would come back soon," Grandma said behind him. He hadn't heard her come in.

"Any more of that pie?" he asked, turning around and smiling broadly, but feeling a bit guilty about deceiving his grandma.

"Why yes, George," she said, turning to the cupboard to get it. She cut off a big piece and handed it to him on a plate.

George took it, thanked her, and headed for the door, hoping she wouldn't notice how much bread and cheese he had.

George ran along the longer route south to the barn to avoid Grandpa, who was carrying water to the chicken coop, west of the barn. Boots, who had been waiting outside, saw him eating the pie and was close at his heels. George knew he would need to find a good hiding place where Boots couldn't get his stored food. He walked into the cow stable, closing the door tightly behind him. Then he climbed up the ladder to the hayloft above and hurried into the granary beside the loft. It was a small room about fifteen feet long with a narrow aisle in the middle, and tall bins full of grain on either side. He packed his bread and cheese in an empty grain sack that was lying around. Then standing on a barrel to reach into one of the bins, he dug a deep hole in the pile of grain and buried the food.

He was back down in the cow stable when he heard Grandpa close the chicken coop door just outside. He grabbed a pitchfork and started to pitch hay into the mangers.

"I'm going on up to the house," Grandpa shouted, opening the door to the stable. "You'd better come too. It's nearly dinnertime."

George just kept pitching hay and thinking. He decided he'd slip away that very night after his grandparents were asleep. He felt sure now that Grandpa wouldn't send the soldiers to track him.

Ideas just kept coming to him. He'd leave a note dated ahead five days. That way Grandpa could take it to Albany when he did his Saturday shopping, and it would be too late for the trackers to catch him. And his grandparents wouldn't be in any trouble either with the Board of Commissioners in Albany. He hoped Grandpa would understand about the date.

He marched along briskly as he headed for the house, with Boots racing along beside him. He wondered how many days it would take him to catch up with the family.

Eleven

George placed the note on the kitchen table.

October 10

Dear Grandma and Grandpa
　I have gone to New York to be with my brothers
and sisters and Mother
　　I am very lonely without them
　　　I took some food. I hope you don't mind.
　　　Thank you for everything

Love
George

He opened the cupboard slowly, hoping it wouldn't creak, and reached for a loaf of bread and some fruitcake. There was some leftover pork roast, which he grabbed too. He carried his food in one arm and his load of clothes over the other shoulder. He'd only taken a couple of shirts, an extra pair of trousers, his winter boots, and a thick wool coat. His mother had left him a bit of money in case of emergency, and he was taking that too. If this wasn't an emergency, he didn't know what was. He headed for the granary to pick up the rest of his food.

George hated to leave his musket behind, but he felt

he had to. In his worn pants and too-small coat, he'd be taken for an orphan boy or a runaway. In either case, there would be no danger. But if he carried a musket, the farmers might suspect he was an enemy. Soldiers might even shoot him. But he did slide his utility knife for hunting into his pocket, along with his flint and steel and a few fish hooks and line.

When George left the granary, he walked briskly down the dark laneway to the road. Looking down, he saw Boots at his feet. He bent over and whispered to him in as nasty a voice as he could, "Go back, Boots. I don't have time and food for you. You stay!" He pointed to the house and shook his head. The poor dog understood and slunk towards the house in bewilderment, his tail between his legs.

George continued quickly along the land he knew so well. His mind raced ahead with plans. He would cross over to the east side of the Hudson River sometime the next day. If he travelled all night, he'd be well past Cooeyman's Landing by daylight — and out of the territory where he'd likely be seen by folks who knew him. By about the next night, he'd make it to Athens, where he'd cross over on the ferry to the town of Hudson. Then he'd keep going south along the east bank of the Hudson from there. He didn't think he'd travel right on the East Road that ran by the river, but he'd keep it in sight. That way he wouldn't get lost.

He might even make it to the Athens Ferry by late afternoon. He'd heard from his grandfather, who talked with soldiers when he delivered food supplies, that the Rebel forces had moved in farther south and built new forts on the west side. He must not risk going that way because they would ask too many questions and might even send him back.

Before reaching New York City, he would stay back from the river and cut across Westchester County through farmland. He knew if he travelled steadily, he'd reach New York before the sloop. It would stay at anchor every night and take at least ten days to make the trip. George felt he could get to the New York docks in about six days. He was a day late starting, but with three days of leeway, there was little risk of arriving there too late.

He walked along quickly, making scarcely a sound — the way he did when he used to hunt with his father. And he wasn't really afraid to travel in the dark, at least not in this area, which he knew so well. He would soon pass the home where he had lived his whole life until that day, over a year ago, when the Rebels had barged into their kitchen in the middle of his twelfth birthday party. He was tempted to stop for a moment as he passed by the trail across the end of the orchard, but he did not.

George had been travelling in the darkness for about two hours when he heard the low beat of horse hooves and the creak of wagon wheels along the road he was following. He hid behind a clump of dogwood and watched as a wagonload of men came closer, and finally passed him. They all rode silently, rifles in hand. Their expressions chilled him, for he suspected their business was grim. Were they looking for him? He thought not. Those men had more important business to attend to. Still, he shivered as he waited to see if another wagon would follow.

It was very dark now. Only a sliver of moon rode through the sky. Then he heard another noise behind him.

He turned quickly and looked up into the burning eyes of a hooting owl.

He must get out of this territory where he was known. The morning light would come sooner than he thought, and many farmers would be up and about at sunrise. He edged out from behind the dogwood and walked on down the road. The night seemed to be getting darker. He had no idea what time it was. Perhaps he should not have left after all. At least he would have been safe on the farm. But now that he *had* left, the thought of turning back was more frightening than going on.

No sooner had he come to this conclusion than he heard steps behind him, very close in the darkness. When he stopped, they stopped. When he went ahead, they started again. Someone was tracking him. But the footsteps were not heavy — in fact, they were almost impossible to hear. It must be someone accustomed to the woods or maybe it was a small wild animal — a fox, for instance. But whatever or whoever it was, he did not like the idea that he was being followed. He stopped again. Maybe he was just hearing things. An eerie silence followed. His legs tingled with fear.

"This is ridiculous," he said to himself. "Why don't I just turn around and see what it is." But somehow he couldn't bring himself to do that. His neck wouldn't move.

Just at the point where George thought he would burst, his pursuer raced towards him. It was an animal all right. It was Boots.

"Boots! What are you doing here?" he said in a low voice. "Boy, am I glad it's you!" Boots jumped up and licked his face. George gave the dog a bear hug.

"Well, it looks as if you're coming with me now. At least I won't be all alone . . . "

The dog and the boy walked on, passing along between the shadows of the night.

Twelve

Waltermyer saw a flickering light in a back window. His rifle ready, he crept over the fallen leaves towards the farmhouse and crouched behind a thick, green spruce. He stared through the crisp night air, waiting to make his move. Was that a black band painted around the chimney pot — a sign that the owner would give refuge to a Loyalist? It was already too dark to tell.

It was October 5, 1778, almost a year and a half since Waltermyer had left his home in the middle of the night with Kruger. A figure moved between the light and the window. It was a man. Then another, smaller one passed by. Did he dare approach?

He had checked the barn and surrounding yard. There were no signs of visitors. Still, he was wary of a trap, for he was carrying a message from General Frederick Haldimand, the Governor General of Canada, who had arrived in Quebec the previous June, to Sir Henry Clinton, the British General in command of New York City. He knew the Rebels would hang him if they caught him. So he waited.

Finally, he approached the door and tapped lightly.

"What do you want?" a low voice said through the door opened only a crack.

"Hudibras sent me," he replied.

"Your name?"

"Hans."

The door opened. "Come in, come in," a small man whispered impatiently. "In the name of Hudibras, what is your full name?"

"Hans Waltermyer," he said as he stepped into the large farm kitchen.

"You can't stay here," the man said. He shifted uneasily even as he spoke. "The authorities have been here once for you tonight. They'll be back." He was slipping on a jacket and reaching for his rifle when they heard the sound of horses' hooves in the yard.

The small man looked then at the younger one and said, "We'll go out the side way. Keep them a while. Act uneasy. They'll ask to search the house. Be defensive and they'll insist. That'll delay them till we get a head start." He turned to Waltermyer and ordered, "Follow me."

Waltermyer followed the man to an inside door behind the kitchen pantry. It led not to the outside but to a dug-out cellar under the house. As he stumbled down the stairs in the dark, he wondered if he was being led into a trap. Still, this was one of the houses in Hudibras' network of Loyalist homes. He had no choice but to follow.

In the jet darkness, the man led him through the main dug-out area and across a second room. Then the man stopped and wrenched open a door. "There are steps here that lead up to the outside," he said in a low whisper.

They crept up quietly until their heads brushed against something. The man pushed it up only an inch. It was the trap door over the outside entrance to the cellar. They looked out onto the dooryard. A small clearing stood washed in the moonlight, edged with shadows from the orchard.

"You go first and if you make it, I'll follow and lead you to a hiding place," the man said.

Waltermyer hesitated again. What if the man shot him in the back? Hudibras would think the Rebels shot him. The man did not seem friendly. But who would be, in these circumstances?

He hesitated no longer. From the top step he ran across the yard and rushed into the grove of apple trees, not the best for cover but better than nothing. He waited. Several lights were flickering throughout the house. He saw shadows passing by windows. Then he saw the small man coming towards him.

The man raced past Waltermyer and beckoned him to follow. Waltermyer was relieved when they cleared the apple orchard and entered a woods thick with spruce, pine, and balsam. The heavy undergrowth made their travelling slower but the cover was better.

"That was close," he said. "To whom do I owe thanks?" He had been directed to the farm but had not been told the name of anyone there.

"It is better that you not know," the man replied.

He followed the man without talking. The moon's light did not penetrate deeply into the woods, but the man knew his way and he held back branches for Waltermyer as he pushed ahead through the underbrush.

After about twenty minutes, they came to a large rock covered with moss. The man began clearing the growth from around the stone. Waltermyer pushed forward to help him. They pulled the stone back, and another of equal size after that. A small cave was behind the stones.

"You'll be safe here," he said as he motioned Waltermyer into the cave. I'll push the stones back after you're inside.

"Wait!" Waltermyer exclaimed.

"Surely you trust me after the way I just helped you."

"I trust you. But I don't trust the bears starting to hole up for the winter."

Waltermyer heard a low chuckle as he proceeded to check out the small cave. "All clear," he said. "Before you go, we need a plan. I can't understand why the Rebels were so close on my trail."

"Peter Sager reported you this afternoon in Albany to the Board of Commissioners, for transporting messages for the British."

"Whatever would make him think that. I *have* been recruiting for Jessup, but now it's impossible to get enough recruits across Rebel territory to Quebec. Jessup suggested I get men for Oliver DeLancey in New York City. Jessup's been fed up with the British ever since Burgoyne's defeat a year ago. He says they won't listen to the Loyalists, and their strategy for winning wars in Europe will not work here."

The man was watching Waltermyer intently as he talked. "So now I'm headed to New York to talk to Delancey."

"Yes, and I'd like to keep you moving," the man said glumly. "Remember, the Commissioners have got men searching the countryside for you around Albany now."

"Have you heard anything about my wife and children?"

"They left yesterday for New York. It's doubtful the officials will waste their time bringing them back. Anyhow, they got a good head start. You'd best hide here till the search blows over."

"No. I want to push on now."

"How?"

"Maybe by canoe . . . "

"Are you crazy? You'd be obvious in a canoe."

"I could hide in the bottom under a canvas and you could paddle me by in the daylight. No one would search a boat passing in broad daylight."

The man thought for a moment, then replied, "You may be right. But my punt would be better. It's true that it wouldn't be safe to bring you food here for very long either."

"I'd like to leave by dawn. We should be passing Albany before noon, and we'll be a good distance beyond there by nightfall. I'd take to the woods then on the east side of the Hudson."

"The river is a mile away. I'll go now and fetch my punt and a few supplies for you. We'll be on the Hudson by sun-up." The man hurried out of the cave, and Waltermyer watched as the stone was rolled loosely back into place.

Waltermyer shivered in the damp cave. The nights were becoming colder now. He crouched with his arms wrapped around himself for warmth. Unable to sleep, he thought again of the message that he carried from General Haldimand. After he had told Jessup he was headed to New York, Haldimand had sent for him and insisted that he take the message to Clinton. There really wasn't much choice. The British were fresh out of couriers. So far they had all been caught and hanged by the Rebels. One courier, Daniel Taylor, was taking a message to Burgoyne from Clinton when he was caught by the Rebel troops. He swallowed the information — it had been hidden in a hollow silver musket ball — but with the help of the army doctor he was forced to vomit it up and when they unscrewed the ball and found the secret message, he was hanged. Waltermyer's hand fell lightly on his dispatch, which he was carrying in a pocket under his clothing. He'd throw the evidence away before he'd swallow it.

Waltermyer had asked Haldimand to tell no one that he carried a dispatch, and Haldimand, a professional Swiss soldier, who had been in a great many wars, agreed. Surely Sager's accusation was just a guess. He was probably trying to win popularity with the local officials.

Then Father thought of Polly and his children. So they were finally on their way to New York — as he had advised Polly a month ago when he visited the farm. He leaned against the damp wall. His exhaustion was overpowering his discomfort from the cold. Before long, he drifted off to sleep.

***

It was about noon. A light rain was falling on the water of the Hudson as a small man in a homespun jacket and a three-cornered hat manned the oars of his flat-bottomed punt. In front of the man, a canvas moved only a little in the October breeze. It was anchored securely by a few bags of grain — a farmer's produce going down the Hudson.

The man looked up as he rowed past the Albany wharves, but he did not alter his steady pace. It was obvious he was not docking there. With unmoving lips, he muttered, "Indian captives, women and children too."

The canvas moved a little. Waltermyer peered out at the shore. He sickened at the sight of men in irons, and women and children without proper clothing or any shelter standing in the cold October rain.

"Put down that canvas," said the man through clenched teeth. "It's my neck too, you know, if we're caught."

Waltermyer lowered the canvas but mumbled, "I must know which tribe. Ask the guard."

"Lie still then," the man replied and without changing direction, he started to steer a little closer to shore.

When the punt was only a couple of hundred feet from the prisoners, the man shouted out, "Where'd you capture those pests?"

The guard smiled. Then he answered directly, "They're Onondagas. We got the chief too."

"Good work," the man replied and returned to his task.

The Onondagas are neutral, Waltermyer thought, and the Mohawks, the Seneca, and the Cayugas are fighting for the British. The Rebels already have the help of the Oneidas and the Tuscaroras. Why can't they leave the Onondagas alone?

Waltermyer remembered his own vain wish to remain neutral. Even sheltered by the canvas, he felt the rain pelting against him and shook with the cold. How must the captives feel with no protection? Then he thought of Polly and the children. In what condition had they left his father's? Had they been allowed to take enough food and clothing? He knew that both were scarce in the besieged City of New York.

He wished the punt would go faster. At nightfall, he would take to the woods behind the road on the east side of the river and cut across country. He might even arrive in New York in time to meet his family. But he knew he must deliver his letter to Clinton first. This would be his first and last trip as a courier — and he'd tell Clinton so when he delivered this message. He would settle his family in, then talk to DeLancey about recruiting men for his company of Loyalists. Somebody had to stop these Rebels and if the British wouldn't, the Loyalists must!

Thirteen

George arrived at the outskirts of Athens exhausted. The bare trees along the river had been no protection from the cold, raw wind or the steady rain. George's clothes were soaked through to his skin, and water was dripping from his nose and chin. Boots was slinking along now with his bedraggled coat of hair clinging to him. When they came over a rise in the road, the small landing dock was only about three hundred feet ahead. Two empty wagons were driving away and the ferry was preparing to leave. George and Boots broke into a run.

"How much to cross?" he shouted.

"Come on, boy," the man at the ferry shouted to him, and he ran onto the ferry just in time.

He sat down on his sack of clothes with his bag of food over his shoulder. Boots sat beside him. Both were puffing heavily.

"Been travellin' a long way?" the same man asked.

"Yes, quite a distance."

"Where's home?"

"Up north of Albany."

"You come from the Saratoga area?"

"Yes, not far from there."

"You're a farm lad?"

"Yes."

"Your farm touched by the battle up there, last fall?"

"No, we are north of the Saratoga battlefield."

"Where are you headed now?"

"Going south to visit my grandpa at Poughkeepsie," George answered without hesitation. He had prepared himself for questions like this.

"At Poughkeepsie, eh? Well, just follow this road on the east side of the river. It'll take you straight to Poughkeepsie. The road on the east side is better than the one on the west. More folks travel on it. You were wise to cross over. You'll probably catch a ride with a farmer along there. Don't know about the dog, though. Why'd you bring the dog? Didn't they need him at home?"

"He's not my dog. He just started following me. I kinda let him tag along for company."

"I see. Say, instead of payin' for the crossin', you could help me unload these bags at the other side."

"Sure, I'd be right glad to."

"I'll call when I need you." The man threw George a large canvas.

George was relieved, for he didn't want to use up his little bit of money if he didn't need to. He pulled the canvas over himself and Boots. The dog was as wet as a sponge, but he was warm. George leaned against a pile of soft bags and fell asleep immediately.

***

"You goin' to help me with these bags?" George opened his eyes and saw the ferry man standing above him. The boat had already docked. He scrambled to his feet and grabbed a sack. He was becoming sturdy for his size, so it did not take long to unload the pile.

"Well done, young man. I can see you're used to work. I need a helper on the ferry. Care to stay and help me for a while?"

"No, thank you, sir. I have to get to my grandpa's place. But thank you for the ride."

George waved goodbye, walked down the gangplank to the dock, and started down the east road. Boots followed close behind, wagging his tail. At times like this George wished *he* was a dog too. They didn't know a war was going on and they didn't need to plan escapes. All they needed to do was follow along.

Once the ferry was out of sight, George climbed through a rail fence into a field. He stepped slowly over the freshly ploughed earth that was being turned into mud by the continual rain. He would keep the river just in sight as he travelled down to Poughkeepsie. Grandpa had told him that the prosperous farms along this river were owned by Dutch families. George didn't think Grandpa would tell the authorities at Albany that he'd run away, but he couldn't be sure. It seemed centuries ago that he and Grandpa had talked by the well. Who knew what he might be thinking now?

As night approached, George felt as if he could not move another step. His feet ached and his eyes were sore. He had walked a whole night and a whole day before reaching the ferry, and his sleep on the boat had been all too short. When it was fully dark, he decided, he would sneak into the nearest barn and sleep.

George travelled some distance away from the river and over the hilly countryside until he finally sighted some farm buildings. The barn was a few hundred yards from the stone farmhouse.

He walked straight into the upper hayloft, so he wouldn't disturb the cows in the stable below. Boots lay down beside him, completely still. Both were asleep in seconds.

***

"Qu'est-ce qu'on a ici?" a voice boomed under the rafters.

George opened his eyes. He must have overslept. The sun was streaming through the hayloft window. Boots was blinking and yawning with sleep, and a very large man was standing over the two vagabonds. Dazedly, they looked at the man . . . a white man with a deep tan, dark hair, and strong, even features. He didn't look Dutch, which surprised George, since he thought he was still in the Dutch farming area.

"What's that?" George asked as he scrambled to his feet. Boots growled a little and George nudged him quiet.

"Why in my barn?" the man asked with a firm voice. He was a sturdy man with alert, brown eyes.

"Only for a sleep," George replied and picked up his bags. "We'll go." Frightened, he pushed past the man to the doorway. It was the second day of his trip . . . October seventh. Already the ground was covered with the yellow leaves of the elm and the red of the maple. He rushed outside blinking in the bright sunlight.

"Come back! I not hurt you. Have meal," the man called out.

George hesitated at the thought of food, fresh home-cooked food, and he stopped. Maybe he could trust the man. He did not know, but he turned and came back. He still had quite a lot of food in his sack, but he would eventually run out. This might be his last full meal for days.

The man led him to a small two-storey stone farm-house. As the door opened, George could smell frying pork and eggs and fresh coffee — and, he hardly dared believe it — spiced applesauce muffins. He paused on the doorstep for a split second, then rushed right into the kitchen. Boots waited mournfully on the back stoop.

Across from the fireplace, where the farmer's wife was hovering over a cast-iron kettle and frying pan, were a wooden table and benches. Two boys about ten years old were sitting at the table, wearing patched, tan-coloured pants and beige homespun shirts. They were sun-tanned like their father and had the same dark hair and eyes. They looked up at George with interest.

Their mother wore a short, straight brown linen gown, with a mattress-ticking petticoat that reached the floor. Her clean white mob cap and fresh white apron made George suddenly aware of how rough and dirty he must look.

George did not feel awkward for long. Her tender brown eyes and gentle smile made him feel right at home as she motioned him to a basin of water. He splashed the water on his hands and face and smoothed back his curly red hair as best he could. Then he sat at the table beside the man while the boys continued to stare at him shyly from across the table.

The woman with the soft brown eyes set a plate of eggs and pork in front of George, who wolfed it down before he could think of his manners. Instantly, his plate was filled again. He smiled in appreciation, since she spoke in a language that he could not understand.

"Where is it you are from?" the man asked, once George was well into his second plate.

"North."

"*Eh bien*, and you go where?"

"South."

"Ah, yes, I understan'."

"Are you Dutch?" George asked.

"No, no? We are French!"

"Mostly Dutch about here, aren't they?"

"Yes, but we have been chase from our 'ome at Kingston. Most of de town is burn last fall. We are coming nort to 'ere. Before Kingston, we live at Wallkill River. Some move up to Kingston. When Kingston is burn, some go much more to de nort'. We stop here."

"Did the others go north to the British?"

"Dis we do not know," he answered and in a suspicious tone added, "Why dis question?"

"I must go."

"Where do you go? Sout' to de British?" the man questioned.

"I must go," George repeated. "Thank you, Mr. . . . ."

"DeJoux."

"Thank you, Mr. DeJoux, Mrs. DeJoux."

"*Attends un moment, s'il te plait!*" Mrs. DeJoux said kindly. She handed George a cloth packet tied together at the top. It smelled like fresh muffins.

"Thank you," George said with delight as he took the packet. Boots, who had just finished licking a dish outside the door, trotted along beside George down the hill towards the east road.

"Well, what a good breakfast that was, Boots," George said once they were out of earshot of the house. "We might not have another one like that for a long time. I wish we could have stayed with that nice family — but we have to be careful. We don't want anybody to find out who we are and where we're going. Besides, we don't have a moment to lose if we're going to reach New York on time."

But Boots didn't seem to be listening. He was trotting happily beside his master, remembering pork bones and mash.

Fourteen

George squinted through the trees to where the river was glinting in the sun. Two days had gone by since his breakfast with the French family, and his food pack was almost empty. He hadn't counted on feeding a hungry dog. Now he was looking for a spot on the riverbank that was hidden from view so he could catch fish. He had made a fishing rod — a sturdy branch to which he attached his line and hook. His bait was a small piece of fruitcake wrapped inside a torn piece of cloth from his shirt. He might catch a mudcat.

Suddenly he realized that he was in plain view of three Rebel soldiers, who were sitting on the limbs of a fallen tree beside the road, playing cards. There was no way of getting to the river without going right past them. So much for the fishing expedition. George climbed back up the hill that sloped away from the road and ducked out of view.

Before long he came to an apple tree that still had fruit on it. It was at the top of a hill, where the apples had been protected from frost by the night breeze. He figured he must be near a homestead, since apple trees did not grow wild. George picked as many as he could and stuffed them into his food sack. Then he found one to eat right away. It was a bit wizened, but it was sweet. Boots wouldn't touch the bite of apple that he offered him, even though he had peeled it first with his hunting knife. So, with regret, he threw Boots his last chunk of pork. It wasn't big, but George had been looking forward to eating it for supper.

George couldn't help thinking about some of the delicious food his mother prepared. He could almost smell her hot chicken with dressing. How he loved to pour the thick, bubbling gravy over his mashed potatoes and turnips. Right now he'd even be happy with the sizzling sausage rolls and fluffy pancakes floating in maple syrup that Mother sometimes served for breakfast. Even a wedge of Grandma's sweet, spicy apple pie would help. Instead he took another bite from the cold, withered apple and wished he had brought his musket.

He stopped and listened from time to time in case there were more soldiers about. He could hear nothing but the occasional scamper of small animals — probably squirrels. Perhaps he and Boots would find a farm where there was a woman like Mrs. DeJoux, who would offer them food.

By early afternoon, George felt as if he could hold out no longer. The chunks of apple that he had gulped a few hours before were not enough. It might have been better to stay with the French family and risk discovery. He might have been eating roasts and pies for the past two days if he'd stayed there. But he couldn't really have done that. What would be the use of coming all this way if he didn't get right to New York City where his family would be soon?

"Besides," he thought, trying to cheer himself up, "I can't be that far from New York myself. If I figured it out correctly, I must be getting near Westchester County — and that's just next to Manhattan Island." George was always bored when they did map reading at school, but now he was glad he'd memorized the map of the Hudson River area.

Just as he was trying to remember where Yonkers was, he came upon a stream. He scooped up the clear water in his hands, and it tasted great. The water along the shore was shallow, but farther out, it looked tempting enough for a fellow to jump right in and wade out there for a swim.

Boots suddenly darted ahead and started barking.

"Quiet!" George commanded and hurried over to see what was the matter. It did not take long to find out. Boots was barking and whining over a dead rabbit caught in a trap. The rabbit was still warm. It couldn't have been dead long.

"Am I glad I brought my hunting knife!" George said, eagerly anticipating a square meal. He leaned over and loosened the rope that had just strangled the animal in the snare. "Get back, Boots," he shouted. Boots may have been devoted to his master, but a fresh rabbit like that would test the loyalty of any pet. Carrying the rabbit by its two feet, George searched for a stick to use as a skewer. He found a small willow branch, peeled the outer bark from the end, and laid the branch on the grass.

Then he collected some small stones and put them together in a circle. Inside the circle he placed a bunch of dry leaves, shaved bark, and dead twigs, then rummaged through his bag for his flint and steel. He struck the hard, grey stone with the small, U-shaped steel tool. At once a tiny spark grabbed the dry leaves and bark. He watched the blaze flare up and catch the wooden twigs. Then he gently added some larger chunks of dry wood.

Now he was ready to skin the rabbit. He hung it up on a low branch and made a cut down the centre of its back, then started peeling the fur off, keeping his knife on the sinews between the fur and the meat. Once he'd finished the skinning, he found a fresh piece of birch bark on the ground, cut the meat into strips about five inches long, and stacked them on the bark. He threw some of the insides to Boots, who gobbled them up.

In less than an hour, he had a good bed of coals, and with his knife, he burrowed a small hole into three pieces of meat. He pushed them onto the end of the willow twig.

The first piece of roasted meat was almost as good as his mother's chicken dinner. He roasted another piece and gobbled it down. Then he gave a bit of raw meat to Boots and cooked the rest. Since the weather was getting so cold, the cooked meat would still be edible for days.

"Now we're going back to that stream we saw," he said softly to Boots. They headed back about half a mile.

They drank their fill of cold, clear water at the stream, then travelled a couple of hundred yards downstream. Seeing all that water made George realize how grubby he felt. He tore his shirt off, then the rest of his clothes, and took a run and jumped in. The water was so cold he lost his breath for a minute. Then he splashed himself over and swam back to shore. His teeth clattered as he put all his clothes back on — including his thick wool coat. Now it was time to look for a warm barn where they could spend the night.

As darkness set in, George was still searching. But there were no barns in the area.

"Well, Boots," he said. "It looks as if we're going to be camping under the stars tonight. We should go back towards the road and the river before we stop, though. There could be wild animals in this unpopulated area."

George was a little confused about the shortest route back to the river. He could see more light ahead to the right, so perhaps the woods ended there. He trudged along towards the light, certain that he would see the road just beyond the trees. To his surprise he looked at a few hundred yards of clearing, with even thicker woods beyond. He dropped his bag on the ground and sat down.

"I'm just too tired to go any farther," he told Boots. He lay down at the edge of a hollow in the ground and stretched out with his head on his bags. Boots cuddled up close, and George put his arm around the dog. He felt warmer in the damp night with Boots acting like a blanket. It was a good thing Boots had come along.

***

"Get up, boy!"

George woke up with a sharp pain in his left leg. In the early morning light, his eyes travelled up a ragged trouser leg and past a doeskin coat to the unshaven face of a middle-aged man who was snarling at him and threatening to kick him again.

George jumped to his feet. Boots barked hoarsely at the man — but he didn't sound very ferocious.

"Stay off if you know what's good for you," the man spat the words out and pointed his gun at Boots.

"Down, Boots!" George yelled, trying to sound as if he wasn't scared. He rubbed the sleep from his eyes and realized there was not just one man, but at least twenty standing before him.

They were not British Redcoats or Rebel soldiers. In fact, they wore no uniforms. But then George remembered that the Rebel soldiers did not always wear uniforms. Still, they could be hunters, for they *were* wearing doeskin coats.

"So, what are you doing out here, boy?" the rough man demanded. "Where are you headed?"

George thought a bit before he replied, "To Grandma's. My grandpa died a while back, and my parents sent me to help my grandma with the farm and all. She needs help getting up the wood for winter. Boots and I are going to help Grandma White."

The men had gathered around and were building a fire. He watched hungrily as they started to saw through a chunk of raw red meat. Looking more closely, he noticed that they wore homespun trousers and woollen leggings, and in each man's belt there hung a tomahawk instead of a soldier's bayonet. They carried homemade wooden canteens and rough linen haversacks. Each man also carried a Hudson Valley fowler — the same kind of hunter's musket his father used to have.

"What happened to your grandpa?" the man asked.

"Died of old age, sir." George decided he had better show some outward respect for this rough bunch. He also hoped that the man might offer him some breakfast if he spoke politely.

The men laughed. George felt encouraged. Strips of beef with sliced potatoes were soon cooking over the open fireplace, and George forgot his fear as the hunger pangs overcame him. He gazed in awe at the freshly cooked beef steaks sizzling in the pan. He had never smelled anything so good before.

"Hungry, boy?" the rough man asked. "It's a wonder your family didn't pack enough food to last you, or maybe they did."

He motioned to the man on his left, who grabbed George's bags and dumped the few clothes he wasn't wearing onto the ground. The pieces of cooked rabbit bounced out, and Boots jumped on them and snapped them down quickly. The withered apples rolled in all directions.

"Boots!" George shouted angrily. Boots crouched and slunk away from him, but continued to gobble the meat.

The men all laughed rudely. George grabbed for his clothes.

"Wait!" the man said. Carefully, he shook out each garment and felt in each pocket. Finally, he came to the piece of fruitcake. He unwrapped it, picked it apart, and started eating it.

"Someone makes good cake," he admitted.

"My grandma," George replied.

"Your grandma? I thought you said you were *going* to your grandma's!"

"I am. I am. I meant to say my mother. She made it for my grandma, but it's my grandma's recipe that my mother made. Now leave my clothes alone." George grabbed his bag and started to stuff his clothes back into it.

"There's nothing there but clothes," the man said as he looked at George, puzzled. "Well, we need a boy," he added. "Lots of work to do back at camp."

George resisted reaching for the hunting knife in his pocket and hoped they wouldn't search the pockets of his trousers.

The men gathered around and picked out their steaks from the fire. The rough man, whom the others called Ben, handed George a small piece. He took it in his hands and chewed off a bit. It was just as good as his mother's cooking. He licked his fingers to get the last taste.

"More where that came from," the man said to George, "but you'll have to work for it. We need a boy back at camp to cook and do chores."

"I can't cook!" George answered.

"You'll learn fast with Jed to teach you," one of the men snapped.

"No, I won't," George said firmly. "Thanks for the breakfast," he said amiably. Then he grabbed his bag and ran. He was barely a few feet away when a firm hand grabbed his shoulder and flung him to the ground.

"You'll stay, boy!" the voice of the man rang out. "Tie him up, Jake."

"With pleasure."

One man kicked out the fire and covered the ashes with dirt. Then he and another man grabbed George and dragged him kicking over to the poplar tree. They tied his hands together tightly and in a few minutes, they had him in a sitting position, lashed to a tree. The rope circled George and the tree trunk many times. His wrists hurt under the chafing rope. Then, to George's dismay, the men all hurried off through the bush, leaving him alone with Boots.

George's bag of clothes was still lying where Ben had dropped it — just out of reach. George started wiggling to get free. He tried and tried, but that just made the rope dig in more tightly. Time dragged on. Through the trees, he could see the sun rise high in the sky.

"Here, Boots!" George called to his dog, who was over at the firesite, trying to sniff out another steak. Boots came over, wagging his tail.

"Oh, you stupid animal," George yelled. "What can you do. You didn't even wake me up. Twice now we've been caught asleep."

Boots cowered and moved away a bit. George stared out into space. Maybe if he yelled . . . No, he decided he'd better not. Boots inched back towards him, then began to lick his hands as if begging to be noticed. "Oh, all right, Boots, I didn't really mean it. You're all right," George said in a forgiving voice.

Boots licked harder and was slobbering all over him now. George was about to yell again, but he noticed the cords around his wrists didn't hurt so much now that Boots was licking them. Then he realized that the wetness made the ropes seem less tight. Perhaps his hands would slip free. He struggled again, but he couldn't get them out.

"Good dog," he said, hoping Boots would keep licking around the ropes. Boots just wagged his tail and then sat still beside him. George began to spit on the ropes until his throat was dry. They did not loosen.

"I'm so thirsty," he told Boots. "If only I could have a drink of water." Boots came over and licked his hands again.

Maybe Boots could go for help while it was still daylight. He shouted, "Go fetch 'em, Boots!" At his grandpa's, he had been training the dog to round up the cows. If he sent Boots out to look for cows, then someone might see the dog and follow him back. George was confident that Boots would come back before dark.

It took some shouting, but finally Boots left and George felt more hopeful as the time passed and he did not return. He was surely out there hunting for help.

***

By dusk, George was no longer hoping. Boots had not returned and George was afraid for the dog and for himself. He leaned heavily against the tree. He had not been able to free himself, and thoughts were racing through his mind. What if these men did not come back? What would happen to him? He could be a good ten miles from any farm buildings. He had hoped a hunter might come through the woods, but no one appeared. Should he shout for help? What if an animal heard him and came to attack him while he was helplessly tied to the tree? Now he didn't even have Boots to help. What had made him think Boots would run and get help anyway? He was a smart dog, but that was asking a bit much.

Finally he decided to shout. "Help! Help!"

His throat felt worse, almost as though it was cracking. He blinked back tears. He could not cry. No boy of his age ever cried. He must act like a man, not a coward. He remembered now asking his father if *he* was afraid. He sure wished Father was here now to get him out of this fix. He could die here and maybe no one would find him for years. And where was God, who was supposed to be his keeper? Had He forgotten all about him?

Then he just sat very still, cramped and exhausted. He watched the evening shadows grow around him and started to shiver. In the silence of the night, he started to hear the sounds of animals scampering around. Then there was a louder sound — a larger animal was running towards him. George tensed every muscle as he listened.

Boots crashed out of the bushes in front of George and headed straight towards him. The dog jumped against him in great bounding leaps, and the rough burrs caught in his hair rubbed off on George.

"Oh, no! You're burrs all over." In the moonlight now, he could clearly see that the dog was a mess. "You were supposed to bring help and not go chasing woodchucks into holes." George's groan ended in a low whimper.

"So this is where your dog was leading me," a voice

shouted out to him as a figure emerged from the woods. "I was sure he wanted me to follow him."

George looked up and saw a hunter standing in front of him on the other side of the firesite. The man strode over to George and began to untie him.

"Oh boy, does that feel good," George said gratefully as he rubbed his tingling wrists.

"Have you been here all day?" the man asked.

"Yes," George answered directly. He spotted the man's water canteen. "Can I have some water, please?"

The man pulled the wooden plug out of his canteen and handed it to George, who gulped down as much as he could drink.

"Now, tell me what happened," the man said.

George was starting to feel better now and a little foolish about his whimpering. "These men came up on me from behind. They were big and mean. Their leader was a monstrous size. They overpowered me."

"Hmm . . .," the man said and cleared his throat.

"It took two of them to overpower me," George added as a final touch.

The man looked away to hide his smile and said, "Boy, I want to know who you are, where you are going, and why. If you don't tell me the truth, I will know."

"How will you know?"

"Well, first of all, about the monstrous man who was the leader of the giants . . . did he wear tattered brown breeches and a doeskin coat, and was he really a little shorter than me?"

"Why, yes," George blundered out with surprise. Then George realized that this man who had rescued him must know the others. Was he their friend or their foe? If this man was their enemy, then George should try telling the truth. And anyhow, telling lies to the others hadn't helped him . . . He made his decision.

"Very well," George said, looking down. He felt a little embarrassed when he thought of his tale about struggling with the men.

"First, where are you going?" the man asked.

"I'm going to join my brothers, sisters, and mother, who are travelling in a sloop to New York City."

"Why are they going to New York City?"

"They're going to hunt for my father."

"What makes you think he's in New York?"

"We don't know. He left over a year ago. We haven't heard from him since."

"Who is your father?"

George hesitated. The man looked sincere even if somewhat rough and dishevelled — and besides, he had helped him.

"Well?" the man asked.

"Hans Waltermyer," George answered. "I'm his oldest son, George." He looked down after he mumbled these words, wondering if he had been wise to give the man his real name. In these times, most people told strangers as little as possible.

George did not see the man's startled expression or notice his quick effort to cover his emotion. The man's voice sounded no different when he said, "George, eh? Named after George III?"

"I don't know," George said glumly. Then he looked up and saw that the morning's crew was returning to the campsite.

"Look out!" he shouted, and the man turned swiftly, rifle in hand.

"It's only us, James," their leader said, and George recognized the rough man, Ben.

"Taken to recruiting children lately, Ben?" James asked.

"Jed needs someone back in camp to help with the meals," Ben said in a tone that told George the real leader was James.

"It won't be this boy," James said with a grim expression.

George looked at the men starting the campfire. They hauled out fresh beef steaks again.

James sat cross-legged on the grass and looked at no one as darkness gathered in around the campsite. He seemed deep in thought.

George decided there was no point in trying to run away. He went and sat beside James. Boots followed. George looked at his sore wrists and silently thanked God that he was still alive.

Fifteen

George rode along the trail bareback on a chestnut mare. The evergreen trees were thick on either side and branches hit at him as he spurred his horse ahead. Ten of James's men rode behind them, and he could hear Boots yelping from inside a box on the supply wagon. George could not help him because he had to use all his energy to keep up with James.

The day after George's capture and rescue he had stayed in camp with James. The rest of the men had spent the whole day away. When they returned, they brought fresh supplies of food and clothing with them. And the clothes were not from a store — they had all been worn before. George reckoned they were stolen. He couldn't help wondering what had happened to their original owners.

The men prepared a quick campfire and warmed up peas for supper. Then Ben ordered George to clean up, and James did not object. While George was busy washing the tin plates and wooden bowls, the men had huddled together on the far side of the clearing. James talked to them in a low voice. George could hear only bits of the conversation — not enough to piece anything together.

George could not figure out who these men were, nor did he ask questions. But he was sure their business was illegal. The leader, James, had protected him against the others, but George didn't feel very secure. Where did their mysterious trips take them? And where were they going now? George did not want to be forced into taking part in a raid of some kind.

A sharp branch cut into him and knocked his breath away for a second. He almost lost his balance. Lowering his head against the horse's mane, he kept the horse more closely on the trail. Then, increasing his speed, he came closer to James, who had stopped at the edge of a clearing.

George looked beyond him to a broad, flowing river. He knew by its size that it was the Hudson. How far would Captain Schoonhoven's sloop be by now? By his figuring they would be almost to New York City. Then fear gripped him. Were these men going to raid a sloop . . . maybe even Captain Schoonhoven's sloop?

George had planned to escape if he came near any inhabitants. Now he was not so sure. If his family was in danger, maybe he could somehow warn them if he was there. He drew his horse up beside James.

"The Hudson looks calm tonight," George said.

James kept his eyes on the water as though searching for something. Then his eyes rested steadily in one place. George followed his gaze and saw the sloop. At this distance, he could not tell if it was Captain Schoonhoven's boat or not. He turned to James and said, "Where's our next stop?"

James pulled his horse's reins to the right, and the horse headed back for the trail. He did not answer. His dark hair and stubble hid his face.

They travelled along for about half an hour in silence. Then George could stand it no longer. He knew they were following the sloop. He spurred his horse on and squeezed in beside James. "Where are we?" he shouted. "I have to know."

James looked then at George, whose curly hair was all blown out around his flushed red face. James's eyes were not unkind as he answered, "Yonkers."

George knew then that it was probably Captain Schoonhoven's sloop they were going to raid. Yonkers was the last stop before Manhattan Island and New York City. A sickening feeling swept over him. He had wanted to join his family, but not this way . . . as a bandit, robbing and stealing. He had not run away for this.

In the dusk, he watched as they came closer to the small settlement of Yonkers. Maybe he should make a run for it after all. What good would he be to his family? It would kill his mother to see him with these men. Maybe she wouldn't know he had been captured. She might think he was one of them.

By the north dock at Yonkers, a few men stood guarding the supplies that they were waiting to load on to the sloop. When they saw the men in the doeskin coats approaching, they ran shouting away from the docks. George thought he heard one of them shout, "It's the Cowboys!"

James and his men watched them go. Their loud laughter echoed in George's ears. He figured this was his time to make a run for it and join those dock guards, who were disappearing between the small wooden sheds. He gave the side of his horse a sharp slap. But not soon enough.

James blocked his path. He nodded to two of his men and they rode up on either side of George. One of them took the reins of his horse. George knew there was no escape now.

He faced James. "Don't do it, James. Please don't do it. Don't raid that sloop. It has my family . . . I'll do anything for you, James, . . . even cook in camp with Jed. Only please don't raid that sloop!" His voice was breaking now with emotion as he pleaded.

"Be quiet, boy," James said in a stern voice. Then he directed his men. "Blindfold him and keep a close watch."

***

Captain Schoonhoven walked restlessly about the deck. The tails of his long, tight blue coat were blowing in the breeze. It was bright against his full pale brown trousers, which were made of sailcloth and reached just below his knees. Although he had hoped for the cover of fog to finish the trip to New York, the day had been bright and clear. Nevertheless, all had gone well. They had made good time, and he was satisfied.

After this trip, the captain hoped to rest for the winter. Perhaps at sixty now, he was growing too old to make the run anyway. Ten years ago, in peace time, he had loved the journey back and forth. He liked to meet new people and made friends easily. The boat would often anchor a half-day here and there on shore, and he would lead the passengers on a tour around the countryside.

The farmers' wives always welcomed the touring passengers. Some sold fresh baking and offered meals. The women and children could speak only Low Dutch, but he could interpret enough to manage. Yes, he missed those trips ashore.

The war had changed everything. He could no longer set his own trip schedules. The Rebel officials in Albany expected him to make the trip from Albany to New York and back to Albany in an exact amount of time. If he didn't meet their deadlines, something might happen to his wife back home — and maybe to his children, though they were all grown up and married now.

And then there were dangers on the river, especially as the sloop approached Westchester County, which had become a no-man's-land. Because neither side held the land for sure, two groups of partisans, the Skinners and the Cowboys, had started irregular fighting all over the zone. At first they had taken food only, but lately they had started more savage plundering. The Cowboys plundered for the British and the Skinners for the Rebels. But neither army admitted any connection with them.

His watchfulness now was probably unnecessary, he decided. All day he had looked with his field glass along the shore and seen nothing. So he'd let his passengers stay on deck. He would invite the folks to come up on deck now for a bit of air before darkness closed in. They would soon anchor for the night, and then the next morning they would complete the short trip to the shore opposite Manhattan Island and meet the bateaux to exchange cargoes.

A short time later, many of the passengers were milling around the deck, stretching their cramped limbs and talking in small groups. Captain Schoonhoven turned to look at the shoreline again. He had to leave a few supplies at Yonkers, so the sloop drew in close to shore. The crew flung down the anchor and put the gangplank across to the landing.

"Are we in New York, sir?" a young voice just behind him asked.

Among the first who had rushed up to the deck were Mary, Leonard, and Tobias Waltermyer. Now Mary was looking up eagerly at the Captain.

"Not yet, Miss Mary," he answered cordially. "We're

picking up a few supplies now, and then we'll push out
and on a bit and anchor for the night. First thing in the
morning when you wake up, young lady, we'll be there."

Mary was glad their trip on the sloop was nearly over.
After spending all her life on a farm where you could run
in the yard and the fields, she had had trouble getting
used to the cramped cabins on the sloop. Catharine had
been sick most of the trip, and the whole family was tired
and cranky.

"Let's watch over here where we can see more,"
Leonard suggested as he pulled Mary and Tobias over to
the edge of the sloop, where one end of the plank was
resting.

"Stay back!" the Captain barked. "No one goes ashore
here. We won't be stopping long enough. We're just
leaving a few supplies and taking a few."

Some men in doeskin coats carried parcels on board
from the shore. The Captain stood staring at the delivery
men. He did not recognize any of them. Tomahawks were
tucked into their belts.

He stepped up to the first man and was about to ask
him who he was when the man shouted, "Everyone
down!"

"Down!" yelled another man, who was standing behind the Captain.

The passengers all dropped to the floor of the deck;
only the Captain remained standing.

"Who's the Captain?" a loud voice called out.

"I am," he said in his deep voice.

"Heaven help us if it's the Cowboys!" an old man
nearby said in a grim voice.

"The Skinners aren't any better," hissed back a middle-aged woman, her teeth clattering.

The leader of the bandits came forward and spoke quietly to the Captain. "We're not looking for trouble. We only want to drop off a boy who claims his family is aboard this ship."

Captain Schoonhoven spotted a red-headed teenager being led up the plank to his boat. With one hand, the boy, whose eyes were covered with a ragged kerchief, clutched the long hair of a lively, golden collie with a star on his forehead.

The leader's voice bellowed out, "This way," and all his men gathered around him, muskets still in hand.

Then James tore the rag from the boy's eyes and said loudly, "When you see your father, George, tell him he owes James DeLancey!" He let out some loud guffaws of laughter as he and his men marched off the sloop.

Captain Schoonhoven stood with his mouth open for a few seconds, then recovered himself and gave the order to raise the gangplank.

George looked around him. Everything looked blurry still and he recognized no one — until three figures ran towards him across the deck.

"George!" Mary screamed. "It's George!" And she hugged him so hard he nearly fell over.

Sixteen

George stared at his brothers and sisters in shock.
They'd all come pelting along the deck, and
Mother was coming close behind, trying not to
break into a run. Boots was jumping around like a young
pup from one child to the next. Tears started to roll down
Mother's cheeks as she embraced her son.

"Thank God you're safe," she whispered. "But how
did you get here?"

A little crowd of people was gazing at them in hushed
silence. Their ordeal over, the crew and passengers were
relieved but still a little stunned. As they watched the
reunion, they started to become very curious and even
suspicious.

The Captain broke into the silence and gave directions.
"Everyone below now. We'll be sure we're safe before
we stop again, and you'll be put ashore early in the
morning. . . . Now, Mrs. Waltermyer, you'd best take
your family below too. We've had enough adventures for
today."

"Who were those men?" Tobias whispered to George
as they climbed down the ladder to the hold. "And what
were you doing with them?"

"Did you run away from the farm?" Mary asked.
"Here, this way to our cabin. You've got to tell us all

about it. You're so lucky. What an adventure! Were they sort of like pirates?"

Inside the cabin, George sat on the only hammock. The children sat on blankets spread out on the floor, which was their bed for this voyage. Mother wrapped a blanket around George and sat down beside him.

"You must be hungry, George — and you look like a wild animal. Here, have some of Grandma's fruitcake," Mother said as she unwrapped the food parcel beside the hammock. "I think you need something to get your energy back. . . . Now, tell us what happened. Did the farm get raided? Oh . . . are Grandma and Grandpa all right?"

"Oh, they're fine," George said, feeling a bit guilty about running away now that he was safe. "At least last time I saw them. I just had to run away. It was awful on the farm wondering what was going to happen to you and thinking you'd all see Father and I wouldn't. So I just left one night."

"And Boots? What ever possessed you to bring Boots?"

"Oh, he just followed me. I tried to get him to stay home, but he just came along. And it's a good thing because he ran and got that man when I was all tied up."

"Tied up?"

"Yes, tied right to a tree. Of course, it took two men to . . . ". Then George remembered how silly he'd felt about his boast last time. "Well, some awful men tied me up because they wanted me to cook for them. Then that man James DeLancey came along and untied me, and luckily he was their leader."

"Wow, George! It sounds like a made-up story. I wish I'd been there," Leonard said.

"Well, I don't know," George replied, feeling tired all of a sudden. "It was pretty scary some of the time."

"Well, George, I'm so glad you're here and safe — but you know you did a very risky thing — and Grandma and Grandpa must be worried sick. Now why don't you curl up and have a nice sleep. In fact, I think we should all go to sleep now and George can tell us the rest in the morning. We have a hard day ahead. I don't know exactly what to expect when we reach New York."

George interrupted, "Well, James must think we'll see Father."

Mother looked worried. "I hope he's right. But anyway we'll be with the British. We must be cautious and stay together. We have seen how the Rebels handle folks they suspect. Now we'll see how the British act. I pray we will be in good hands."

Before she slept, Mother bowed her head to pray for their safety.

The children sprawled out on their blankets on the cabin floor and were soon asleep. Boots lay quietly at George's back.

***

"This is as far as I go, folks," Captain Schoonhoven announced as his crew put down the gangplank. "My men will put your baggage on the shore. You may arrange to cross over to Manhattan Island by bateau. Several of them are bringing my cargo and will be glad to have a load back. But there'll be a charge. Nothing is free in New York anymore."

George and Boots were among the first off the sloop. The small docking area was crowded with a small bateau unloading barrels and bags on the flat, pebbly shore. George was looking for the family's baggage and furniture. Leonard had caught up to him and yelled boisterously, "Everything's here . . . even Mother's table!"

The whole family breathed a bit easier once they'd found a flat-bottomed bateau that would take all their furniture.

When they were ready to leave, George looked for his mother and saw that she was talking to the Captain. "Thank you, Captain Schoonhoven, for making our trip as pleasant and safe as possible. The way you responded to those Cowboys may have made all the difference in George's safety and ours. We owe you a great deal."

Captain Schoonhoven smiled. "I'm glad things worked out for you. It's terrible what we have to deal with in the line of duty these days."

"You're more loyal to your job than most," Mother answered. "Be careful, and have a safe trip home."

"Thank you, Ma'am." Captain Schoonhoven waved to the children, who were waiting at the bateau. They all waved back. Smiling again, he shook his head as his eyes lingered on George and Boots.

Seventeen

George's father walked across the wide lawn towards Sir Henry Clinton's mansion. It was dusk, so he could barely see the gardens where flowers had bloomed in the summer. Nothing was growing there now, except some rose bushes that had lost most of their leaves. He looked up at the stately home ahead of him. It was no taller than many of the houses Waltermyer had seen in Albany, but it was much wider and more magnificent, with a large verandah running along the front and sides. Lights twinkled from its many windows. On the roof there were four chimneys and a balustrade. It was hard to imagine that this luxury existed in the middle of besieged New York.

The British soldier who had permitted Waltermyer to pass through the locked gate spoke with some urgency, "Sir Henry Clinton wants to see you immediately."

Waltermyer felt somewhat uneasy as he entered the large house and followed another soldier along the hallway over the deep red carpet. The soldier knocked on one of the big oak doors at the end of the hallway. It was opened by another soldier who said, "Sir Henry is available. Come in."

Waltermyer entered and approached the desk. He bowed to the young General, who was only half a dozen years older than himself. With relief, he handed over his package.

The keen-eyed General tore open the message and motioned Waltermyer to a chair. He studied the message for a full five minutes. Then he looked up at Waltermyer, who was still standing.

Hans Waltermyer stared back at the general. "I have delivered the message from Governor Haldimand," he said. "Now I have other pressing duties." He bowed again and turned to go.

The general spoke out firmly. "But you must wait. I need to send an answer. It is urgent that it reach Haldimand before the snow flies. Tracking a courier over the snow would be too easy. And if we wait until spring to send the message, it may be too late."

Waltermyer replied, "I am sure there are many in your service more experienced in the ways of the military who could deliver your message. I have personal business to attend to. I must be on my way. Good day to you, sir." He turned again to leave.

The General continued to speak. "There are none who know the woods and the countryside better than you, Waltermyer. And Governor Haldimand needs to know the enemy's planned feint in order not to withdraw his troops in the face of a real attack."

Clinton hesitated. The son of a governor, he had started as a captain while still in his twenties. At forty now, he was accustomed to being obeyed and, after all, he was in command of all the British forces stationed in New York City. He resented the bluff independence of this tall, rugged man with the unkempt red hair and unshaven face. Still he would need to win the man's loyalty or he would not be sure his message would be delivered.

Although Waltermyer was not intimidated by the General himself, he felt ill at ease in this grand house. He was uncomfortable too because he had not taken time to clean up before he came, and he was anxious to hunt for his family. He stood waiting to be dismissed.

There was a knock on the door. General Clinton called out, "Come in."

A young officer entered and asked, "Shall I bring her in now, sir?"

The General nodded.

"I have arranged for you to see someone," the General explained to Waltermyer, whose back was still to the door.

Turning, Waltermyer could not believe his eyes. Then Polly was in his arms. ". . . the children?" he stammered.

"They're fine. They're waiting out front. They'll be so happy to see you." For a moment they forgot those around them.

The General cleared his throat, and they were aware of his presence again. "I realize and understand your concern for your family, Waltermyer. But concern yourself no longer. I have soldiers ready to take them to living quarters in the city."

"I am most grateful for your help," Waltermyer began. He knew how scarce adequate accommodation was. "Now I would like to see my children."

"You may. I will not hold you. But if you agree to deliver this message, your children should not see you. It is best they have no knowledge of your whereabouts."

"I have not agreed."

"I am very aware of that. Let me remind you that accommodation in New York is very expensive. The price of victuals is rising almost daily, and with winter coming . . . How many children did you say you have?"

Polly was still holding his arm. How he wanted to escape from this room and this General and be alone with his family! But the General was right. He had little money to provide for his family. How he would hate to leave them in the refugee camp depending on handouts! Prices would increase as winter came on, and he did not receive regular pay for hunting for recruits. He needed a steadier income. Perhaps he could do both at the same time. While he carried messages, he could be talking to Loyalists about joining his Company.

He replied very slowly, "I have reconsidered."

"Good!" The General was pleased. "I offered you two shillings and six pence a day while you were carrying dispatches. Now I will add to that a reduction in the accommodation for your wife and children."

"I would like a short time alone with my wife before I go."

"That can be arranged, but you must leave within the hour. Your children are waiting for your wife in a wagon outside."

Waltermyer looked at his wife, who nodded. He walked to the window on the other side of the room and drew the lace curtains back, but he could not see beyond the high wall surrounding the house.

The General led them to the sitting room next to his office and leaving the door ajar, he went back to his desk.

"I'm so thankful that you are safe, Hans," Polly began. "What is this gentleman saying about messages?"

He hesitated, then decided to tell the whole story. "I am working for the British now. I carry messages sometimes."

"Oh no, Hans, don't! Not for any money. It isn't worth it. What if you are caught?" Polly was shocked as she realized the meaning of the deal she had just heard her husband make with the General. The colour drained from her face.

"Polly, I've hunted in these woods since I was a boy. They won't ever catch up to me. I'll just never stay still long enough, and with these long legs . . . " Sitting now, he sprawled his legs out in front of him.

Polly saw how ridiculous he did look on the velvet chair with his legs stretched across the room. She smiled and said, "I miss you so much, Hans. We all miss you."

"The sooner British communication improves, the faster we'll have this war over and we'll be together again. Somebody has to carry messages for the British. I don't plan to do it for long, though, just till I get enough men for a company."

About fifteen minutes later, there was a tap on the half-closed door. It was the General. "My aide tells me your children are growing restless."

Polly looked at her husband. "I must go but . . . "

He drew Polly to him and kissed her gently. Then he held her close for a few minutes before they walked to the door together. She turned and smiled through the tears glistening in her eyes. Then she was gone.

Waltermyer stood silently for a minute, staring at the closed door, before he turned to the General.

Sir Henry Clinton handed him a small package wrapped and waterproofed in oiled cloth. Waltermyer attached it securely to a thong under his shirt.

"Your family is being moved into the third floor of Barracks VII. I believe you've been there before."

"Yes, but I was never beyond the first floor."

"My soldiers will take you back to the refugee barracks now, and you can set out in the morning."

"They can drop me on the edge of town. The less I'm seen with the Redcoats, the safer this mission will be."

The General did not argue but said, "I do not think it wise for you to have further contact with your family at this time."

"I'm starting on your mission now," Waltermyer replied. "You have my word." Waltermyer drew himself to attention.

The General nodded his dismissal and Waltermyer left.

Part Two
Coping

Eighteen

The Waltermyer children trudged along to the only charity school in New York City at St. Paul's Church, where their mother had managed to enrol them. George was happy to see that fresh snow had fallen over the gravel street and that the buildings did not look as drab as usual. Their own home had two rooms. It was the third floor of an old house that had a soldiers' barracks on the first floor and an old soldiers' hostel on the second. Boots had a place behind the house in the back shed where the soldiers sometimes left bones for him.

Watching a sleigh passing, George almost bumped into a water carrier. "You clumsy idiot!" the man shouted, and George stepped back just in time. More than his feet would have been wet if he had collided with that man.

"Help!" shrieked Anna. A ragged bully from a group of ruffians at the side of the street had grabbed Anna's toque. He stood now leaning against the wall of a cooper's shop, leering at George as he dangled the hat from his extended hand. A shock of brown hair fell down over his forehead.

"C'mon, George," said Tobias. "We can't fight that bunch. We're outnumbered. Besides, they're bigger."

George stood his ground. "They're a sick-looking bunch next to my buddies the Cowboys!"

"I think we'd better go on," Leonard said as he eyed the biggest bully still snarling at George.

"I want my toque!" Anna wailed.

Catharine grabbed Anna's arm and started to pull her along the street. Mary stood right beside George.

The big bully was smirking as he twirled Anna's hat around his thumb.

George lunged at him. Smiling, the bully stepped aside, and George landed against the hard stone wall of the cooper's shop.

Then, before he could turn, George felt someone on his back. Struggling to throw off the weight, George could hear more scuffling and shouts from Tobias and Leonard and the other ruffians.

The load forced George to the ground, but still he held the bully's hands as they were pushing upward towards his neck.

Then Mary jumped on the bully, yanked his hair with both hands and bit his neck.

"Owww!" the brown-haired fighter yelped as he let go of George and flung Mary to the ground.

George was on his feet in an instant and faced the bully again. He was sure he could beat him now. After all, he had lived with the Cowboys and survived.

George lunged out and struck the bully's jaw at almost the same time that the bully hit him.

George staggered from the blow, and blood spurted from his nose. The warm taste was in his mouth, but he lashed out again. This time he missed, and the bully grabbed him and pushed him to the ground. George's arms were pinned behind him now and the bully's hands were around his throat. He could hear Mary yelling. He gasped for breath. Those vise-like hands were tightening . . .

Then the hands were wrenched away, and someone else was fighting the bully. Still gasping for breath, George looked up. It was not Tobias or Leonard. The boy's white-blond hair blew out in the wind. He landed a strong blow on the jaw of the bully, who fell to the ground and stayed there.

Still watching his defeated opponent, the blond-haired boy said to George, "Are you all right?"

"I am now," George said as he looked up into the face of his best friend. He scrambled to his feet.

John Bleecker turned then and recognized George. He clapped both hands on George's shoulders and yelled, "George!"

Suddenly all the ruffians but the leader turned and ran. A watchman appeared. "What's been going on here?" he demanded.

"Those bullies took my sister's hat and attacked my brothers," Mary said. She smoothed back Anna's hair as she put her toque back on.

The watchman grabbed the bully by the collar and made him stand up. "So I've finally got you," he said. "This one has been causing trouble for a long time." He left, taking the bedraggled boy with him.

The Waltermyer children all gathered around John. His face flushed red, he beamed at his friends. "How long have you been here?"

"Almost two months," said George. "And you?"

"We came right after Dad . . . right after the funeral."

Mary and Catharine had moved up beside John. "Are Lucy and your mother here too?"

The light left John's eyes then as he frowned, "Yes."

"Where do you live?" John asked.

"The attic of Barracks VII. Do you know where that is?"

"Yes. We're only a few blocks away on Murray Street."

"That's great, John. Can we go now to see Lucy?" Mary asked. John looked down in silence.

George saw his friend's jaw tighten and he knew there was a problem. "We can't now, Mary. We have to go to school. But why don't you meet us afterwards and come home with us. Could Lucy come too?"

John was smiling again. "I'd like that," he said. "We'll wait inside the cooper's shop here."

"At four then," George said and hurried to catch up with the others, who had already started down the street.

***

John and Lucy were waiting in front of the cooper's shop when the Waltermyer children hurried up to them. They were both smiling eagerly at their old friends.

Lucy spoke first. "I could hardly believe it when he told me. It's so great to see all of you, even you, George." She giggled and reached out to give them each a fast hug. She was taller than Mary now and seemed even thinner, with braids long enough to sit on.

George shifted a bit uncomfortably from one foot to the other as she gave him his hug. He guessed that in wartime like this an old friend looked pretty good even if she was a mouthy girl. But did she need to carry it this far?

John and George sauntered along behind the others. John was thinner too now, but he was smiling and obviously happy to be with his old friends.

"You sure came at just the right time," said George.

John beamed with pleasure. "Oh, you had the stuffing knocked out of him before I got there. I just had to sorta finish up."

"Well, I'm glad I wasn't the one who got finished up."

Up ahead Mary and Lucy were both talking at the same time. They had a lot of catching up to do. The others were joining in from time to time.

"How's your mother, John?" George asked.

A silence followed. Then John said, "Fine."

"Are you living with relatives?" George asked. He hoped that wasn't the wrong question, but he did know that the money from the sale of the Bleeckers' store had all gone to the Rebels. They couldn't have afforded their own place. Looking sideways at John, he noticed the same frown he'd seen on John's face before.

"You could say that," he said. George thought that he should not inquire anymore. If his friend wanted to share whatever was bothering him, he would.

"So you go to school even now?" John asked.

George nodded. "Mother found the only free school in New York City. I suppose it's something to do. But I could think of more exciting things — like my trip alone down the Hudson."

"You mean, you didn't come with the rest of the family?"

"No, I ran away and joined the Cowboys." George was starting to feel better now than he had just after being defeated by the bully. "It was great fun, John. I just wish you could have come with me."

John was looking really eager now. "I wish I had," he said. "Tell me all about it, and don't leave anything out."

For the rest of the walk home, George told of his

adventures. He spent a long time describing the meal with the DeJoux family, the Cowboys' campfires and delicious steaks, and the adventure of joining the sloop.

Finally John asked, "George, weren't you afraid at all?"

George looked at his admiring friend, who was still staring at him in wonder. He was quite ready to say, "Not at all, John." But something in his friend's trusting expression caused him to hesitate. Then he said, "At times, I was scared stiff, but it turned out all right."

As they came up the steps of the Barracks, Mary turned to John and George and said, "Lucy wants to see Boots. How about you, John?"

"Sure," said John, and they all tramped around to the back shed, where they found Boots curled up sleeping.

"The star is clearer than ever," said Lucy. Boots woke up and wagged his tail as though he were greeting old friends.

George was certain that he remembered them. "I told you he's a smart dog," he said to John. "Boots brought help when I needed him."

"When was that?" Lucy asked. She looked at George wide-eyed as he told his story again. Lucy wasn't so bad after all, George decided, as they headed upstairs to their rooms.

"You sure were brave, George. I wish something exciting like that would happen to me sometime," she said. "But Mother hardly ever lets me out of her sight ever since Dad died. And she hasn't been any better since she married again either."

George shot a quick glance at John. He was looking down and frowning.

Nineteen

*I*t was Christmas Eve. The snow fell gently on George's wool coat as he walked to church with his mother and the rest of the family. This night New York City seemed a little quieter than usual.

"I miss the church bells," Catharine said.

"Me too," mumbled Mary.

"The bloody Rebels took them all before they left, to make cannon."

"George! Watch your language!" Mother exclaimed.

Joy to the world! the Lord is come:
Let earth receive her King . . .

The congregation was already singing as they entered. For a moment George felt as if everything was normal again and there had never been a war. Of course, this huge Church of England Cathedral wasn't anything like the small crowded church he had gone to with his family back home. They would always sit in the pew just behind his grandparents and Uncle Jacob, and after the service they would go over to their house for a while. After they opened their grandparents' gifts, they'd all pile into the back of the sleigh with the bearskin robe over them while Father and Mother sat up front. With the bells on the horses' harnesses jingling, they would sing carols all the way home. George could almost hear Father's strong voice leading the others.

No more let sins and sorrows grow,
Nor thorns infest the ground . . .

George looked over at his mother, who was sitting beside him in the pew with Jacob in her lap. A tear rolled down her cheek, but she brushed it away and kept singing steadily. Mother did worry a lot, George thought, but he still admired her courage.

He rules the world with truth and grace,
And makes the nations prove
The glories of His righteousness . . .

George doubted that God was ruling the world just now with truth and grace. He looked at the people around them. Then he spotted John with his mother and sister, and John was frowning. He wondered what John was thinking just now. Lucy sat between her mother and John, singing steadily, but she too looked sad. Her braids were combed out now and her long hair floated around her shoulders and down her back. George noticed how thick and soft her hair looked.

O come, all ye faithful, joyful and triumphant,
O come ye, O come ye to Bethlehem;
Come and behold Him, born the King of angels . . .

Then people of different languages joined in singing the Latin version of the first verse.

Adeste fideles, laeti triumphantes,
Venite, venite in Bethlehem;
Natum videte, Regem angelorum . . .

Following the verse, their voices blended together into
a great volume as they sang the chorus:

Venite adoremus,
Venite adoremus,
Venite adoremus Dominum.

George thought about the Baby Jesus, and Mary and
Joseph, who had no place to go. He bet he knew just how
they felt. But then even Jesus had Joseph there to care for
the family. Where was Father tonight? He had always been
with the family on Christmas Eve until that awful day a year
and a half ago when he had run for his life. George looked
across at John. He was not singing, and he looked grim.
Suddenly George felt very badly for being so angry at God.
He began to sing with the others.

When the service was over, a lady named Mrs. Norman, wearing an ostrich-feather hat, bustled up and
asked the whole family to go downstairs for a minute.
There she handed them a parcel marked for the Waltermyers from St. Paul's. Mother thanked her, and George
took the parcel to carry up the stairs. He was making his
way into the crowded hallway when he looked up and
saw a familiar red curly head and broad shoulders standing out above the crowd.

"Father!" he shouted above all the noise of the people
in the vestry and nearly dropped the parcel. Hans Waltermyer turned and smiled, and the family pushed through
the crowd to surround him.

***

Christmas dawned bright and clear and cold. George crawled out of bed. He could see his breath in the air, and as he looked out the window, his breath froze on the windowpanes. He thought of Boots in the cold shed out back. Then he remembered Father was home. Would he dare sneak past his parents and bring Boots in?

He walked over to the door. He could hear his parents' and Jacob's steady breathing. They sounded fast asleep. He opened the door, walked through the main bed-sitting room to the outer door, picked up his boots that used to be Tobias's and flung his coat over his shoulder. In the outer hallway, he put his boots and coat on quickly and made his way to the main entrance. All was quiet. Even the soldiers seemed to be sleeping in this morning.

On the main floor, he turned and headed for the back door. As he stepped outside, he blinked in the bright sunlight and walked briskly along the path. The snow was not deep, but it was bitterly cold. He opened the door and tiptoed into the shed. A shaft of light fell on Boots, who was huddled in the far corner on straw that George had arranged for him there. At first Boots was so still that George was afraid he had come too late, and the dog was frozen. But when George squatted beside him, the dog lifted up his head sadly and licked George's hand.

"Good boy," George said, rubbing the dog's fur back and forth and hugging him.

"What am I going to do with you Boots?" he said aloud. The dog was up by now and wagging his tail.

Intent on his dog, George did not notice the far outside door behind him being opened and a hand stealthily slipping around the corner, to pick up a stick of wood. But Boots did. With a low growl the dog came to life and bounded towards the man, who was now aiming to knock George on the head. Just in time, George turned and missed the blow that was intended for him. The man hit Boots instead, and the dog lay out cold on the floor. George caught only a glimpse of the ragged man's face before he fled.

George ran out the door, but in the small yard he could see nothing of his assailant. He went back into the shed, took his coat off and wrapped it securely around Boots. The dog was so thin that he was not heavy to carry, so George picked him up in his arms and walked back through the sunny courtyard to the barracks.

When he reached the upper hallway, he set Boots on the floor outside the door. He gave him another little rub and walked into the front room, where Mother was already up, frying something in the iron spider. It smelled like pork strips. Father was leaning back in his high-backed easy chair by the fireplace.

Father looked healthy and tanned from spending so much time in the outdoors, but he had developed deeper lines around his eyes. The laughter lines of his mouth were drawn tight now, and frown lines had appeared on his forehead.

"How's your dog?" his father asked. Mother had told him about Boots.

George replied, "Not so good. He's half-frozen. A man broke in the shed and tried to jump me. Boots stopped him and the man knocked him out with a stick."

"Where is he now?"

"The man got away, and I brought Boots upstairs and laid him down in the hallway."

"He might still be too cold out there . . . go bring him in, George. It's Christmas Day, after all."

George rushed back out to the hallway, hardly believing his luck, and gently carried Boots inside.

"Put him down on this, George," Father said.

He laid Boots on the coat his father had put on the floor just inside the door. Father examined Boots, feeling gently around the wound. Then he pulled back the dog's eyelids and looked very carefully at his eyes. Next he took the dog's legs in his hands and, one at a time, moved them easily.

"He's going to be all right," he told George. "But I think he shouldn't go back to the shed just yet. We can make a place for him in the upstairs hallway for the severe weather and he can stay in here now until he's warmed through."

To George's surprise, Mother didn't complain and even gave him some pork strips for Boots, who was soon able to gobble them down.

As George sat quietly on the floor beside his dog, he looked at all the boots lined up by the door. He was irritated because he had started wearing his *younger* brother's hand-me-downs a few weeks before. Looking at his father's boots, he wondered if he would ever be big enough to fill them. He picked one up to see just how big the foot was compared to his own. Then George noticed what appeared to be nicks cut in the edges. The heels had been cut underneath, and the flat soles had the identical shape at both the back and the front. The other boot was the same.

"Father, why are your boots the same at the front and the back?"

"George!" Mother exclaimed. "Put down your father's boots."

"Don't worry, Polly. George isn't going to tell," Father said quietly. But Mother grabbed Father's boots and tucked them under the side cupboard.

"I carry messages for the British sometimes," Father said, "and I can't be tracked as easily if the enemy doesn't know whether I'm coming or going. I just toe in or toe out as the need arises. What do you think about that, George." He tipped his curly head back and laughed heartily.

George was glad to hear Father's laughter again.

"It's no laughing matter," Mother interrupted in her worried voice.

Father grew more serious. "Remember, George, no one must know, not even your brothers and sisters. The fewer who know the better. But you are the oldest. Now you're going on fourteen, you're old enough to be aware of the danger and my need for secrecy."

George nodded. "I'll remember," he promised, feeling proud that Father had confided in him. Tobias might be bigger than George, but now George really felt like the oldest again. It was good to have Father home, George thought as he patted Boots. His poor pet was fast asleep now, snoring loudly with his head in George's lap.

***

"What are you gonna call her?" Leonard asked as he held up the new rag doll with the acorn head, just above Anna's reach.

"Give me *my doll*!" Anna reached up to get it from

Leonard, but with a smile he held it even higher. She turned then and grabbed Jacob's wooden doll and started moving its joints back and forth. Jacob started to cry.

George yanked the doll from Leonard and handed it to Anna. She took it eagerly, dropping Jacob's doll. "Smarten up, Leonard," said George. He grabbed Leonard's new sweater that Grandma had sent and started to wrap it around Leonard's neck. Leonard grabbed George around the legs and hung on. In a second they were both down on the floor rolling over and over.

"Pick on someone your own size, George," Tobias yelled.

George was furious. He pushed Leonard away and swung at Tobias.

Turning with the iron pot from the fireplace, Mother shouted, "Stop this minute, George! Stop — all of you! George, how can you behave this way . . . and on Christmas Day too." Leonard smirked at George as he picked up his new sweater.

"I saw it all," said Father. "Leonard started it by teasing Anna. I see you need something to do, Leonard. Help your mother with supper."

George was glad that Father had noticed, but he figured it wasn't much of a punishment for Leonard. He could see Leonard eating up all the meat left on the pork bone that should go to Boots.

Just then Mary set a big plateful of bread and meat on the centre table. "These are sandwiches, Father," she said. "Mrs. Norman told us about the Earl of Sandwich when we first arrived, and how he is the Lord of the Admiralty in charge of all the British ships. He invented the sandwich."

"Yes, I've heard the story, Mary," he replied. To Polly,

he mumbled, "They say the great need for this new meal arose because he couldn't pull himself away from gambling long enough to eat at the table."

"Hans, what a thing to say about the Admiral," she replied.

"I'm afraid it's true, Polly. And this war is just another game to them. It's not their homes, their livelihood, their very lives and those of their families . . . as it is to us."

"Surely it's not a game to all of them?"

"No, but to many it is. Two years ago after General Howe captured this city, he just sat here in New York. General Washington fled with his Rebel army to New Jersey, and they almost perished that winter from the cold and lack of supplies. Howe could easily have taken them and ended this whole bloody mess! We could have been home long ago!"

"After the great fire, though, wasn't General Howe busy building up the city again and helping all the refugees?"

"Busy, my foot! Did he rebuild the burned-out areas? No! He could easily have sent soldiers down there to do just that, but he didn't. He had a great time with the women of New York. Or maybe I should say his officers did. He brought his lady friend from Boston. They all had a great holiday — partying all winter."

"Hans . . . the children."

"They might just as well know. Howe did the same thing again last winter. Our scouts told us that Washington's Rebel troops were even worse off then. They were almost overcome by cold, famine, and sickness, and had to stay put, just twenty miles outside Philadelphia. Meanwhile, Howe sat in Philadelphia with his officers and troops and had another winter's party. He left Sir Henry

Clinton in charge here in New York — and Clinton followed Howe's example by having a party of his own."

"Is there no hope, Hans?"

"In spite of everything, I think there still is. I believe deep down that Americans want to remain loyal to the King. We are starting to unite. DeLancey's brigade has three battalions, and I hope to be a captain if I can recruit enough men. The British know we're fighting to regain our land and our homes, and their leaders are starting to listen. They're starting to recognize our abilities and our sincerity. At first, the British soldiers treated us like country bumpkins, but that's starting to change . . . "

Father looked up and saw George staring at him. George was thinking how exciting his father's life must be. He wished he could carry messages. No one would expect a boy to have anything valuable on him. His size could even be an advantage. And was this Oliver De-Lancey any relation to James?

Before George could say anything, Father motioned his family to the table. "Well, we can't let this meal go to waste," he said.

"Am I ready to eat!" said Leonard.

"Just a minute," Father said and bowed his head. The children quickly followed his example. After the blessing, Father passed the sandwiches around while Mother left the table to open a parcel. She returned with a beautiful cake that looked just like the kind that Grandma baked for them every Christmas. She set it in the middle of the table.

"How did you manage to bring all these things from Grandma?" George asked.

"I have my ways," Father laughed. He seemed his old jovial self again.

Boots was attacking the pork bone when Mary said to Father, "We lost Curly right after you left."

"He followed me, Mary, when I first left the farm. I found a place for him with a family of Loyalists who fled to Canada. When I was there I hunted him up. He's living with a French family now near Machiche in Canada. I couldn't bring him back."

"I'm glad he's fine, and Boots is a great dog, Father," George interrupted Mary. "He followed *me* when *I* left the farm. I was supposed to stay with Grandma and Grandpa."

"They told me, George," Father said. "They sent the soldiers after you the next day."

"I didn't think they'd do that. I thought Grandpa would give me more time."

"He was afraid for you, George. The soldiers wouldn't have hurt you. They would have taken you back to the farm. I can't speak for Father, though. You might have got a good tanning. He was pretty upset. I still can't understand how you ever made it safely all that distance."

"I wouldn't have if it hadn't been for James."

"James who?"

"James DeLancey. He said you owe him for helping me."

George retold the whole story.

Father listened intently to George, smiling occasionally at some of the tall tales, but only at the end did he laugh loudly when George told him about James DeLancey's comment as he left the boat.

"James is okay. Not nearly the monster the Rebels make him out to be. He's Oliver DeLancey's younger brother. I see him occasionally in my travels."

"Do you travel much, Father?" Catharine asked.

"All soldiers travel, Catharine. Some more than others."

They had all finished eating now and Father picked up the Bible that Mother had set by his plate. He began reading rather haltingly, for it had been a while since he had read to his family.

And the angel said unto them, Fear not: for, behold, I bring you good tidings of great joy, which shall be to all people. For unto you is born this day in the city of David a Saviour, which is Christ the Lord. And this shall be a sign unto you; Ye shall find the babe wrapped in swaddling clothes, lying in a manger. And suddenly there was with the angel a multitude of the heavenly host praising God, and saying, Glory to God in the highest, and on earth peace, good will toward men.

George was thinking that there wasn't peace or good will, just as he had thought in the church service that God wasn't really ruling with truth and grace. Was God really in charge?

Father looked up from the Bible at his family. It almost seemed to George that Father had read his mind. "He is in charge," Father said as he looked around the table, "and He will take care of us. It's difficult to understand now, but we have His many promises." George could tell that Father really believed what he said. George hoped he was right.

***

Christmas Day ended too soon, it seemed to George.

After supper, they gathered around the fireplace and popped corn in a kettle over the fire. Grandma had remembered how they all loved popcorn, and Mother put out butter in a dish for them to scoop into.

They sang many carols again, ending up with "Joy to the World":

He rules the world with truth and grace,
And makes the nations prove
The glories of His righteousness . . .

George felt better this time as he sang the words. When they were finished, they all left the fireside to go to bed, long after their normal bedtime.

The children were sleeping quietly on their straw mattresses in their attic room when George threw back the quilts and crept over to the window. He looked out over the moonlit snow that covered the street below. A few figures and a single sleigh were passing by. For a few short moments it looked as if peace really had come to the world.

Twenty

George turned onto Murray Street. It was another street like their own, with tall drab houses all touching each other. The wind blew fiercely but the waggoners drove their sleighs with the same reckless speed as on calm days. George hadn't heard from John in two weeks now and he hoped he had come to the right house.

He stood there stamping his feet with the cold. No answer. He tried again. Still no answer. He stepped back and thought he saw the curtain at the window move a little. So someone was there. They just weren't answering the door. Well, he'd wait even if he was late for school. He knocked again much louder.

"What's all that noise," shouted a gruff man as he opened the door. George looked up into the face of a burly man with dark hair. "Well, whatever you want, boy, we don't have none. Now be off with you." He started to close the door.

George was not going to be put off so easily. "I want to speak to John Bleecker. Does he live here?"

The door opened again and the man spoke in a lower voice. "It's John, you want, is it? Well, the lad's at work, which is more than I can say for the likes of you."

"I'm George, John's best friend from Albany, sir. May I speak to him, please?"

Then George saw John's mother come up behind the man and stand beside him. She was much thinner and paler than George had remembered. Her hand trembled a little as she put it on the man's arm and said, "Let him in, please, he's an old friend."

The man opened the door, and John's mother led George through the hallway to the kitchen. She motioned him to a chair and looked nervously at the man. "George, meet my husband, William MacKenzie."

The man peered sharply at George and said, "Good day, George. I'll fetch John." His whole manner had changed after John's mother had come. A big muscular man, well over two hundred pounds, he thumped out the back door.

"Have a muffin, George," John's mother said. The familiar smell of apple-spice muffins reminded him of Albany days.

"Thank you," George said. He put down his books on the floor beside his chair. "I've come to see if John can go to school with us at St. Paul's. I know he's always wanted to be a merchant like his . . . Well, he'll need to study more, Mrs. Blee . . . I mean Mrs. MacKenzie. He'll need to polish up his figures, Ma'am, and I thought he could go along with me."

An awkward silence followed. George was glad when Lucy came through the back door into the kitchen. She carried two large buckets of water and looked up with surprise when she saw George. He jumped up to help her.

"Thank you, George, but I can manage fine," she said as she set them on the floor. Then, one at a time, she lifted them onto a small table at the side of the room. She was almost lost inside John's baggy pants and old homespun shirt.

John came rushing in at that point, and panting a little,

said, "George, I'm surprised to see you." He was frowning.

"I've come to take you to school with me. Our teacher says there's still room for a few more." John stopped frowning and looked at George with new interest. "You always liked school better'n I did," George continued, "and it'll be more fun if you're there, John."

"Do you think I could go too?" Lucy asked.

"My stepfather is a waggoner," John said, "and I have to help him load and unload. I doubt he'll let me go to school, but I'll sure ask."

"It's free," George said.

Then they heard the loud thumping sounds of someone coming. Mr. MacKenzie pushed open the back door and shouted, "Get out here, boy. I'm ready to go." He turned abruptly and was gone.

John turned red. "I'm sorry, George," he mumbled with embarrassment and rushed out the back door.

"Do Mary and Catharine go to school?" Lucy asked.

"Yes, even Anna goes. I think you'd like it, Lucy."

Lucy turned to her Mother then. "Can I go, Mother . . . I'll change real fast and go with George now . . . Please!"

"I don't know, Lucy." Mrs. MacKenzie was so pale that George thought she looked sick. But before she could refuse her daughter's request, Lucy rushed out of the room. Her mother brought the plate of muffins over to George and he readily accepted another one.

Before George had finished eating the muffin, Lucy was back, dressed in a long, full, striped petticoat and a short linen gown. She threw a hooded wool cloak over her shoulders and motioned George to the door.

"What about your lunch?" John's mother asked.

"They give us lunch," George explained.

John's mother was close behind them as they reached the front door. "What time will you be back?"

"School is out at 4:00. We'll walk home with her and we should be here by 4:30 or sooner. St. Paul's isn't far."

George looked back just before they turned off Murray Street and saw John's mother still standing in the doorway, watching.

"Turn around, George," Lucy said, "or she'll change her mind." She was walking in fast strides and George had to move fast to keep up to her. "Mother never lets me go anywhere. She probably won't let me go to school either. But I'm looking forward to going — for today."

A little farther on, George looked sideways at Lucy, who was rushing so much she was puffing. "I think we could slow down now," he said. "We're out of sight of your house."

Lucy smiled then and looked up at George. "You're right," she said. "I was just so glad to get out of there, I wanted to run."

"John isn't happy either. Is there anything wrong, Lucy?"

"Is our stepfather mean to us? Is that what you're asking me, George?" Lucy demanded in an abrupt tone.

Lucy always was direct about things, George remembered. He was feeling uneasy now about asking, but he figured he might just as well continue. "Well, is he?" he asked.

Lucy almost bumped into a couple who were carrying large round baskets covered with cloth. They reminded George of the farm people around Albany, and he remembered taking their own produce to Mr. Bleecker's store and the jovial welcome there. John's stepfather was sure different.

"He's not real mean, but he makes John work awful hard . . . a lot harder than he did in Albany for Dad," Lucy said. "And it's heavy work. I help Mother, and she hardly lets me out of her sight. It's a wonder she'd even let me come today. She's been this way ever since Dad died."

They walked on in silence. A street porter passed them as he carried a heavy load in a wood frame on his back. His long, tattered coat fell way past his knees but didn't quite cover his leggings, which were made of old blanket pieces tied around the legs.

"Do you think your stepfather will let John come to school?"

Lucy was walking quite slowly now. George supposed she had tired herself by rushing so much at first. She hesitated before she answered, "I doubt it. Mr. Mac-Kenzie used to have slaves helping him in the business, but they ran away. He needs John to help."

"Slaves get their freedom if they join the British army," George said, "so they'll not likely be coming back."

They walked on in silence. Suddenly George saw a waggoner racing down the street. "Look out," he yelled as he grabbed Lucy and pulled her back from the street just as they were starting to cross. They felt the raw cut of snow across their faces, thrown up by the speeding sleigh.

Another sleigh was close behind the first one. Safe at the side now, George looked up to see the driver, lashing the horses as he pushed ahead at a rapid speed. In the midst of a whiplash of wet snow, George caught a close glimpse of the driver, who was looking straight ahead. It was John.

Twenty-one

A sk your father," Mother said. "You know I don't approve of the theatre, Mary."

"But, Mother, this play is different. It was written by William Shakespeare, the great English playwright, over one hundred and fifty years ago. Our teacher says it still has meaning for today's world."

Mother's mouth tightened firmly. "I'm surprised Miss Bonisteel gave you those tickets."

"Mother, it's a good cause. Look at the ticket, please. It's to raise money for charity."

"And it might help us with our school work," George said. He wasn't interested in Shakespeare, but he figured anything would break the deadly boredom of the long, cold, winter evenings. Besides, school was no fun either — and it didn't help that John and Lucy hadn't been allowed to go or that John was always so sad. When John and Lucy visited the Waltermyer children, which they did a few times, John seemed almost like his old self. Most of the time, however, he was very quiet and withdrawn, and he never invited George to his home.

The winter had been a bitter one. The price of wood had continued to rise and the army had ordered people not to cut trees — but that did not prevent smaller trees around the city from disappearing overnight. With Father's savings, the Waltermyer family was able to buy enough wood to keep the chilling cold from their bigger room. But at night, the other room was so cold that the children had to drag their mattresses close to the doorway between the two rooms to get any heat at all. It was March now, but the bitter weather showed no signs of letting up.

Father opened the door and walked in quietly. He bent over his wife and said quietly, "I've received my marching orders. I leave in the morning . . . I may be gone for months."

George overheard and he was even more eager to be off too. He was almost fourteen now, and others had joined up at his age. At his first chance to speak to Father alone, he would tell him his plans.

Mary rushed to her father first. "I have tickets for a theatre performance. It's going to help us at school."

"Oh, really? Here, let me look at them," he replied.

After he had examined the tickets, he turned to his wife and said, "Well, what do you say, Polly, my girl? Shall we go out this evening?"

"I don't think we should, Hans. The children could pick up bad ideas. They say the language in some of those plays is not the best."

"I doubt that one performance will corrupt them. Anyway, the language on the streets these days is not the best either. We're not isolated anymore. Besides, we haven't had much excitement lately. Let's go."

Polly knew her husband wanted to make the children happy on his last night at home, so she nodded and said, "Very well, but who'll look after Jacob and Anna?"

"I will," Tobias volunteered.

"Me too," said Leonard, who thought the play would be too much like school.

Father smiled. "Then it's decided," he said. He sat

down in the easy chair by the fireplace. As he watched Polly carry the steaming kettle to the table, he savoured the moments he had spent with her and his young family. There were long months of loneliness ahead. How he would miss her! They had married while still in their teens, almost fifteen years and seven children ago, but she was still very beautiful. Her deep blue eyes were as clear as ever, and the ruffles of her mob cap framed her rosy face, flushed just now after her work over the hot fire. In spite of the hardships of late, she still had the same deep dimples when she smiled. But she was not smiling now, for she was worried about the next day.

His wife and children were strong and they would survive this war, Hans convinced himself. He wished there was some way he could have spared them this pain, but there was no way out. The most he could do now was to get on with the job. He'd keep fighting for their property and for peace. This bloody war couldn't last forever! He gazed sadly into the blazing flames of the open hearth and prayed that peace would come.

***

After supper, the Waltermyers, dressed in their best, walked briskly towards the theatre on John Street. Their teacher had explained to the girls that it would be crowded and difficult to obtain a seat if they were late. She said the rich people sent their slaves or servants as early as five o'clock to hold their box seats until they arrived.

The Waltermyers arrived around 6:30, but the congestion was already bad outside the theatre. Grandly dressed ladies descended from their carriages.

There was one lady right in front of them dressed in a long, royal blue velvet gown with a mink fur cape over her shoulders. Her hat had a bright red ribbon around it that tied in a bow and hung down the back. At its front, there were two huge soft yellow feathers that curled out and forward. As she walked, the feathers of the hat swirled about. She took her gentleman friend's hand as she climbed down from the carriage, and held her petticoat up, showing just the tip of the toe of her brightly painted shoe.

The officer with her was no less splendid in his bright red jacket with black lapels and his snow-white trousers. White lace frills showed at his neck and wrists when he held out his hand to help her. George liked the look of the red British coats better than the dark forest green of the Loyalists, but Father explained that, in battle, green was a safer colour.

"Well, let's go." Father gave Mary and Catharine a gentle push. Like George, they too were staring at all the sights.

Outside, the building was not too unusual, just a large, plain, red brick building. It was about sixty feet back from the street, with a covered archway made of rough wood leading to the entrance.

Inside, George could not believe it was the same place. The lobby had fine floor coverings with bright red, white, and blue flags hung on the walls. Vases of real and homemade flowers adorned the tables.

When everyone was in their seats, an elderly violinist came to the front of the stage. His clothes were so old-fashioned they looked like something out of the 1740s. He had a full-sleeved coat, a long-skirted vest, and a long, full-bodied wig. But his music wasn't out of style. The crowd gradually became quieter as he played

Bach's "Air on a G String." Then the tune changed suddenly to a different but very familiar one. The audience rose to sing the national anthem. The Waltermyers all sang loudly — the children with enthusiasm, their parents with solemnity and some sadness, as they knew what it was costing them to sing it:

> God save Great George our King,
> Long live our noble King,
> God save the King:
> Send him victorious,
> Happy and glorious,
> Long to reign over us:
> God save the King.

When the violinist left the stage, everyone sat down, and an actor came to the front of the almost-empty platform. "Now is the winter of our discontent . . . ," his voice boomed through the theatre. Then the strange-looking, hunchbacked man started talking about all his problems and his great desire to be important.

"I can't understand this stuff much," George complained.

"Hans, do you think this play is going to be violent? We have enough violence around us now without coming here to see more," Mother protested.

Before Father had a chance to answer, a lady behind him whispered loudly, "I can't see." She tapped Father on the shoulder and said, "I can't see over you. Do you suppose you could sit down a little?"

Father nodded and slid forward to the edge of the seat, his legs stretched in a cramped position far under the seat ahead.

"There's a lady in this scene," Catharine whispered. "Oh, look, Mary, she's in mourning, poor soul."

Father spoke out instantly. "Poor soul, nothing! That's a British officer wearing women's clothes. Can't you tell that's a man's voice?"

"Father, everyone knows some of the women's roles are acted by the men. But there's a new lady actress for this play. Her name's Maria Turner. My teacher said she'd be acting tonight."

"Quiet!" a man hissed behind Mary.

Continuing in a softer voice, Mary explained, "All of the male parts are acted by British officers. Our teacher says Major André of the Guards, and Major Moncrieffe of the Engineers are the favourite ones."

"British officers! I can't take this anymore. I'm going."

"Hans! Wait!"

"Polly, I'll be waiting outside when it's over!"

Father untangled himself slowly from his seat, then strode out into the darkness.

"This play is crazy!" George said. "First that man wants her to kill him with the sword. Now he wants her to marry him. I think I'll go look for Father." George started to leave his seat.

"Sit down this minute, George. You don't know where your Father has gotten to by now. He'll come later to meet us."

"Quiet!" yelled several from behind.

"Too bad children are allowed to come to these performances," another person said.

"They just don't seem to have respect for their elders the way they used to when I was young," an older woman's voice added loudly.

George was glad it was dark. He stayed for only a few more minutes, then slipped out quietly to look for his father.

Hans Waltermyer was still standing by the lamp-post when George reached the street. He stood beside his father for a minute without speaking.

Then Waltermyer turned to his son and said, "It's too cold to stand here. Let's walk around a bit." At first, George was finding it difficult to keep up to his father's long strides. Yet he had to keep up with him. He could not lose this time to talk. Back at the apartment there would be no privacy for a conversation. "I need to talk," he said, " . . . before we get back home."

His father turned then, as though just realizing his son was there. He slowed his pace to a crawl. "You heard, didn't you?" he said.

"Yes, I know you're leaving in the morning. I want to go too. I'll be one of your recruits. I know there are fourteen-year-olds in the army."

"Yes, there are, George. Some of them are orphans and some have followed their fathers, but you have a family who need you here. Your mother needs you. I can't be with them, so you have to stay. Please promise me, George, that you'll not run away and leave them."

Suddenly George's resentment flared. Why should he have to take care of the family? That was his father's job, not his. He turned to his father and said, "I'll stay if I must. I'll not run away the way *you* did!"

A silence followed. George had not intended to say those words. But he wouldn't take them back now. After all, they were true. Finally, he looked sideways at his father.

There was no anger in his father's face or in his voice

when he spoke. "I had no choice, George," he said. "I didn't . . . I don't want to be on the run all the time the way I am."

"No choice! You could have joined the Rebels like all our neighbours!"

"Could I? Could I ignore what they did to Vandervoot, a good man, and our neighbour too? Could I pretend the British had done us harm?"

George felt the emotion in his father's voice and he looked down as he said, "There were atrocities on both sides. Grandfather told me about some of the Redcoats' murders."

Father replied quietly, "I believe that, but they did not happen on my doorstep like Vandervoot's hanging. I could not be a part of that. I did what I had to do. Afterwards I no longer had a choice. Life often doesn't have as many choices as we think it's going to."

George did not answer. They walked on in silence.

Finally his father spoke, "Some day you'll understand, George."

George doubted that, but he didn't answer. There was no point in arguing any more. After all, his father was leaving in the morning.

***

When Mother, Catharine, and Mary stumbled out of the theatre, it was pitch dark. Only the occasional lamp cast light on the streets. Some had gone out and no lamplighter was in sight. Father and George were waiting for them. Keeping close together, they hurried noiselessly along the crowded streets.

When they reached their rooms, they found them

quiet. The door to the children's bedroom was closed. This was the first night that the weather had felt a bit milder.

"Let's sit for a bit by the fire," Father said as George and the girls started to head for bed.

George sat cross-legged on the floor. Catharine sat on a nearby chair, and Mary sat on the floor leaning against Father's chair. Without looking up, Mother poked the fire and added a large chunk of wood to last for the night.

Father gave them the news very simply and directly. There was no easy way to tell his family. "Tomorrow, when you wake up, I'll be gone. I have my orders."

"Where will you go?" Mary asked.

"I can't tell you. Those are army rules. In fact, I won't know the details myself until I report in. It may be some time before I see you again, but one day this war will be over, and we'll all go home again."

"Really home or to Grandfather's?" George asked, for Father had told him that a new tenant, a Rebel sympathizer, had taken their old farm.

"Really home, George."

Father stared into the flames. Mother and the children gazed at him sadly, knowing that they might never see him again.

Twenty-two

"Can you use an extra hand, John?" asked George, who had hurried out of the stifling hot attic rooms just after sun-up. It was mid-August, and the family had not heard from their father since he had left in March.

John was sitting on an empty wagon in his stepfather's backyard. Surprised to see George so early, he tied the horse's reins to a post and jumped down beside George. "How come you're offering to help on a day like this? It must be a hundred in the shade even now. I can't imagine how hot it'll be by noon." He mopped his brow with a big red kerchief.

John's stepfather came rushing out of the house then, and seeing George, he shouted, "No time for play. We have to haul all day down to Cunningham's prison-ship by the southwest shore."

"Well maybe we could use some help. It would speed things up," John said. He frowned at his stepfather as he waited for an answer.

"You could be right, John. But mind no playing on the way. Keep those horses moving," Mr. MacKenzie ordered as he looked sternly out at John from under his heavy dark eyebrows. "Is that dog going too?"

"I was counting on taking him, sir . . . if it's all right with you. But I could run him home first."

"I guess it's all right. But mind don't let him run around loose at all. The waggoners wouldn't take kindly to havin' their teams spooked. I couldn't be responsible for what they might do to the dog — or his owner either for that matter."

John was still frowning. "C'mon, George," he grumbled under his breath, "before he changes his mind." He unwound the reins from the hitching-post and jumped back up on the wagon. George leapt onto the wagon with Boots right behind him. John lashed the horses and they were on their way. John explained, "First, we have to go up to the north of Manhattan Island to the military post to pick up supplies."

The boys sat cross-legged on the empty wagon with Boots sprawled out right beside George. "He'll behave," George said. "He's too hot these days to do anything else."

"Yeah . . . like the rest of us," said John. "What I wouldn't give just to take the day off and go fishing."

George thought back. "Remember that time you came out to the farm and we fished off Cooeyman's Landing and you caught such a big fish he pulled you in?"

"Yeah, and nobody believed me. They just thought I wanted to be the first one to go for a swim that year."

George laughed. "And you *were* the first, John." He looked sideways at John and was pleased to see that he was smiling. So George thought this might be a good time to ask. "I'd kinda like to drive that team. Mr. MacKenzie wouldn't need to know. I miss the farm animals."

"They're not the easiest team to handle. I have to be rough sometimes to control them. It's the way they've been trained."

"Well, you're right here to take over if I need you."

John handed the reins to George. Then he reached back and patted Boots.

George lightly whipped the reins against the horses' backs. "If we go fast now while we're travelling empty, we might have extra time later."

"It doesn't make any difference, George. Mr. Mac-Kenzie will just have an extra job waiting for us."

The boys and the dog bounced up and down as the wagon sped over the rough gravel road.

"I wasn't figuring on getting back any earlier . . . just kinda falling in the river after we unload by the prison-ship," George said. "In this heat we'd be dry again before we reached home."

John sat upright and his eyes sparkled. "Of course! Why didn't I think of that?"

"You can have a swim too, Boots," George said. The dog sat up and George was sure he understood.

They could see the Redcoats on patrol by the northern barracks and George drew the horses to a halt. "You better take over here, John. You know your way around."

John took the reins. "I've been driving for Mr. Mac-Kenzie for two years come October. I ought to know my way around by now."

"Did you come right to New York after . . . ?" George asked. He was reluctant to mention John's father because he knew his friend was still hurting.

"No. We went to my Uncle Peter's at Wallkill, but they were in enough trouble with their neighbours because their two sons had joined the British. So we didn't stay long — only a few days — and caught a sloop on into New York."

"Did you know anyone in New York?" George asked.

John drew the horses to a halt and handed the Redcoat

the delivery order his stepfather had given him. The
soldier motioned them to a big grey stone building. John
said, "We gotta load this wagon now, George."

Half an hour later, the boys were on the road back
down to the city. John hadn't continued telling George
about how they came to New York, and George wondered if he should bring up the subject again. John had
visited them only about once or twice a month since
they'd come to the city, and even then he'd been so quiet
it almost seemed that John wasn't his best friend anymore. But today John seemed more relaxed, almost like
his old self. So George said, "You came to New York that
same summer . . . "

John spoke freely, "Yes, George. We came to the
Refugee Camp. We were dependent on handouts. It was
barely enough and very crowded."

"So how did your mother meet Mr. MacKenzie?"
George hoped John wouldn't mind his asking.

"She didn't!" John said.

"What?"

"I was the one who met him — I offered to help with
the work around, and the Redcoats got me loading wagons," John said as he let the reins go loose on his lap.

George noticed John's thoughts were not with the
horses. "Will you let me drive again?" he asked.

John handed him the reins and continued. "Well, Mr.
MacKenzie asked me to work for him. He paid me a little.
I had to work awful hard . . . same as now, but I didn't
mind, and the money helped us. Then this one night we
were late, and Mother was waiting for me. From then on,
Mr. MacKenzie was coming by every Sunday and asking
us to go for a ride."

George looked at John, who was looking down and

frowning. John continued, "Then a month later, he asked Mother to go alone this one Sunday, and she came back and told us she was going to marry this man we hardly knew — the very next Saturday! After that, we moved into his house."

There was silence for a minute before George said, "You have a whole house to yourselves, John. That's nice for your mother and Lucy."

"Yes, I think she musta married him for the house, but how could she? So soon after Dad died. And he's nothing like Dad. All he ever thinks about is his work . . . He doesn't pay me now either. And it's all my fault he met Mother." John looked completely dejected.

George could tell how much his friend missed his father, and feeling guilty over his mother's marriage wasn't helping any. "It's not your fault, John. She probably would have just met someone else."

"But Dad was only gone a little more'n three months."

"I'm sorry, John." Boots wiggled in between them then and John reached out to pat him. He left his arm around the dog as they rode on with George steering the horses carefully past people in the crowded downtown. To their right, the Hudson River was very still today. It was really not a river this far south but a narrow inlet of the sea.

George handed the reins to John again as they drove into the military post. Once again John showed papers to the soldier at the entrance and drove through the gate. Then another soldier motioned them on. They followed a wagon just ahead, then drove past three large buildings and turned a corner that brought them to a halt parallel to the shoreline. Six wagons were ahead of them in line. A wagon wheeled in right behind them with another one after it.

"I can bloody well see our swim-time's gone!" John

exclaimed. "If each one takes twenty minutes to a half-hour to unload, that could be a wait of two to three hours. He slumped down on a bag of sugar. George sprawled out on a flour bag and glared at the line-up ahead. He wondered if it might go faster than John figured.

It didn't. Time seemed to drag. George looked down the slope to the still water. It was so inviting. Just then Boots jumped off the wagon and ran down to the shore. "Come back, Boots," George yelled and ran after him. Boots paid no attention. He jumped right in and swam in circles by the shore.

"That's a great idea, Boots," George said. He threw off his shirt and jumped in with his long trousers still on. The water wasn't even cold, but he ducked right under to cool his head a little. It sure felt better than the hot sweat dripping through his hair and down his back.

When he came up, there was John swimming right beside him and laughing loudly. It was the old John with the loud laugh that George remembered.

Then George thought about the horses. "John . . . what about the horses?"

John laughed again and pointed to the wagons. An old man was sitting on the load, holding the reins loosely as he watched the boys swim. "He's with the load behind us," John explained.

The prison-ship was not far away. A large ship with no sails, it seemed to tip a little to one side. "Think you could swim that far?" George asked.

"I can beat you there," John said and he was off. George and Boots followed, but John swam up first to within a hundred yards of the ship. Then he turned back and met George and Boots coming towards him and the ship.

George could hear moaning coming from open windows at the side of the ship as he and Boots stopped to tread water. "Let's swim around to the far side," he suggested.

On the other side they could see a guard patrolling on the deck. Then he disappeared. George figured he went below to cool off. The prisoners, their shoulder blades protruding in their bare backs, were washing the deck under the blistering sun. George could not believe how incredibly thin the men were. Only one man stopped to look over the railing at the boys. George just stared and forgot to tread water.

"George!" John yelled as he grabbed his friend. George gulped a mouthful of salty water. He started swimming back at once, for he was uneasy in the deep water and in sight of the prisoners.

When they reached the shore, John said, "I'm taking them those watermelons we've got on board. Let's hurry back or we won't have time."

Reaching the shore again, they pulled themselves out of the water. Boots came out behind them, a bedraggled mass of dripping hair. There were three teams ahead of them in line. The line was moving faster than John had predicted.

"I don't think this is such a good idea, John. What if we're caught?" George mumbled. He was feeling tired now and he didn't like the idea of swimming out there in the deep water again.

John reached the wagon first. "Thanks for watching the team. Could you manage a little longer?" he asked the older man.

"I guess so," the man said. "You gonna take another ducking? Why'd you come back? You haven't got a lot of time, you know. Only three ahead now."

"I got a kind of a nasty job to do," John said as he grabbed a bag on the edge of the load. "I almost forgot. The waggoner told me to drown these kittens while I was down here."

The older man shook his head. "Yeah. I hate doing that myself. But it has to be done. Not enough food for people, let alone animals. You're lucky he let you keep the dog."

"That's not my dog. He's my friend's," John said as he lifted the bag lightly and started down the hill.

"Mighty quiet kittens," the man mumbled. "They've probably suffocated already in the sack."

George reached out to give John a hand. "Not yet," John said. "Kittens aren't heavy!"

"I still can't understand why you're doing this, John," George said.

John did not answer. At the edge of the water, John said, "Well, are you with me?"

George nodded and jumped into the water. They swam with the bag of watermelons between them. George knew if the guard was back they would have to let the bag float away. Anyway, how would the prisoners ever get the bag aboard?

On the far side of the ship, they kept treading water while they watched a guard taking a turn around the deck. "It's too hot for him to stay on deck long," John said. When the guard was out of sight, he gave a sharp, piercing whistle like a waggoner calling his dog.

A prisoner on the deck turned and looked down over the ship's side. George thought there was something familiar about the thin face that peered at them. Still treading water, they tried to hold up the bag to show the prisoner they had something for him.

The prisoner nodded. He dropped a rope over the

ship's side and lowered it down — a full twenty-five feet to the water. It dangled there very close to the ship. John started to swim towards it, pulling the bag and George with him. George pushed ahead too, for he wanted to finish this job.

"Hold up the end of the sack," John ordered as he grabbed for the rope dangling back and forth. Finally he caught hold of it and came back to George, who was struggling to keep the watermelons in place. John managed to tie the rope to the bag.

George saw the bag slowly going up towards the ship. He didn't wait any longer. He headed for shore. It wasn't far, but he didn't want to be caught there. He hoped John had enough sense to follow.

George looked ahead once as he swam, just to make sure he was going in the right direction, and he saw Boots sitting on the shore. He's got more sense than we have, he thought to himself. He could hear a splashing sound behind him and knew John was catching up to him.

They crawled out of the sea water together and sank down full length on the gravelly shore. "Did they get the watermelons?" George asked.

"They sure did," John said. He was panting like a dog. "I looked back . . . just before I came round the end . . . of the ship. There were three fellows . . . spitting out watermelon seeds over the deck railing."

"C'mon," a man shouted. It was the man watching their wagon. He'd driven right up to the loading zone. Gasping with fatigue, they ran up the knoll.

"What took you so long?" the man asked.

John smiled at him. "It was sure right neighbourly of you to help us out. Thanks a lot, mister."

"Hey, waggoner up there. Get to work unloading. We

don't have all day to wait," a soldier shouted at the boys. Some of the waggoners behind were pacing along beside their vehicles and looked up with envy at the two dripping wet boys jumping up onto the wagon and reaching for the bags and barrels.

George felt so tired he wondered how he could ever help unload. But John had already started. The bags hit the landing with sharp thuds as John threw them down without a break. George started to roll barrels across the wagon and off onto the walkway.

"Get that dog," a soldier shouted. George looked up to see that Boots had knocked over a teetering barrel, and the impact had loosened the lid. Sticky black molasses was oozing out over the ground.

John reached the barrel first and set it upright before much was lost. "Take it out of my pay," he said to the angry soldier. George grabbed his dog just before the soldier reached him. Boots still struggled to go over to lick up the molasses.

The soldier stepped back. "Very well," he said to John and started to figure out how much he would dock John's pay.

George dragged Boots by the long hair of his neck towards their wagon. "Sit," he said in a nasty voice. "Bad dog!" Boots sat still with his head down. He knew he was in trouble.

Then George heard John explaining further to the soldier. "I'm sorry, the sack of watermelons just rolled off the back. I guess we were trying too hard to make time," John said. "Anyway, the watermelons smashed all to pieces. We had to throw them away."

"That does it," the soldier said. "You'll get nothing for transporting this load."

John jumped up silently onto the empty wagon and whipped the horses away. The man behind them who had held their horses was shaking his head as the team raced out past the guard and through the open gate.

"You better not race them too long in this heat," George advised.

John handed the reins to George. "You're right," he said. "How would you like to drive for a while?"

George was glad to help after all the trouble Boots had caused. And he didn't have any money to pay his friend. "I'm sorry about the molasses. I don't know what got into Boots. When Father comes in the fall, I'll pay you back," George promised in an apologetic tone.

"That's okay," John said.

"How can your stepfather take it out of your wages when he doesn't pay you?" George asked.

"Well, he did today," John laughed. "He'll be out of pocket when he doesn't get payment for this load. You might say I got wages." George looked at his friend. His merry laugh and red face, burned by the summer sun, reminded George of John's father.

"Why did you help those men on the boat? After all, they were Rebels," said George.

"Didn't you recognize him?" John mumbled.

George shook his head, but then the face of the man who had leaned over the side of the ship flashed before his eyes again. George gasped, "Simeon!" He was the older brother of Reuben, their classmate.

John nodded. George put his arm around his dog as he tried to control the sobs that were starting to shake through him.

Twenty-three

George recognized the Yonkers dock and the woods beyond, into which James DeLancey had vanished almost a year before. Again the leaves were in full colour on the elm and maple, making the spruce look even deeper green.

"How much farther do you think?" John Bleecker asked. He was carrying a large packsack on his back, and as he spoke he shifted it to his shoulder.

"I can't be certain," said George. "But I think about three miles north and then a little east. We're lucky it's a sunny day. It's easier to get our directions straight."

"What if that man in town wasn't really one of James's men?" John asked.

George reassured his friend, "He was James's man all right. But I'm not sure he gave us the right directions. His name's Ben. I'll never forget him."

"Are you so sure they'll let me join them?" John asked.

George looked around at John. He figured his friend was not as eager as he had been a week ago when they had planned his escape from home and New York City. "You changing your mind?" he asked.

"Not about leaving home. But I wonder if it might be better for me to go to my uncle's farm at Wallkill — west of the Hudson."

"West!" George said. "They're inside enemy territory. Are you sure they'll even want to see you, John?"

"Uncle Peter swore allegiance to the Rebels because Aunt Jane wasn't well enough to travel. He's too old for battle anyway, but his two sons are both fighting for the British. They'll need an extra hand on the farm."

"I don't know, John," George said thoughtfully. "I'd hesitate to travel alone into that occupied territory. It's not far from the Rebels stationed at West Point."

George studied his friend. He knew John was not an outdoors type like himself and he likely didn't know how hard farm work could be. "Don't be concerned about Ben's appearance. He does what James says. And James is okay."

"How do I know he'll help me?"

"He knows Father." They were into the woods now. "Let's just rest for a minute," George suggested. He set his heavy pack on the ground.

Each leaned against a large maple tree and reached into George's bag for a sandwich. In his free hand, George picked up a large red maple leaf and crunched it as he thought of the note he'd left at home. He hoped his mother understood that he had to help his friend and that he'd be back in a few days. Surely they could manage without him that long.

Anyway, Father would soon be back for the winter again, though they had only received one message from him all summer. Oliver DeLancey had brought it to them in August, along with Father's pay. George grimaced at the thought of that DeLancey. He and John had travelled to his Loyalist barracks on Long Island to ask him where to find James. He had claimed he had no knowledge of his brother or his activities. He'd almost acted ashamed of James.

"I guess we'd better keep moving," John said, standing suddenly.

George jumped to his feet. "Sure, John," he said.

As they strode deeper into the woods, George said, "We could go back to New York. Are you sure you still want to go on?"

"*Yes.*"

"How do you think your mother will take it?"

"She'll adjust quickly. Just like she did after Dad was gone." They were following a trail now, and John was leading at a swift pace.

"I don't see my father much, John," George said. "And he's not the same. It's like the war has taken him too."

"When it's over it'll be the same again. But not for me. Be thankful he's still alive, George!"

George felt the strong emotion in his friend's voice and he did not reply. But he couldn't help wondering if anything would ever be the same.

Zingggg . . . pufffffff. A loud crack followed by a cloud of smoke filled the air around the boys. Instantly, they threw themselves flat on the ground.

Afraid to breathe, George lay still as he heard footsteps breaking the underbrush nearby. Before he could roll to the side of the path, he was looking up from the toe of a boot into a dark, bearded face.

"It's him agin," Ben said. "Git up, you pest!"

George jumped to his feet. John, only a few feet away, sat looking in dismay at Ben, who was still holding his gun.

"We need to see James," George said sternly.

"Yeah. What do you want to see James fer?" He set his musket against the tree. John's colour began to return.

"That's my business," George snapped.

"Your business. I see. Well, it's not my business to take boys where they're not wanted. Now make tracks back the way you come. And be glad I'm lettin' you go."

John was already starting down the trail when George said in a friendly voice, "My friend really needs help. His father was Janse Bleecker, a Loyalist who died a year ago. He's all alone now, Ben, and he'd even be willing to help cook."

"Come back, boy," Ben called out in a voice that was a bit less gruff.

***

At dusk James looked up with surprise as he saw George and John following Ben into the camp. "Couldn't stay away from our beefsteaks, eh, George?" he laughed, digging into the pan to get one steak for each boy.

They took the hot meat in their bare hands and ate greedily. George wished he could have brought Boots to enjoy the bones. The men sitting on the other side of the fire paid little attention. Two horses were tethered just outside the circle of firelight — James's mount and the mare that George had ridden the day they'd "raided" the sloop.

The meal finished, James turned to George. "Now tell me, George, why were you stupid enough to come back here into no-man's-land?"

George was shocked by James's abrupt manner. He had remembered him as a kind hero who had rescued him. Now he was talking almost like an angry father. "I came to help my friend," he said.

"How?"

"He wants to join up with the Cowboys."

"We don't need boys," James said impatiently.

John was shifting about restlessly on the stump he was sitting on. "I don't need your help. I'll live alone in the woods," he burst out.

"Live alone! In these woods? Don't you know the dangers?"

"What dangers?" George asked.

"The Skinners! Rebels! Scavengers! Wild animals! Any or all of them," James shot back.

John turned pale.

Sitting there by the campfire, George started to feel quite brave: "Well, the Skinners wouldn't be a problem. I'd just pretend to be a Rebel. And I didn't see any wild animals when I came through here before."

James couldn't help smiling at George. "Well, you were lucky," he said. "They are here — bears and wolves even."

"Well, the human wolves would worry me — the Scavengers," George admitted. "I don't know how I'd handle them."

"So you'll go back then," James said with relief.

John was still very pale but determined. "No. I won't go back and face my stepfather. I'd sooner face the Scavengers."

"Very well, if you'll work in our camp, you can stay."

John looked relieved. "I don't care how long. I'm not going back."

James turned to George. "I'll take you to the edge of Yonkers, and I don't want to see you back here again. I'm too busy. Why didn't you ask your father for help?"

"He's never home this time of year. Anyhow, if you see him, maybe you shouldn't mention about my being here." George looked uncomfortable.

"I see. Well . . . your father travels swiftly and alone. Sometimes I envy him. I have a hard enough time with my men as it is without . . . George, when you reach New York, stay there!"

"I hope I don't have any trouble on the sloop. That skipper asked a lot of questions when we came aboard."

"I know the skipper that's sailing in there tonight. We better make tracks to catch that boat. The others aren't too friendly."

George filled his sack with bones for Boots. Then he turned to John. "I just wish I could stay with you. But I can't leave the family. They need me."

John nodded. "Look out for Lucy," he said. "She's okay, but Mother keeps her in so much, I'm afraid it isn't good for her."

"I'll look in on her, John," George said. Then, putting his hand on John's shoulder, he said, "When this is all over, come back to visit us."

"Where?" John asked.

"At Cooeyman's Landing . . . back on the farm."

"Come on!" James yelled from his mount.

George dropped his arm and turned and leapt onto the mare, and without looking back, he followed James into the woods.

Twenty-four

C ome quickly, George," Mother called. George rubbed the sleep from his eyes and stumbled into the front room in his night clothes.

Catharine's reddened face was darkening and she was gasping for breath. Mother motioned him to lift Catharine from the bed to the armchair beside a pot of water boiling on the hearth. She inhaled the steam for about five minutes before her choking gasps subsided, but her breathing was still laboured. George stayed and held her there.

Mary came rushing out then and asked, "May I help?"

"Yes, steady Catharine while George and I move this bed closer to the steam," Mother said.

It was mid-January now and they had all been sick by turns since Christmas. An epidemic of agues and intermittent fevers had spread throughout the city. They had all responded well to the herbs that Mother had brought from the farm — all except Catharine. And her coughing was growing worse. George hoped that Father would soon come back. They had not gone for a doctor, since half the city was sick, and it was hard to find a doctor free to come to their home.

George lifted Catharine back into the bed that was now near the fireside. She rested a little more easily against the pillows. George and Mary sat on the bedside opposite the fire.

"Father will come one of these days and take us all back to the farm, and you'll get better real fast," Mary reassured her sister.

"I hope so," Catharine whispered, still weak from her ordeal.

George was afraid this wasn't going to happen. Another Christmas had come and gone and they had not heard from Father. He was starting to worry about what had happened to him.

New York had been hit with one of the hardest winters ever. The cold and repeated storms had come with a vengeance. In early December, Sir Henry Clinton had issued orders allowing people to cut down trees for fuel, with the exception of spruce trees. The bark from the spruce was used to make beer and other drinks that helped ward off scurvy. Fresh produce was very scarce and beyond the means of most families. In spite of the precaution, Manhattan Island and nearby Staten Island were soon stripped of all their trees. The farmers to the north of the city objected in vain. The General promised compensation. But since a number of his promises had not been kept, the people had started to distrust him and had little hope that they would receive payment for their wood.

The crisis passed, Catharine was breathing easier now, but she suddenly put her head in her hands and started to sob until her shoulders shook.

Mother and Mary had gone into the other room to wake the others. George said awkwardly, "Please don't cry, Catharine."

"I'm not crying because I'm sick . . . It's . . . because . . . I want to go home. I want to see the roses and the lilacs and the garden and our own clean room and the swing and . . . Father. Why doesn't Father come, George? . . . Why?"

"He'll be here any day now, Catharine. You just rest."

***

George was thinking about Catharine as he walked to school. He would find a flower for her even if it was winter. He didn't know where, but he would find one.

"What do you think has happened to Father?" Mary asked. She and George were walking just behind the others.

"He's busy. If he were sick or worse, they would have told us." They walked on in silence. Then George said, "Mary, where do you suppose I might find a flower, any kind of flower?"

"Now?" Mary asked with surprise.

"Yes, now . . . for Catharine."

"There were sewn flowers in the lobby of the theatre, and you couldn't tell the difference at a distance."

"That's it, Mary. I'll go to the theatre."

"Let me go too," Mary coaxed.

"No, Mary. I'll go alone," George said.

Mary smiled as she looked up, for they had reached the school and a teacher was standing in the doorway. "Not without being missed you won't," Mary said.

"And how can you help?" George grumbled.

"I'll pretend to be sick and ask to have you take me home," Mary smiled confidently. "But only if you promise to take me with you. Do you promise, George?"

"I promise, but be sick early, Mary. We have a test this morning."

***

The pupils in Mr. Inglis' crowded class quietly bowed their heads. They had just finished singing "God Save the King" and were starting the Lord's Prayer. Some were speaking out loudly; a few were mumbling. George kept his eyes open. He was waiting anxiously for the morning exercises to be over.

Our Father which art in Heaven,
Hallowed be Thy name.
Thy kingdom come.
Thy will be done on earth, as it is in heaven.
Give us this day our daily bread.
And forgive us our trespasses, as we forgive those
who trespass against us.
And lead us not into temptation, but deliver us
from evil:
For Thine is the kingdom, and the power,
And the glory, for ever and ever. Amen.

The boy across the aisle whispered to George with a smirk, "I studied all evening. I'm not worried about this test at all." His hands were resting on his desk as he waited for the teacher to hand out the papers.

"Good for you," George hissed back.

Mr. Inglis looked up just then. "George! You should be using this time to look over your history notes. Why are you talking to Raymond?"

"Sir, I was just . . . ," George stammered.

Mr. Inglis picked up the foolscap as he spoke. "Well, George, I'm waiting," he said.

A knock came at the door.

George watched with relief as Mr. Inglis walked to the door.

In a moment, he came back and went straight over to George. "Your sister Mary is sick, George. You are to walk her home. You'll be given a different test next week."

Tobias immediately waved his hand in the air, hoping to be let out too. But George was out of the room and on down the hallway before Mr. Inglis could answer Tobias.

"Tobias and Leonard know you're 'sick,'" George told Mary. "They overheard Mr. Inglis. So I guess we'll have to tell them the truth after school when we meet them with Catharine's flower. They probably won't tell on us.

"Now where is the theatre?"

"It's on John Street. We'll follow Broadway straight on down to John Street to the theatre. It's not far."

"We may have to spend the rest of the day somewhere. We can't wait outside the school all day," George said.

"We can worry about that later. Right now, I'm trying to remember the way to the theatre. It was dark when we went last winter." Mary didn't need to be quite so bossy, but he wasn't sure where the theatre was himself, so he went along with her orders.

As they hurried towards John Street, the snow crunched under their feet. Sleighs passed them. The horses' breath shot out of their nostrils as their drivers whipped them ahead. Mary and George stayed close together. The streets were busy, and they did not want to be separated.

A big man bumped into Mary and almost knocked her over. As quickly as he came, he was lost in the crowd. Struggling to keep her balance, Mary dropped her few books and scattered them all over the side of the street.

George and Mary stooped to pick them up, but another man tramped over them before they could snatch them out of the way. Mary's work sheets were torn, and the copy of *Gulliver's Travels* that her teacher had lent her had a huge, dark footprint on the front cover. Mary brushed the snow from between its pages and put her ripped work sheets inside it. She clasped it tightly with one hand and hung onto George with her other hand.

George was almost fifteen now, and he was nearly five feet nine inches tall. At last he was no longer small for his age. With his sturdy frame, he was not buffeted about by the sudden wind that had started swirling around them. It circled by and then blew at their backs and pushed them on down the street.

"Anything look familiar?" George asked.

"No, it's hard to see in this storm."

"Keep looking. It's probably only a squall. It should pass soon."

"Let's ask someone."

"Okay." They stopped beside an elderly man huddled in a doorway. He clutched his light coat tightly around him. His reddened face was leathered with wrinkles from the weather and his age.

"Which way to the theatre?" they asked.

"Over that way," he answered, waving his arm around in a southerly direction.

They kept going south. Between gusts of wind and snow, they could see the buildings distinctly. George thought he would be able to see the theatre from Broadway. But he was not sure. The theatre had been a short distance from Broadway, on John Street.

The wind seemed to be growing stronger and Mary pulled her woollen toque tighter over her ears.

George shouted above the noise of the wind, "This can't be the theatre area."

"Why not?"

"Look!"

They waited for another lull in the wind to look about them. They realized at once that they were no longer surrounded by a crowd. There were some passersby, but not nearly as many as before. And the roadway did not have as much traffic. Horses occasionally went snorting by, and then the noise of the storm isolated them again in their own small, white island.

As a partial clearing in the snow came, they could see that the buildings were different. They were made of frames, covered with flapping pieces of canvas. In other places the snow so weighed down the sagging low roof-tops, that the children could only guess that the roofs were covered with canvas or sailcloth. Between some buildings heaps of snow were visible, suspended between the crumbling walls.

"This is Canvas Town, Mary," George said abruptly. "I've heard the soldiers in our building talk and laugh about visiting this part of town."

"I don't know why they laughed. It's a dreadful place. A lady at the barracks told us about the very poor people who live here."

"Well, we've come too far. We'd better turn around."

"George, my legs feel numb. Couldn't we just get warm somewhere before we go back?"

"I don't think so. There are no stores along here."

"Let's find a shelter somewhere behind the canvas."

"It might not be safe, Mary. We don't know who'd be there. I've heard that desperate people hang around here."

"I'm so cold." The white wind blew all the more fiercely and a small group of people bumped into them. They caught one glimpse of ragged children with their snow-covered hair blowing wildly about their faces. They were smaller than George, but they were fast. They grabbed Mary's toque and were out of sight and sound in the whiteness of the roaring storm.

"Oh, no!" wailed Mary. She had given up holding her hat so she wouldn't lose her books.

"We'll look for a shelter," George said. He grabbed his own cap and pushed it down on Mary's head. His red hair blew out in the wind. Then he took Mary's books in his other hand, so she could hold his hand and keep her toque on her head.

They stumbled along, searching for a pathway or entrance not completely covered by the falling snow. Finally they found a spot where the edge of a canvas had blown open and flapped about.

Since there was no door, they couldn't knock. They struggled to pull back the tarp and crawled inside. More snow was piled up at the entrance. They drew back more canvas, walked a few steps farther, and stamped the snow from their feet. The cold still froze them through, but they were sheltered from the wind. George rubbed his ears while Mary slapped her legs to restore feeling.

"It's most likely warmer farther inside," Mary suggested.

"I'll go first," George said and started to go on alone.

"Oh, no, George, I'm staying right with you."

George pulled back the canvas before them. Then he stood perfectly still, blocking Mary's way.

"Well, George, you're in my way," Mary said, moving

around George and looking into the partitioned area beyond.

At first, in the almost complete darkness, George could see nothing. Then, as his eyes adjusted to the dimness, he saw figures huddled together, partially covered by a ragged quilt. Beside them was a small, blackened lantern that no longer gave light or warmth.

As his eyes continued to adjust, he saw the faces more distinctly . . . the face of a man . . . the man stealing wood on Christmas Day . . . with two small children . . . still . . . without breath or movement . . . like frozen statues!

His sister's scream was drowned by the sound of the howling storm outside.

Twenty-five

Mary and George rushed back into the outer canvas area. "We can't stay here, George," Mary insisted.

"Well, I can't go out in that storm either. Not without a hat." George went to the doorway. He could not even see across the street with the wind and the snow flying. Still there were a few people coming and going.

"We must get help," Mary said.

"They can't be helped now, Mary."

"Are you sure, George?"

"Yes."

They waited and shivered, not knowing what to do.

"I'm going back to see if I can find anything for my head — maybe even a cloth of some kind."

George found a small blanket near the entrance of the room. He did not look at the bodies again, but tore the blanket in half and doubled it over his head. He tied it securely at front and back.

In the outer area again, he said, "We'd best stay a while. The storm may subside."

They waited. Neither one suggested returning to the inner area. They could not even bring themselves to go back to grab the lantern. It was too near the bodies.

The day dragged on. They kept looking out of the opening to see if the storm was dying down. It was not.

Finally, George said, "Mary, I think we should go now. The day is wearing on, and it won't get any warmer. We don't want to spend the night here."

George directed Mary as they emerged. Already their tracks had been wiped out. "I hope we're headed the right way," George said as they faced into the wind.

"I think so. The wind was in our backs coming down."

"Let's ask someone," Mary suggested.

"Not yet," George replied. He felt it would be better not to let anyone around there know they were lost. He had heard of people being robbed in Canvas Town. Even their clothes could be valuable in this storm.

Facing into the wind, they kept going as steadily as they could. Occasionally, in the white world around them, someone would bump into one of them and pass on along the street.

"George, we've got to stop soon," Mary choked out breathlessly.

"Look up, Mary. I can see a blue patch in the sky. The storm's going to break soon."

Mary struggled on as George kept pulling her through the knee-deep snow. It seemed as if they were always going two steps forward and one step back. When the storm finally let up a bit, they could see sleighs running past again. They shrank back to the buildings to get out of their way. The wind was less raw now, and George was certain that the storm was dying down.

They no longer felt alone. There were a lot of tall buildings around them. Mary looked down the street ahead and yelled out, "That's it. That's John Street. The theatre isn't far."

"Perhaps we should just go home, Mary," George said.

"It isn't far, George."

They turned down the street. It was early evening, and carriages were drawing up to the theatre entrance. There were officers in brightly coloured uniforms and ladies in long, flowing cloaks.

"Maybe it's not such a good idea, George. There are too many people around now. How can we afford to buy a flower anyway?"

"I thought I could offer to pay with my hunting knife. It's worth more than a flower."

Mary looked doubtful. "I don't know, George." Then she became more hopeful. "I have an idea. *I'll* offer your knife. They're more apt to give a flower to a girl than a boy."

George was relieved. He was starting to feel self-conscious about asking for a rose. When Catharine was crying to go back home, it had seemed like a good idea, but now he was starting to feel a little foolish. "That's a great idea, Mary," he said. Smiling, he handed over the knife that he had brought.

"I think it would be better if you waited here, George," Mary said, and ran under the wooden archway that led up to the main entrance.

From the doorway, a harsh-voiced attendant waved her back. "Children are not allowed in the theatre without parents."

Mary felt in her pocket for George's hunting knife. As she drew it out, the doorman shouted, "Look, no rough stuff."

He pushed her hard, and she fell backwards and sprawled across the entrance to the theatre. Just then, a long gown swished across Mary's legs and feet as the lady wearing it skilfully avoided stepping right on her.

"Grab that girl," yelled the doorman. "She tried to knife me."

"No, I didn't," screamed Mary. "I wanted to trade the knife for a flower for my sister who's sick."

George came running over. "Leave my sister alone, you big bully!" he shouted.

By then, people were gathering around and staring. The woman who had almost stepped on Mary said to her, "Just a minute." She opened a small basket on her arm and took out a deep red rose. She handed it to Mary.

"You may have it. It's not real, though. Samuel couldn't find me a real one. He says there are no real flowers in all New York City. I don't believe him. He just didn't bother, and he knows how I like genuine pieces. You might just as well have it." She pouted prettily at the young officer beside her, who shifted uneasily in his polished black boots.

"I'd let the girl go," the officer said quietly to the doorman.

"Oh, thank you," Mary breathed as she stared at the flower she held in both hands. "If only I can keep it safe until I get home."

"Here," the lady said as she offered Mary her small round basket. "It came in this anyway."

The lady and her officer friend quickly walked on into the theatre. George and Mary turned and raced away, fearful that the lady or the doorman would change their minds.

They walked at a stiff pace, and it wasn't long before they passed the school. Its doors had been shut tight for the night. Soon after that they found themselves back home.

At the top of the stairs, Boots bounded out to greet them. George gave him a fast pat as he followed Mary into the apartment. He didn't want to miss seeing Catharine when they gave her the rose.

Mary burst into the room and rushed directly over to Catharine. She pulled the rose from the cold, snow-covered basket. A few flakes of snow were resting on the rose itself. As she lifted it from the basket, the drops melted and glistened like morning dew.

"Oh, Mary, it's beautiful!" Catharine said. Her whole face was alight with the familiar smile that George had not seen for weeks as she reached out for the rose.

Twenty-six

G eorge! Mary! Where were you?" said a stern but familiar voice.

George turned to see his father standing behind him in coat and boots. His long, tousled, curly hair and thick beard were as messy as a bird's nest. He leaned on his tall cane, a disguised sword that he now carried on all trips.

"Father!" Mary ran over and hugged him. "We got lost in the storm."

George stared at his father in silence.

"I've worried myself sick over you two ever since the others came home without you," Mother scolded. "Your father just got here, but he was leaving to hunt for you."

George reluctantly told them the whole story. He was surprised that Father seemed to understand, but Mother was still very cross.

"New York is no longer the place for my family," Father said.

Catharine had been listening. "Can we go home now?" she asked.

Father looked up from where he was stretched out in front of the fireplace and said, "Not yet, Catharine."

"Where then?" George wanted to know.

"To Long Island. The ice is frozen hard enough to cross over. Oliver DeLancey's troops are stationed there, and he'll know who needs help. Most of you are old enough now to do your share of work. There is a severe shortage of labour for the farms on Long Island. Most of the men have enlisted with the British or run off with the Rebels."

"Back on a farm . . . it would be like home," Tobias said.

"No, Tobias, it wouldn't be like home. It would be hard work for all of you, but you would still be allowed time off to go to school. I'd see to that."

"Oh no," sputtered Leonard. "Another new school!"

"And John Bleecker is going to be on Long Island," Father said.

George was surprised. "But John is with the Cowboys," he blurted out.

His father looked at him sternly. "George, you were not wise to travel into enemy territory. And warfare among the partisans is too severe for a boy of fifteen. He's joining DeLancey's troops on Long Island. James sent him back with me."

"I'm going over to see him," George said and jumped up to grab his coat.

Father interrupted, "Don't, George! He's already gone to Long Island. He plans to visit his family after he's joined up. That way they can't stop him. His mind's made up."

"It would be better for Catharine on a farm," Mother said, then turning to George and Mary, she said, "Now you two, drink some of this tea before you get a chill."

Exhausted, George and Mary sipped the hot herb tea and cold sandwiches that Mother had prepared. When he'd taken his last bite, George went back out to the hallway landing to sit with his arm around Boots. He buried his cold hands in the dog's warm coat of hair. Boots snuggled contentedly up against him and stretched his long thin nose across George's knees. He could hear Mother and Father talking about the move to Long Island.

George was disappointed that Father wasn't discussing the moving plans with him. He felt that he was really more in charge than Mother these days. She stayed inside all the time now and hardly knew what was happening inside New York, let alone out in the countryside.

He was sure she hadn't heard of the Cherry Valley massacre of the farmers and their families by the British troops and their Indian helpers. Even the British soldiers in the barracks were furious about that brutal slaying of women and children. He knew they were bracing themselves for the revenge that would follow. There was no more partying in New York. A sense of doom had gripped everyone as they waited for the bloodshed that would come in the spring.

By the end of January, Father found an estate on Long Island where the family would live and work — and Boots was allowed to go too. He would be able to stay in a warm barn at night and run around in the fields during the day.

The owner of the farm was a widow, Mrs. Lloyd. Her sons were away, one fighting for the Loyalists and the other for the Rebels. Her young slaves had run off to join the British army and be free. Their wives and families had gone too. Only two elderly slaves had stayed. She needed help badly.

When the family arrived in early February, the house was spacious, but dirty and dull. It didn't smell as bad as the attic had when they first arrived there, but Mother said it needed some soft soap and elbow grease. Mother could hardly wait to start.

George was glad that he would be in charge of the barn and the livestock. He hated being around when Mother was housecleaning. Lately her spotless ways seemed to make life even more miserable. But Father did not seem to mind. He just tried to keep out of the way.

Catharine was given a room on the main floor that had its own fireplace. It was at the opposite side of the house to Mrs. Lloyd's room because she was afraid that Catharine might have consumption. Father got a special army doctor to come and check Catharine over. The doctor told them that with fresh air and proper food Catharine would be fine in a few months.

Catharine still kept the rose on top of the basket beside her bed. As she improved, she was able to do a little needlework again and was more cheerful than she had been all winter.

The children would be allowed to go to school in the winter months when there was lighter farm work, and Father explained to them that he had registered them under the name Meyers instead of Waltermyer. He said that he now used the English version of his name, John Walden Meyers, since he wanted to have a separate identity from the rest of his family, who were all Rebels.

The first day of school, the children were all ready to go when the family received word that the school had been closed. A smallpox epidemic was sweeping New York City, and many people, weakened by the flu, were dying of the dreaded disease. Schools, theatres, churches, and almost all stores had been ordered to close to reduce the risk of people infecting each other.

Fear of the disease spread rapidly. Mrs. Lloyd confined herself to the far side of the house, and the family rarely saw her. She insisted on giving Mother instructions in the open air from a distance. Mother said they all had to put up with this so Mrs. Lloyd wouldn't send them back to New York. As time went on, however, Mrs. Lloyd stopped worrying because all of them, including Catharine, got better again.

***

One morning in early March, George was busy in the barn throwing down hay for the cattle when his father opened the side barn door and came over to him. George stuck his fork upright in the hay and turned to his father.

As he approached his son, Meyers suddenly realized how much George looked like himself at that age. "I'm leaving today," he said. "A message came from the Barracks."

George looked up in silence. His father continued. "I don't know just when I'll be back. This war has taken some unpredictable turns. Now that France has joined the Rebels, the British have a harder fight on their hands."

George looked his father straight in the eye. "The soldiers back in New York think there'll be more revenge and massacres against the British in the spring. The Rebels can never forget the Cherry Valley massacre." He wondered if his father would deny that the British had killed helpless women and children right along with the farmers.

"The so-called massacre was *not* the way you heard it," Father said. "Still, the bloodshed will increase. And vengeance will bring more. It's a never-ending cycle. But now that the British are taking this war more seriously, it may soon be over."

"And will we go home then with all our neighbours hating us?"

A shadow seemed to cross his father's face as George asked that question. "They aren't all our enemies, son. How do you think I manage to travel through the countryside without being found?" Then he brightened a bit and said, "Perhaps we'll go to Canada. There's a lot of good unclaimed land there, much like the land around Albany."

Surprised by his father's suggestion, George asked, "Haven't the French joined the Rebels?"

"France has, but not the French in Quebec. I'm confident they won't."

"Why not?" George asked.

"They have been fairly content under British rule and they are happy working their farms. They won't risk losing them to take on someone else's battle."

"Will you be stationed in Canada *again* this summer?" George said in a slightly bitter tone. He thought his father wasn't really doing much up there.

Father did not tell George that he had been kept there last summer for the purpose of carrying the news to New York if Quebec had fallen. And Haldimand had feared just that, for Canada had been ill-prepared to fight off an attack.

"Perhaps . . . my orders come only at the last minute. I'd really like to see some action if . . . " Father stopped as he saw the angry look on George's face.

George grabbed the pitchfork and started throwing down the hay again at high speed. "Yeah, I know the feeling. Some of the rest of us would like to see some action too."

"I'm sorry, George. But your mother needs you. I'm going up to the house now to pack and leave." He reached over and clapped a hand on his son's shoulder. "You're in charge, George, really in charge now."

George did not reply. He just pitched the fork loads harder. His father dropped his hand to his side and stood watching for a few minutes before he walked away. He closed the barn door silently.

George worked with a fury for about half an hour. He realized then that he had thrown down enough hay for a week. He stuck the pitchfork upright in the hay and headed for the house. He couldn't let Father leave without wishing him well.

On the front step, Mother, who was usually so strong, was clinging to Father. George hung back. Finally, his father's jaw tightened firmly as he pulled himself away. He started for the road. George came forward then and put his arm around his mother's thin shoulders.

Father did not look back until he reached the road. Then he turned and stared back. With his free arm, George waved. Hesitating there, Father gave a single wave and was gone.

Twenty-seven

At dusk three men slipped into a crowded tavern on the north side of Schenectady. The tallest man worked his way cautiously through the crowd. As he bent over the bar, the slightest bit of red hair showed under his large three-cornered hat. His two companions were close behind him.

"Is the tavern keeper in?" he asked.

"And who kin I say is askin'?" said the bar attendant with narrowed eyes.

"Hudibras," said John Walden Meyers in a hoarse voice.

The attendant started for the back room.

"Who's waitin' on folks here?" a big red-faced man shouted as he banged the counter. The bartender turned back to serve him, and the three men took a side table in the shadows.

Only one of the three faced into the room, and his hat, pulled well down over his forehead, shaded his face. They listened as they waited.

In spite of the fresh June air coming in at the doorway, the room was filled with smoke and so noisy that it was hard to pick up separate voices. George's father, the tallest of the three, thought of his family back home. It was over a year now since he'd left them. Last fall, he was relieved to get word from a courier that all was going well on the Long Island estate.

Snatches of conversation drifted to them as they waited.

"Finally got the leader of that pack!" a voice said.

"Yeah, the Cowboys will be useless now," said another voice.

Meyers felt a light tap on his shoulder. The attendant handed him an ale with a note under it. It read, "Come around to the back door."

A few minutes later, after they had all downed their drinks, they sauntered out the front doorway, then hurried around to the back. The door was already ajar, and they entered without knocking.

Inside, an elderly grey-haired man recognized Meyers instantly and gave him a nervous smile.

Before he could speak, Meyers said, "We need supplies."

"Schuyler's men have been hunting for you around Albany," the tavern owner said. "He's got half his militia out. He claims he'll get you this time."

Meyers turned to his Loyalist recruits, both in their early twenties. "We're a good piece ahead of him."

Hank smiled back, "And we'll keep it that way." The young recruit had stayed true to his word and joined up with Meyers again. After the defeat of Burgoyne in 1777, he'd gone back to work on his family's farm, but Rebels had burned down the house and barn in the summer of 1780, and Hank had barely escaped with his life. Now, a year later, he was back at the side of the now-legendary Meyers.

Then, turning to the tavern keeper, Meyers said, "I'm

not worried about Schuyler, but what's this news about the Cowboys?"

"Their leader, James DeLancey, is waiting execution six miles north of here at Ballstown jail. They just caught him yesterday, but they won't wait long. Schuyler's bound to call off his hunt for you to place extra guards on the jail."

Meyers did not look pleased. Taking the sack of food the tavern owner gave him, he said crisply, "Thank you." The three stepped back out into the street.

They did not have far to reach the woods, for the tavern was right on the edge of town. They passed a large apple orchard where a few crab apple trees were blooming.

Meyers led them off the beaten path to a rougher trail that led into the Adirondack Mountains. The green underbrush became thicker, and wild raspberry branches tugged at their homespun overalls.

After they had travelled along for half an hour at a rapid pace, Meyers said, "Let's eat." The men needed no urging. They soon found a dry stone to sit on and tore open the sack. Munching on the pork sandwiches, they felt their strength come back.

"We're to meet ten more recruits just this side of Ballstown. Now you men have a choice. You may come with me or continue on alone to Canada and I'll meet you there."

Hank did not hesitate. "We'll go with you," he said.

"You may change your mind," Meyers said, "for I plan to raid the Ballstown jail this night. A friend of mine is there."

" . . . You what!" the other recruit spoke out in shock.

Meyers rose to his feet. "I'm leaving now. Suit yourselves. Whichever you decide is fine with me. We can meet in Canada. Just remember to tell the officials that you're my recruits when you sign in."

Meyers was not far along the trail to Ballstown when he heard his recruits following close behind.

***

Meyers gathered his twelve followers the evening of June 4th. The mosquitoes hummed steadily around them as they waited until dark to make their attack.

Just before dawn, Meyers had visited Ballstown alone to assess the situation. He was familiar with the area, for the family of a friend, Joseph Bettys, still lived there. Bettys' father ran the tavern in the centre of the village, which was made up of about half a dozen log cabins and a few frame houses.

His main concern was the local militia unit. But he was surprised how small the company was, and he figured that the tavern keeper in Schenectady may have been right. Maybe they had launched a manhunt for him around Albany.

Now, with his men huddled around him, he was drawing a map of the jail and area, pointing out where the sentries were stationed and where the guards would likely be found inside the jail.

The moon was only a sliver in the sky as the men stole out of the woods that night and approached the village. A sentry was standing at the roadside just before the first house. Meyers jumped him and knocked him out with a single blow. His men tied him to a tree and gagged him so he could not warn the others when he came to.

Another two hundred yards ahead two more sentries could be seen pacing in the shadows through the trees at the edge of the town.

Meyers looked at his young recruits. "Good practice for you men," he said.

They rose to the bait, and the two new prisoners were soon tied and gagged as the other had been.

Stealthily the thirteen armed men crept into the sleeping village. There were no lights at the tavern as they passed. They hurried around the corner to the jail. It was a small frame building with a stone basement.

Meyers looked through the open window. A guard was leaning back in his chair with his feet on the desk. His musket was resting on the table beside him. From their vantage point it was impossible to tell whether or not he was sleeping.

Meyers mumbled to his men, "It'll be better to surprise him. He'll go for his musket, but when he sees we're armed he'll surrender. Even if he did get one of us, we'd be sure to get him. He won't risk it."

They approached together. To their surprise the door was not locked, and they rushed inside with their muskets aimed.

The guard had been sleeping, but he lunged for his musket. Before he could grab it, Hank held him at gunpoint.

"Good work," Meyers said. Hank smiled in triumph.

Meyers took the key from the guard, a Rebel private, and leaving four men at the door with him, he and the other eight headed for the cells below.

Meyers knew that most of the prisoners were minor offenders and Loyalists, for more serious crimes were tried in Albany. He was surprised they had not already taken James DeLancey to the Albany jail.

The basement was dark, stinking, and damp as they crept along, but cheers went up as one by one the prisoners were released. In one cell there were ten men.

Altogether, Meyers and his men released twenty prisoners from the small basement and followed them under guard up the narrow stairs.

Meyers looked closely at the men. In their filthy condition it was hard to recognize them. Finally he asked, "Has anyone seen James DeLancey?"

"They took him down to Albany jail this afternoon to hang tomorrow," the guard said.

Meyers stared at the guard. "Then why'd they leave you here?"

The guard looked smug. "Short of local men. You can't think they'd be stupid enough to leave a notorious outlaw like James DeLancey in a small rural jail with only one Rebel soldier to guard him."

Meyers knew the guard was right, but the man's need to convince him made him wonder. He turned to the prisoners now under the control of his men. "Did anyone see another prisoner?"

A Loyalist he knew spoke out then. "I couldn't even see myself in that hole let alone who else was there. I'm sorry but I couldn't tell."

One of Meyers' men was growing anxious, "Let's get out of here before the whole militia wakes up."

Meyers made a decision. "Tie and gag the guard and take him with you. The rest except for Hank take the prisoners to the edge of town the way we came in. I'll meet you soon."

The men moved out the door. Meyers turned to Hank, "If you hear anyone coming, hoot three times like an owl, then get out. I'll know the signal."

Meyers grabbed the guard's lantern and headed back down the stairs. He would not leave this jail until he had examined every corner and crevice.

Searching in an empty cell at the far end, he noticed marks on the one wall. He brushed back the straw from in front of it. It was a door. He forced it open slowly, for it was stiff from lack of use.

Meyers held up the lantern. On a pile of straw, a bearded man sat with his hands to his face, blinded by the sudden light.

"James," Meyers said in a loud whisper. "I'm Meyers. I've come for you."

James jumped to his feet in an instant and rushed to the door. "I'm with you," he said.

In a few minutes, they were on the main floor.

Meyers handed James the guard's musket and cartridge pouch and they rushed into the street with Hank. The three men advanced stealthily in the darkness.

As they approached the meeting place, they saw the other men waiting. Meyers separated the Loyalists whom he knew from the others. "These men can be trusted," he said. "And these, I don't know. For now, keep them under guard. I still have plans." Turning to the freed Loyalist prisoners, he said, "Does anyone of you know your way to the officers' quarters?"

"Yes," two men spoke out at the same time.

"And that house is separate from the rest of the militia stationed here," another added.

"How many are there?" asked Meyers.

"Just three men."

Meyers looked pleased. "We'll take them with us to Canada as prisoners."

"I'm with you too," James DeLancey said, as Meyers began to pick men for the raid.

Pleased, Meyers nodded to James. In five minutes, ten of them were on their way. It was not far, for the house was at the edge of the village. Even if they did rouse the militia, they could disappear into the woods almost immediately.

***

Half an hour later, Meyers returned with three Rebel officers as prisoners and his nine men laden down with food supplies, muskets, and cartridge pouches for the Loyalists he had freed. The whole motley group followed Meyers along the trail for an hour. Then Meyers stopped.

As the men rested on the ground, Meyers said to the Loyalists he knew, "I invite you all to go with us to Canada and fight in my company. But if you want to go home or elsewhere, then that's your choice. I'll not hold you."

Three of the men chose to go home. Meyers gave them some of the supplies and wished them well.

"What about us?" asked a Loyalist who was unknown to Meyers.

Meyers thought for a minute. "You have the same choice. But you'll travel with us for another hour." He reasoned that if someone decided to go back to warn the militia in Ballstown, he and his men would still have a good head start that way. Then he called a Loyalist he knew from Ballstown to lead while he fell back to guard the rear.

The three Rebel officers and the captured guards, all tied securely, fell into step between the other men. The group moved ahead at a steady pace.

James came up beside Meyers. "I'll be cutting across the country here to my men," he said.

Meyers filled James's wooden canteen from his own

and handed him a sack of food. James took it gratefully. "You saved my life. I owe you," he said.

"Your men would probably have rescued you if I hadn't."

James shook his head. "If they had heard, they would have tried, but I'm often off scouting for a few days. They seldom talk to folks in town. I'd probably have been strung up before they even knew I was taken."

Meyers put out his hand. As James shook it vigorously, Meyers said in a husky voice, "You saved my son, and he means more to me than my life. I can never repay that debt."

"I hope you've warned your son about any more trips into occupied territory."

"He should realize the danger is worse now that I am a wanted man."

"Does your son know that?" James asked.

"I don't know," Meyers said. "I never discuss my work, and it's over a year now since I've seen my family."

"I'll tell him if I see him, but that may be too late," James warned.

James waved as he cut into the bushes. "Godspeed," George's father called out behind him. "I must get word through to my family somehow," he thought as he broke into a run to catch up with his men.

***

On the morning of June 5th, two miles south of Albany, the famous Rebel General Schuyler awoke with a start as he heard galloping and shouting outside his mansion.

He had worked late the night before and had given orders to his wife not to call him until nine in the morning.

He jumped up and threw on his breeches over his nightshirt. He walked out of his room and looked over the railing to see his wife receive a soldier at the front door.

"Wait!" he shouted. He was not a young man, but he came down the stairs at a fast clip. He took the scroll from the courier.

"Waltermyer has freed all prisoners in Ballstown jail," the message said, "including James DeLancey. He has taken captive — the officers of the Ballstown militia."

"That troublesome fellow again!" Schuyler grumbled under his breath. "He must be stopped!"

Twenty-eight

George's father looked out from the entrance to the cave. The moon was full, and he could see well across the familiar fields. He was not far from Cooeyman's Landing and his own farm, which was now in the hands of that Rebel sympathizer.

It was early August and he hadn't been able to send a message to his family since he had rescued the Ballstown prisoners two months before. There were no couriers available and he'd been kept too busy to get back to Long Island himself.

The crickets chirped loudly. At the faint sound of a dog's bark in the distance, Meyers tensed instantly. Perhaps he should alert his men in the cave. He hesitated. The sound grew fainter until he couldn't hear it at all. There was no need to alarm his men.

He had good, reliable fellows on his team. Four of them were Loyalists who had left home some time ago. Three of them were from this very area and the other was Hank. And there were the two British regular soldiers that Governor Haldimand had forced on him for this assignment. The Governor was in charge of the British troops in Canada.

Like the rest of them, the soldiers were dressed like farmers so they would not arouse suspicion if they were

stopped. Meyers warned them to remain silent, however.
Their Cockney accents would give them away.

He also knew that they weren't eager to take orders
from a Loyalist who didn't have their army training. Still,
at Haldimand's insistence, he was making the best of it.
Meyers was still hopeful he'd soon have enough recruits
for his own company, but in the meantime, he'd accepted
this job. He looked forward to the excitement and chal-
lenge and planned carefully.

This mission was very important to Governor Haldimand. It was not a traditional military tactic. He had
chosen three especially talented men for the job of kidnapping three Rebel leaders from New York State. Meyers had been honoured and thrilled to be given the task
of kidnapping General Schuyler from his home just south
of Albany and just north of Cooeyman's Landing. Haldimand had allowed him to pick his own Loyalist recruits.
Only the British regulars were forced on him.

The other two kidnap victims also lived nearby. Haldimand had instructed Matthew Howard to capture John
Bleecker, a cousin of Janse, who used to run the General
Store in Albany. Joseph Bettys was scheduled to capture
Dr. Samuel Stringer, who lived in Ballstown. All were
told to attack between midnight and dawn of July 31,
1781.

The unsuspecting Rebels would be taken off guard
because kidnapping was not a traditional strategy for the
British. Furthermore, the Rebels would be forced to
search for three kidnap victims at the same time, which
would make the escape easier.

Those were the plans, but matters had not progressed
as Meyers had hoped. He had sent out Hank, who was

not known in the area, to scout around. He came back with very disturbing news only two days before the planned attack.

Howard had been captured at Bennington and it was rumoured that plans for the kidnapping had been found on his person. How much the Rebels could extract from Howard, Meyers did not know. When they had learned of the capture, Meyers and his men had been staying in the barn of a former neighbour, John Ver Plank. Although he was still sympathetic to the Loyalists, the elderly man had been forced to swear allegiance to the Rebel cause.

Once this news was out, Ver Plank asked that Meyers and his men move on. Meyers had quickly complied. He did not wish to cause trouble for his old friend. When he had led his men all safely into this secret cave, he felt a measure of relief. He was thankful that Ver Plank had given them a good supply of food. From their hiding place, they could see Rebel soldiers swarming all over the countryside.

Many questions were racing through Meyers' mind. Had Howard kept papers telling of the three kidnap ventures? Had they really been taken by the enemy when he was captured? Were Meyers and his men being hunted down? Meyers did not have the answers. So he waited.

After almost a week, the hunt appeared to be over. Meyers wondered if the enemy had really abandoned their search or if they were just regrouping to start again. Finally, he sent out his scout. Hank travelled back to the farm and returned with shocking news.

The soldiers had been hunting for Joseph Bettys. Meyers had asked why they were hunting for Bettys, who had been given orders to attack some distance north of there at Ballstown. He shouldn't have been in that area at all.

It turned out that Bettys had completely neglected his duty. He had travelled down to visit his old girlfriend, who lived only a couple of miles from the Schuyler residence, Meyer's target. Then she had run off with Bettys, and her irate father had immediately reported the incident. In the meantime, Bettys' men, left without their leader, had attacked ahead of time and bungled their attempt to kidnap Dr. Stringer. They had all headed north, with an infuriated father and the Rebel army scouring the entire countryside for Bettys.

Meyers was furious. Bettys had a brilliant war record, but now his unprofessional behaviour was inexcusable. He didn't care about the man's personal affairs, but he had no right to mix them with his duty.

Meyers knew he must make a decision. Would he attempt to kidnap Schuyler now that the other two attacks had failed and the enemy were on guard? He sent Hank out to scout again. Hank came back with the report that all was normal about the countryside. The search for Bettys appeared to have ended.

Meyers wondered if they should all just return home. His men would follow his orders on the kidnap mission, he knew, but they were jumpy. From their cave, the sight of Rebel soldiers searching the fields for Bettys made them completely aware that they were surrounded by the enemy.

Meyers knew too that his men would prefer to head straight back. But here they were, so near their destination. They would pass right by Schuyler's home on their way. He decided that if there was no sign of the enemy, he would try to carry out their assignment. Tomorrow would be exactly *one week after* the date that they should have carried out the kidnapping. But they would still have to try.

"My turn for watch, sir." One of his men interrupted his thoughts.

"Thanks, Dan," Meyers replied. He went farther back in the cave and stretched out his full length. Sleep did not come easily, for there had been little room for recreation of late, and his men were restless. He had decided about tomorrow, however. He had a job to do and he was going to do it.

***

The day dawned clear and hot. Meyers did not waken until near noon, nor did his men. They stayed well back in the cave by day, so there was no need to rise early. Meyers generally did not sleep late, but he had tossed and turned most of the night, disturbed with thoughts of the home he had built nearby and of his family so far away on Long Island. Finally, as the late morning light crept into the cave, sleep claimed him for a few hours.

When he awakened, he was alert at once and called over his scout, Hank. No need to worry the others with his plans just yet.

"Look over the area, especially around Schuyler's. If the troops have gone, we strike tonight," he explained briefly. Hank ate quickly and left.

Gradually, the other men started moving about. As time wore on, they grumbled about their food and their miserable hideout. Meyers finally decided that the excitement of his news might just straighten them out. Almost anything would be better than this dragging monotony and constant bickering.

"We're kidnapping Schuyler tonight if the soldiers have gone," Meyers told them.

In the middle of an argument, they were suddenly quiet. After a long pause one fellow asked, "Isn't it still too dangerous?"

"I don't think so. The soldiers were looking for Bettys, not us. The news is that he's escaped. So they've left."

"What about the papers your friend says they found on Howard? Did they expose our plan?"

"Probably not. The instructions were strict. We were not to take any papers. Even Haldimand does not want to be connected with the incident. Kidnapping is not routine army practice."

"Then why did your friend say that?"

"Rumours. They always brag about how much they find on spies when they catch them. Probably all false. Besides Hank is out there now. If he sees any sign of Rebel soldiers or anything suspicious, we'll wait longer."

One of the British soldiers burst out, "No, let's go no matter what. I don't think I can take this bloody cave another day."

The men had no further questions, and they sat more quietly than before. Their squabble, whatever it had been, was forgotten. They were soon to face the common enemy.

Meyers was alone again near the entrance of the cave. Not too far away the water of the Hudson River flowed by quietly. He wished he could dive out into it to relieve the tension and refresh himself for the task ahead. Instead, he sat and waited. Finally, he saw Hank coming across the fields and then up the shoreline.

"All's clear," Hank reported.

"Great! We'll have our chance," Meyers said with zeal. He had waited long enough for an important job like this. "You rest now. But first see to your muskets and cartridges. We'll leave a little after dark. That way we'll have the full night to travel back with Schuyler. By morning, the whole Rebel militia will be after us."

***

Meyers halted his men in the undergrowth across from the clearing. From there, they could plainly see in the moonlight the back entrance to General Schuyler's residence. They waited silently and watched for over an hour. They could detect no unusual movement.

One by one the flickering lights went out in the Schuyler house. There still remained a small light, high in the attic room. Meyers knew that it was the nursery. Burgoyne, the British General who was defeated early in the war, had been a prisoner there. He'd made a detailed map of the house and given it to Haldimand. Meyers had studied it thoroughly. Meyers pulled up weeds and brush and cleared a small area on the ground. With a stick he started to draw a map of the Schuyler house. He dug the lines clearly into the dirt. The men needed to know their way around once they were inside.

There were not enough of them to surround the house, so Meyers posted one man as sentry. He led the rest stealthily towards the back entrance. Soundlessly, they reached the back door. The lock was firm.

One of the British soldiers quickly smashed it with the butt of his musket. They waited. All was silent.

Meyers and his five men crept through the hallway to the next door. It too was barred securely.

Suspicious, Meyers hesitated, then drew his men together. With a prearranged signal, he indicated that he suspected a trap. He knew that even generals were seldom that cautious. This area was well behind the Rebel lines. Unless he had been warned, the general would not likely have barricaded his double entrance so securely.

They stood back, alert and ready for action as Meyers shot through the back door lock.

Immediately, they were in the middle of gunfire and blows.

Meyers slashed out in the semidarkness at the bodies before him as he pushed his way into the inner room. Two guards lay at his feet and more kept coming.

Meyers did not have time to reload. He lunged forward at the wild face before him, pushed the man backwards with a single blow, and felt him fall.

Two musket shots sounded sharply in the night air outside.

The glass in a window near him shattered. Then he heard a command from an upstairs window. "Surround these men!" Was that Schuyler himself, shouting to his men?

Meyers looked about and saw only his own men with their prisoners. They had taken muskets from four guards. "Lock these men in the basement," he barked to the British regulars. They left promptly.

Meyers rushed through the house to the hallway. "Keep guard here," he shouted as he started up the stairs.

Without permission, Hank stepped up behind him. Meyers was glad he was there. Together they rushed up the first flight of stairs. Only their own shadows were reflected on the opposite side of the stairway.

They could hear a light scuffling of feet above them, but when they reached the landing of the stairs, all was silent. They crept up the remaining steps one at a time.

On the second floor, the long hall was bare, and closed doors gave them no clues as to Schuyler's whereabouts.

Meyers flung open the first door and stood back waiting for gunfire, but none came. Then, rushing in, he searched and found no one.

Hank kept watch as Meyers checked each room to no avail. Just as he opened another door to a long narrow staircase, his guard shouted from the foot of the stairs, "The Rebels are coming." A musket sounded and smoke filled the air.

"Let's go," Meyers shouted to Hank. They rushed to the bottom of the stairs.

Back down in the front hallway, Meyers ordered Hank to call the men guarding the prisoners.

The men came quickly and two of them started to run, but Meyers yelled at them, "Come back here and help with the wounded."

They dragged out one wounded British soldier while Meyers took care of the other one. They met their sentry, who had two of Schuyler's guards with him as prisoners.

In an instant they were all back in the undergrowth. Meyers looked at his men and noticed that no one was seriously wounded. Then, as he looked more closely, he said abruptly, "Dan's missing."

"He fell with the first shots. I think he's dead," a British regular replied.

"We can't just leave him," Meyers exclaimed. "I'm going back."

Meyers could hear the commotion in the house as he crawled around to the side window. As he stretched up to look into the room, he saw Dan's motionless form lying still on the floor.

Then a guard bent over Dan and said, "Well, this one's sure dead. By morning the others'll join him. The militia will be here soon."

Meyers ran back to the others. He gave them the news directly. "Dan can't be helped. We must make speed now while we can travel in the dark."

Bullets had grazed each of the British soldiers, one in the arm, and one on the left hand. But Meyers felt their wounds should not keep them from travelling fast. Thoroughly familiar with the countryside, he led his men forward at a rapid pace.

Finally, one of the regulars spoke out. "My arm is paining badly. I just can't go on."

Desperate to move ahead, Hank and the others looked at their leader.

Meyers made a fast decision. "You three move on and take the hostages with you. Return the way we came. I'll take the British regulars with me by a different route."

Relieved, they turned and sprinted away through the bush.

Meyers sat briefly with the wounded men, then said to them, "Let's go."

They gave him a startled look but did not move.

"Remember," Meyers said, "if we're caught, we'll all be hanged as traitors. You don't have your uniforms or any proof you're British soldiers. You won't be kept as prisoners of war. You'll be hanged right along beside me."

"Let's go," the most hesitant soldier said, jumping up.

Meyers led the way at a brisk pace. The British regulars started off behind him at great speed, with no further complaints.

If he had not been so bitterly disappointed by the foiled kidnapping, he would have smiled.

Twenty-nine

*T*he rumour's true. Your father's a captain now," General Oliver DeLancey told George, who had come to see him at the Loyalist Barracks on Long Island. Two and a half years had passed since his father had left them and the only way they got news of him was by asking at the barracks or through the few courier messages that reached them.

"Isn't he connected with your troops anymore?" George asked.

"No, he's been a captain in the Loyal Rangers corps since May. That's the battalion headed up by Ebenezer Jessup's brother Edward."

George seemed surprised. "Do you mean since this past May?"

"Yes, George," the Commander said. He turned to his desk piled high with work.

George was determined not to be dismissed so easily. "Sir, I just have a couple more questions."

Oliver DeLancey looked impatient but said, "Well?"

"Are the rumours about Father really true?"

"What rumours?"

George was uneasy now. He knew that Oliver DeLancey would tell him the truth, but he hated to bother such a busy man with talk of the men from the barracks. "Did Father almost kidnap General Schuyler last summer?"

"He attempted it."

"Really?"

"That's what I said. And you may have heard another rumour and it's true too. Your father did free the prisoners from Ballstown Jail and capture the officers in charge of the militia there. That was a daring feat. Your father is very courageous. No wonder he's been given his post as a Captain even though he didn't manage to enlist the required number of his own recruits. Now, young man, I have work to do. Good afternoon."

George hurried out the door. He was still thinking about his father's feats when he almost bumped into John Bleecker, now one of DeLancey's Loyalists stationed at the barracks. He couldn't help feeling a twinge of jealousy seeing John in his brick red coat just like the Redcoats. George was over six feet now and could have easily passed for one of the soldiers. He had thought many times about joining them, but he knew his family needed him. Still he wouldn't wait forever!

John was speaking to him. "I'm off duty tomorrow. Would you like to go into the city with me?"

George hesitated. It was late August and they were very busy harvesting the crops. Even his seventeenth birthday in July had gone by almost unnoticed because they were too busy with the farm work. "I sure would like to," he said, "but I can't leave just now."

John looked disappointed but he said, "That's okay, George." John had been stationed with the troops on Long Island as long as George and his family had been there. He had a job keeping track of supplies for the men at the barracks and running their small store. It was something like a merchant's job — which John liked, since it reminded him of the old days back in Albany.

George knew he wouldn't have been so content if he'd been assigned John's duties. He was looking forward to some real action when he joined up.

"I hear your father's a captain, now," John said. His big old grin was spreading across his face.

George smiled. "Yes. I just found out from General DeLancey."

"I'm afraid the action's almost over, though," said John.

George frowned. "Why would you say that?"

"Well, as you know, the British under General Cornwallis were defeated in the south last fall. In the north, General Haldimand has withdrawn his troops from fighting on the frontier. What a shock to find out the Royal Yorkers and the Mohawks were ordered back! And the British are starting talks in Europe to negotiate a peace."

"A peace? It sounds more like a surrender!" George exclaimed.

John did not appear as upset as George. "We are expecting the British to arrange for the return of the Loyalists' land and property. So all will not be lost."

"So you'll go back to Albany then, John?" George asked.

John frowned. "No, George. I don't want to go back." Then he brightened a bit and said, "I may move north to Canada."

"Well, the war's not over yet. I'd still like to see some action," George said. "I doubt I ever will. For one thing, I have to get home now to help my brothers with the chores. I'll look you up again next time I'm here."

"Goodbye, George," John said a bit sadly as he turned and headed back to the barracks.

Hurrying along the pathway to home, George was

thinking of his mother, who would be quietly waiting for any news of Father. When he was younger, he had taken his mother for granted. But now he wondered at her steady fortitude and seemingly limitless energy. All the same, she never laughed anymore and did not talk about Father except in the family prayers. He wished that his mother would share her feelings. When she was upset, she just cleaned the house more vigorously and became more silent.

He turned into the laneway of the estate and circled around to the back kitchen door. Mother would be busy in the kitchen preparing the evening meal, he thought, but he walked into an empty room. The cutting board was out, and there was a pile of husked corn on the table, but no one was there. Voices were coming from the front room.

Stepping to the door of the parlour, he could see his mother, with Mary and Catharine beside her, talking to a soldier. The man was in his mid-fifties and was dressed in a well-worn, almost shabby green coat — it was the uniform of an officer of the King's Rangers. But its decorative trim still showed that he was a captain. George watched, unnoticed from the doorway.

The Captain readily accepted the chair offered to him. "I'm John Dafoe, a friend of your husband and a courier for the British. I have brought a message from your husband." Captain Dafoe handed over a single scroll. Mother read the letter silently and then aloud.

June 11, 1782

My dear Polly,

It is urgent that you see Sir Guy Carleton to arrange passage for yourself and all our children

to the garrison at Halifax, where you will be safe.
I can arrange passage from there by ship to Quebec. We'll meet there.

Hans

Sir Guy Carleton was the new Commanding General,
who had just that spring replaced the very unpopular Sir
Henry Clinton. The new General was already showing
much more concern for the people, and hopes were
rising.

"Thank God he's alive," Mother said with relief in her
voice, "but is Hans really well? Why has he been away
so long?"

"John suffered a serious bout of malaria, but he responded well to the medicine. The army had a supply of
quinine on hand, which works much more effectively
than the herbal remedies. He is fine now, but he is
stationed in Canada and could not come through to see
you."

"Why couldn't he come to see us after so long a time
away from his family?" Mother asked directly.

"He's a captain now, in the corps of the Loyal Rangers.
The Major-Commandant is Edward Jessup, and he will
not free him from his duties up there. So John sent his
message with me as I had other business in New York.
Now, back to his instructions. John says that you
shouldn't think of going overland, even though it's the
shorter route."

"It *is* much shorter and we could avoid all the travel
by ship that way," Mother replied. "Many Loyalist
women have been allowed to pass through to Canada. In
fact, we obtained permission to come down through

Rebel territory to New York. We had no serious difficulties."

"That's all true, Mrs. Meyers, but everything is different now."

"Why?" Mary asked anxiously.

Captain Dafoe looked away and hesitated before he said more. After a brief pause, he continued, "It is best that you know. Your father is the Rebels' most wanted Loyalist spy. You would be recognized and held as hostages until he gave himself to them. Then they would surely hang him."

There was silence after that. They had known Father's work was dangerous. After all, war is unpredictable for everyone. But not that dangerous!

Captain Dafoe spoke again, "The British are starting talks in Europe to negotiate a peace. We Provincials are still urging them to negotiate for the return of our lands."

"If not, is all lost?" Mother asked.

"Here perhaps, yes, but we can build new homes in Canada. It's a fine land with experienced men in charge. Though it isn't official yet, we who have served feel confident that the British will reward us with land grants."

"I see," Mother mumbled, dazed by all this news.

"I must go. I will speak to Sir Guy Carleton on your behalf. I have a message for him from John. Let me strongly urge you, Mrs. Meyers, to make an appointment to see the General as soon as possible. Obtain your passes to go by ship to Halifax. He is too busy to contact you. Keep trying until you get passage."

"I'll go to New York tomorrow," Mother replied.

"Also, under no circumstances let any of the children go by land. Go by sea, and go soon."

"Thank you. I hope we'll meet again," Mother replied.

"I trust we will . . . in Canada."

As Captain Dafoe strode quickly from the house, George brushed past Mother and out the front door.

"Wait, sir," he called.

Dafoe turned. Something about this man reminded George of his father. Was it his fast stride or his look of firm resolution?

"Captain . . . Captain . . .," George stammered.

"Dafoe," said the Captain.

"Yes, Captain Dafoe, excuse me, sir, but I am John Meyers' son George, and I overheard you speaking to my mother. I could join my father's company. I could be ready to leave in minutes."

A smile of recognition spread across the Captain's lined face. The red hair, the height — there was no mistaking that this was John Walden Meyers' son.

"I'm afraid that would be impossible, George."

"Come now, younger fellows have fought and died for the cause. We're not beaten yet. I'd like to be in the action. Why not?"

"One very good reason, George. If you were spotted, and you would be, you'd become a target for the Rebels."

"Why?"

"You are the very image of your father. They'd recognize you in a minute. You do not have the knowledge, skill, and experience to evade the enemy as he has. They'd use you to get him. He'd surrender to save you, and they'd hang him in a day!"

"I didn't know he was that well known."

"Trust me, he is. His two attacks a year ago made him much talked about by the Rebels."

"I see."

"Even the Rebel women warn their small children to behave or Hans Waltermyer will eat them. He has become notorious among them."

George thought about his peace-loving father, who was forced to take sides in the war, and he protested. "But my father is not a violent man. He has never harmed a woman or child in his life. In fact, I never even thought he fought much in battles either."

"We know that, but the enemy doesn't. He is known by the British as a daring and enterprising soldier, but not a cruel one. Although, mind you, when your father is on assignment, he is a force to be reckoned with. The enemy would do anything to put him out of action, and you would be the perfect target. And what would the family do without you? They need you. It will be a long rough trip to Quebec by ship."

George looked down, a bit embarrassed that he'd blurted out his request without thinking of the consequences to his father or his family, but not quite ready to accept the fact that he would never fight in this war.

"You have a big job ahead of you, getting your family to safety. That's the most important thing now . . . Well, I have another message to deliver before dark. Good luck, Meyers. I may see you in Quebec."

George turned back to the house. There was no question, then, of winning the war, and he would never be a part of it. But Quebec — that would be a journey to talk about! He was ready to go. His father was already there, waiting to see them all again. Did he really look that much like Father now? Everybody said he did. But he could hardly remember what Father looked like. He hoped that, before long, he would see him.

Captain Dafoe continued on his way, relieved that he

had completed his task. He hoped he really had convinced George that it was foolish to enter enemy territory. He could not imagine the wrath of John Meyers if he were to return to him accompanied by his son, having crossed enemy lines. As daring as Meyers had been for the cause, his family had always been his main concern. Throughout the long separation from them, he had remained faithful to his wife and proud of his children. No, he wouldn't be the one to risk the life of any member of the Meyers' family, let alone the eldest son.

Nonviolent Meyers might be, but heaven help the man who let harm come to his family!

Part Three
North to Canada

Thirty

S ir Guy Carleton looked at the next file on his desk
and frowned deeply. It had been a long day. As
usual, he had been up before four o'clock. He had
ridden about ten miles on his tour of inspection and then
returned to his office to begin his regular duties.

It was now May 1783, and ever since last fall when
the news had come out that defeat was almost certain,
the number of destitute people coming under his care in
New York City had grown every month. Under the terms
of the peace treaty that was being negotiated, the Loyalists had not been given enough protection, despite Sir
Guy Carleton's objections. So now they were flocking
to the city, which was one of the last British strongholds.
Carleton had resolved that as long as he was here, he
would do what he could for these people who had suffered so much.

With a sigh, the General took some papers from the
file in front of him. It was a request for passage by ship
to Quebec for Mrs. John Walden Meyers and her seven
children. Quebec was much closer by land, he thought.
Why the request for ship passage?

Then he remembered as he looked through his papers. He'd looked at this request last year — at the end
of the summer. It was from the wife of John Walden
Meyers, who was a special courier for Sir Henry Clinton.

Governor Haldimand in Quebec had also used Meyers for courier service. In fact, it was evident that Meyers had been kept in Quebec the entire summer of '79 for the sole purpose of taking the message to New York if Quebec had fallen. If Meyers was chosen for such a trusted duty, he must be one of the most valuable couriers for the British. But Carleton had still made inquiries between Mrs. Meyers' last visit and now. There had to be a good reason for going to the expense and trouble of sending a refugee family by ship. The General turned to the first report.

He read about Meyers' escapades the summer before last — the Ballstown attack and the attempted kidnapping of General Schuyler. Meyers may have failed, but he had made a brave and daring effort, and he had fared better than the others who were sent on similar missions. With time, even Haldimand had admitted that. And during that summer of '81, John Walden Meyers had earned for himself the eternal hatred of the Rebels.

The General then started to read the report from Oliver DeLancey, head of the Secret Service in New York. According to this document, Meyers was one of the spies most wanted by the Rebel leaders. The man had an uncanny ability to escape from the middle of enemy territory despite his conspicuous red hair and large frame, and that talent had demoralized some of the New York State Rebels so much that they thought Meyers had a kind of supernatural power. The Rebel leaders would have liked nothing better than to hang him — if only to stop such rumours. DeLancey recommended strongly that Polly Meyers and her children be given passage from New York by sea. If they were identified by the enemy, he felt the consequences would be tragic for both Meyers and his family.

That settled the matter. Sir Guy Carleton decided he would give this woman the attention she needed. He motioned to his secretary and said firmly, "Send in Mrs. Meyers."

Polly Meyers came forward at the invitation of the army officer and curtseyed.

"Please be seated," the General said in a polite but formal manner.

Polly accepted and quickly made her request for passage. Then she handed him the letter her husband had sent the preceding summer. She had not taken it with her on her previous visit.

The General accepted it and read it. He did not tell her that he had made a thorough investigation since her last interview. She was not aware that he knew more about her husband's war activities than she did.

As she looked up into the face of this man with the bushy eyebrows and deep-set eyes, he frowned even more. But in spite of his sober appearance, he answered favourably.

"You will receive passage soon now," he promised. "In the meantime, I would like you to move into the city to the refugee camp. At present, I have your family scheduled to leave in July. Should passage come sooner, you would need to be here and ready to leave on short notice."

Polly hesitated. She did not want the General to think she was ungrateful, but she dreaded the long wait in New York. They also had an obligation to Mrs. Lloyd.

"Since our passage is for July, could we stay on the farm a little longer? Perhaps June will be soon enough to come into the city."

"I don't think that's wise. Washington will want to enter New York soon, and I don't have the troops to keep him back if he chooses to use force. Don't forget that your husband is a wanted man among the enemy."

"But surely they will not seek revenge on women and children, especially when the battles have already stopped!"

"I'll do my very best to protect and evacuate everyone, but I urge you to come soon. Of course, it's your choice. Notify me when you're staying here in New York." He picked up his next file abruptly.

"Thank you. I will," Polly replied and curtseyed before she withdrew.

Outside on the front steps of the General's headquarters, George was waiting.

"So what did he say?" George asked eagerly as his mother approached.

"He said we can sail for Quebec in July. We'll stay on the farm until the end of June and then move into a refugee camp here in New York so we can sail at a moment's notice."

"So we really are leaving! I thought that was never going to get settled." George had been ready to leave as soon as they'd received the message from Father last August, and he was getting more impatient by the day. Recently, he'd been getting even more restless than ever — since he'd heard that John had been chosen to go with a group of Loyalist soldiers to the Halifax garrison to set up a place for the large number of Loyalists who would soon arrive there. He and Mother were going to the docks now to say goodbye to him before they took the ferry to Long Island. John had obtained a leave of a few weeks to visit his family before his departure. But today he was sailing from New York.

Down at the docks there was a large ship and a crowd

of military men with baggage blocking the passageway to the bateaux.

George led Mother around to one side, and there they could see Sir Guy Carleton himself with the men. Taller than most, George kept looking over the heads of the crowd for his friend, but he could not leave his mother to search more thoroughly.

Finally, a silence fell over the departing soldiers and the crowd of people on the docks behind them.

Already, people respected this General. They knew that in spite of his stern appearance, he cared for ordinary folks as well as his own troops. They realized he was doing everything he could to ease the shortages and to prepare for their departure.

The General bid farewell to his men.

"Gentlemen, you are to provide an asylum for your distressed countrymen. Your task is arduous. Execute it as men of honour. The season for fighting is over. Bury your animosities and persecute no man. Your ship is ready and God bless you."

A look of pride and purpose brightened the soldiers' faces. Then they started passing along towards their ship. George was watching carefully as each stepped by him onto the gangplank. John was nowhere in sight.

Then he spotted a tall girl with wind-burned cheeks and long, thick blonde hair blowing out below the large kerchief wrapped around her head. Her lips parted, she called out and hurried over to touch the arm of a soldier just as he stepped onto the gangplank. He turned and faced her, but she shook her head and turned away.

It was then that George recognized her. "Lucy!" he cried out and pushed through the crowd to reach her.

She turned at the sound of her name and the crowd

cleared between them for a moment. "She's beautiful," George thought, then pushed the idea out of his mind.

"George, is that you?" she said, a broad smile spreading across her face. Then she turned and hugged Mrs. Meyers, who had followed her son. "I've come to find John," she said.

"*Find* him! I thought he'd be with *you*." George could now see the fear in Lucy's eyes.

"He was — but only for a day. He wanted to say goodbye to Uncle Peter and Aunt Jane at Wallkill. They lost both their sons in the war, you know. And John was always their favourite nephew."

"Are you saying that he went back into enemy territory?" George asked.

"He was given a pass, George. After all, we aren't at war anymore — or haven't you noticed!" Lucy snapped.

She hadn't really changed that much after all, George decided. Just as abrupt as ever — and for no reason. George didn't see why she was so worried about John. The war was over, and he did have a pass to go through what used to be Rebel territory.

George, Lucy, and Mother waited a few more minutes at the dock, but there was still no sign of John. Finally the ship set sail without him. "He'd have to go to the barracks to pick up his gear," George told Lucy. "He's probably still there. He's just missed the boat."

"I hope he's in the barracks, George," said Lucy, her mouth quivering just a little as she looked up at him. George suddenly realized that Lucy was not as strong as he had thought.

Mother put her arm around Lucy. "He'll show up. You'll see."

Lucy turned to go. "I'll have to tell Mother," she said.

"Tell her he's at the barracks," George said. "He probably is."

"I hope so, George," she said. She turned then and was soon out of sight in the crowd.

***

Shortly after he and Mother arrived home, George slipped out the side door of the house and headed to the barracks. When he arrived, he found they were not as crowded as usual because many had sailed that day for Canada. The remaining men were quiet and preoccupied. Most were settling in for the night, resting in their bunks. A few played cards by candlelight on a small table in the corner. They did not notice George until he spoke. "Did John make it in time for the ship?"

"John? I don't know. He didn't come back *here*. And I doubt he'd leave without his kit," a soldier replied.

An older man remarked, "He might have if he had to choose between making it back here and missing the boat. You could ask Captain Dan. He'll probably know. He went to see the fellows off."

Captain Dan did not have good news. "He didn't make it," said the Captain. "I watched for him, but he didn't show up. I've had no word at all."

George stood stunned for a moment. Then he turned back towards home. Had John been taken prisoner? Surely they would not kill a Loyalist after peace had been declared! Perhaps he had met with an accident. If his aunt and uncle had died, John would have no one there to help him.

Well he would go to help John! He had travelled that Hudson River before and he could do it again. Wallkill was the other side of the Hudson, but what did that matter? He was bigger and stronger now than when he first made the trip, and his friend needed him. He'd hide his red hair under a hat so no one would know he was his father's son. After all he'd heard about Father's escapades, he figured his father would understand.

Thirty-one

George and Boots stepped briskly onto Captain Schoonhoven's sloop. George had cut short his mass of thick, curly hair, and his three-cornered felt hat, pushed down low over his brow, covered the remaining hair and shaded his face. He was not the small boy of thirteen who had boarded that sloop four and a half years ago. He didn't think he would be recognized. Anyway, if he was detected, he trusted Captain Schoonhoven to be as tolerant as ever.

He had hesitated considerably about bringing Boots, in case the captain would remember him, but Boots had grown to be a great watchdog, and George felt people were less suspicious of a boy with a dog.

The Captain eyed them closely as they walked up the plank and boarded the boat. "Where are you headed?" the Captain asked.

"To my grandparents at Newburgh," George replied.

"Do you realize this boat has to pass inspection by Washington's troops?" the Captain said with some suspicion in his voice. "They're stationed next to Westchester County now."

"I haven't been in any army. I thought the war was over, and besides, my grandparents are for the Rebels, though Grandpa was too old to go to battle."

"What's their name?"

"Clinton, sir."

"Wasn't there a British General by that name?" the Captain asked.

"I heard there was. There was also a governor and captain for the Rebels in New York by the same name. I'm a cousin on my mother's side."

"And what's your name?"

"Way, Thomas Way."

"I've heard that name on both sides too. But you're right. This war is over, and the sooner folks realize that, the better it will be for all concerned." The Captain waved George onto his boat.

On deck, George followed the cabin boy. First they tied Boots in a storage area with a few other animals, then they headed for George's berth. The accommodation would be a little better than before, but he was still going to be sharing. He didn't look forward to that, since that meant he would have to be on guard at all times.

He heard loud voices coming from the cabins as he entered. Five men were already sprawled out on their bunks, singing a loud, tuneless version of "Yankee Doodle." It was obvious they had been celebrating. They looked up when he came in, and one young man shouted over to him, "You headed home too?"

Although they were dressed only in worn homespun farm clothes, George decided that they were soldiers returning to their homes. "Yeah," he answered. He gave them a boyish smile and tried to look happy.

George sat down on his berth. He knew he must get out of there before they asked any more questions. He had brought only a small bag of food in a backpack, and he wondered if he dared leave it behind. He'd hate to lose it so early in his trip. But he wanted the soldiers to feel that he trusted them. So he left it on his berth and headed for the door.

The same young soldier shouted to him, "Wait. I'll go up with you."

George had no choice. He stood waiting as the fellow crawled out of his berth. George couldn't tell his exact age, but he knew he wasn't too many years older than himself. He was extremely thin, but his clothes looked newer than those of the other soldiers.

"Were you in the army long?" George asked. He thought he might better be the one asking the questions.

"Long enough. I was seventeen when I joined and I was sent south. I was taken prisoner when Howe took New York. I nearly starved to death in a British prison-ship. Most of the men didn't make it."

George remembered the thin men in rags who were brought out of the prison-ship, *Wallabout*, docked by Long Island. Folks around had been shocked last summer at the sight of the emaciated figures of the men with rags of clothes falling from their bodies. Sir Guy Carleton ordered them brought to the island for fresh air and exercise each day. Some of the Loyalists had complained at Carleton's extravagance in ordering them new clothes, but most pitied the prisoners.

"Where was the prison-ship stationed?" George asked.

"In New York Harbour on the southwest corner. A soldier called Cunningham was in charge. The old General never came near us. But a new one arrived. I'll never forget. He came right on board and treated us like human beings. We'd almost forgotten we were, what with living that way for so long. After that we were sent food and new clothes. I'm still wearing the clothes." He looked proudly at his trousers, waistcoat, and coat.

"Then were you freed on an exchange?" George asked.

"Yes, but they'll all be sent back soon. Where did you serve?"

George had been expecting this, and he was ready. "The *Wallabout*. I was a prisoner on the *Wallabout* by Long Island."

"The same treatment, I expect."

"Well, they didn't treat us like guests, but we understood it was better than in New York Harbour. We heard prisoners there were ordered to carry their dead up to the deck each morning."

The young man turned deathly pale, and George was afraid the soldier was going to faint. "Let's not talk about the war," George said. "You have a family near here?"

"No. They're away up north of Albany around Saratoga. They got word through to me after I was released. My parents and sisters will be waiting to see me."

"Any brothers?" George was becoming interested.

"Yes. One made it, and one didn't."

"Killed in action?" George asked.

"No, worse. He joined the Loyalists and fought for the British."

George came back to the present reality. Surrounded by Rebels, he must guard his every word. Just then he noticed that the sloop was headed for shore. He could see a number of uniformed men waiting, and he remembered the Captain saying that the ship would have to pass inspection.

He watched the soldiers crossing the gangplank onto the boat. He had told the Captain he had never been in the army. That was quite a different story than the one he had told his new friend. What would he tell the inspector if he asked? He thought about returning to his cabin, but if he went now, he might just draw attention to himself.

The officials and Captain Schoonhoven were walking slowly along the deck towards him and the young soldier. They stopped to speak to other passengers. As they reached the fellows across from George, he still couldn't figure out how to make his two stories fit together. Sweat started to pour from his brow. He was glad there was a cool breeze on deck.

A Rebel officer was speaking to the Captain. "We're busy preparing for Carleton to meet General Washington at Tappan. The war's over at last."

The young soldier pulled off his hat, and George gingerly did the same, clamping his hat back down on his head as fast as possible. His red hair could still give him away. The officer questioned the young soldier: "Name?"

"Gilbert Van Vlack. I've been a prisoner in New York," he replied proudly and started to produce his papers. The officer hardly looked at them and then turned to George. "And you?"

"Thomas Way, sir. I was a prisoner on the *Wallabout*." He pushed his hand in his pocket for the papers he didn't have. He would act surprised that they weren't there.

The officer did not wait for them. He moved on to the next passenger. But George felt Captain Schoonhoven's sharp eyes upon him. The Captain followed the inspector and said nothing.

***

After the inspection was over and the others were all asleep, George was just starting to relax when he heard a soft tap at the cabin door. He hurried to open it. It was Captain Schoonhoven, who motioned him to come out. With growing apprehension, George followed him.

When they reached the Captain's quarters, George was relieved to see that there were no others present.

"Sit down," the Captain said abruptly but not unkindly.

"Thank you, sir," George replied in a feeble voice.

"Well, George," the Captain began, "what are you doing now?"

George faked a surprised look that had no effect on the Captain.

"George, I'd know that dog anywhere. Not to mention that red hair of yours or what's left of it. Now tell me, how is your mother?" the Captain said in a very low but firm voice.

"We are all fine but Father. He was sick with malaria the last we heard. We haven't seen him for three years now."

"No doubt you've heard of his work. All New York State has. It amazes me that you would be out here. I can understand why you are using an assumed name."

"My grandparents are on the Rebel side," George reminded the Captain. "How are they? Have you seen them?"

"They are well, George."

"Uncle Jacob stayed with the Rebel side. Do you know if he made it through?"

"Yes. He did. Your grandparents received word that he was coming home. But your father was the first-born. He was always important to them."

"Maybe we'll be able to visit them soon."

"That wouldn't be wise, George. There's a lot of bitterness. It takes time for such deep wounds to heal. The physical ones heal faster than the other kind." The Captain looked down for a minute, and George was aware that the Captain must be fighting grief of his own.

George did not want to disturb him, so he sat silently until the Captain spoke again. "It is not safe for you to be travelling. Where do you think you're going?"

"My friend went to say goodbye to his aunt and uncle at Wallkill and has not returned. Because he was a Loyalist, I'm afraid for him. I've gone to find him."

"It isn't safe for you," the Captain repeated. "How did your mother take to your leaving?"

"I told only Tobias and he's going to hide it from her as long as possible. He'll tell her I went to New York for supplies."

"What did your friend look like?"

George gave him a detailed description.

"I remember him," he said. "He had an official pass to return to see his relatives. He was safe on my ship, and I did not give away his identity, but on shore folks make their own laws. Washington is against further hostilities but has also made it clear that he hasn't made any promises to protect Loyalists. If your friend's true identity were discovered, he would not be safe."

"His uncle lived on a farm near Wallkill," George reminded the Captain. "He visited there regularly before the war and made friends with a number of neighbours. Do you think anyone would remember him?"

"They'll remember all right. And they will not be his friends. I do think that is the most likely place to look for him. He probably passed unnoticed till he reached the neighbouring area next to the farm."

"Thank you, Captain Schoonhoven," George said. "May I go now? The men in my cabin might miss me and suspect something."

"The way they were celebrating this evening, I doubt they'll waken before we're well into tomorrow. Now,

George, I hope to lift anchor well before dawn, which means we should reach Newburgh by evening. I advise you to travel to Wallkill while it's still dark. Then you might have a chance to find the boy's uncle's house before morning. Do you know the way?"

"I think so. John talked about his uncle's place so often, I'm sure I'll recognize the farm when I see it."

Captain Schoonhoven shook hands with George before letting him leave. "Remember me to Grandma and Grandpa," George said. "One other thing. Please tell them we're all well and tell Grandma I'm almost as tall as Father."

The Captain smiled. "I'll tell them more than that. I'll tell them you're the spitting image of your father."

***

George's day had not been easy. Gilbert had stuck with him and talked constantly. Fortunately Gilbert didn't expect him to say much, but he did have to listen enough to nod his head from time to time. He also had to be on his guard, and he had no time to plan. When they reached Newburgh, the Captain sent for Boots. Before George knew it, he and Boots were on the shore.

"We'll be returning this way in two weeks' time," the Captain shouted. "I'll look for you." George nodded and waved. George realized that the sloop travelled longer and farther each day than it used to.

Boots was wagging his tail. He was glad to be out of the close quarters in the boat and walking along with his master again. George took off his hat as he walked along now in the darkness. The two looked as though they belonged to each other, the large golden collie and the big, fair-skinned youth.

Just before dawn, George saw a small flickering light burning in the upstairs window of a farmhouse not far off to the left. The maple to the right of the front door . . . the hill sloping away to the left . . . the gabled windows . . . this had to be John's uncle's farm. He decided to creep up to the house and try to look inside. It was possible that John had never reached his uncle's, or maybe even they had turned against him.

George and Boots sat down in an apple orchard a safe distance from the house. They would wait until the light came on downstairs. George knew farmers rose at dawn at this time of year to tend to the chores and cattle around the barn so they would be ready early in the day to work in the fields.

He didn't have long to wait. A light shone out from the kitchen. Then another flickering light started heading for the barn. Now was his chance.

"Quiet, Boots," he said. The dog understood and crept along beside him.

Looking through the low window, George saw an elderly woman working over the table. She was not preparing breakfast as he had expected. Instead she was tearing pieces of cloth and laying it on the table. Then she went to the stove and dipped a ladle into a boiling pot. She gently emptied the ladle onto the cloth and then repeated the process. George was puzzled until he saw her fold the corners of the cloth in and over the centre. She was preparing a poultice.

George waited no longer. He rushed up to the door and tapped lightly. Boots stood quietly at his heels.

The door opened only a crack. "Who is it?" the old woman asked.

"A friend of your nephew," George said.

The door opened a bit farther. A thin, stooped woman, with grey hair tied back in a tight bun, peered out. "How do you know my nephew?" she said nervously.

"Your nephew is John?"

"Yes."

"Did he reach you?"

She hesitated before she answered, "Yes. But who are you?"

"George," he replied and removed his hat. "Is John still here?"

"Yes," she said as she stared at George's short red hair. "John said you might come. Step in." As he entered the kitchen, George heard the low whine of his dog. He knew someone was approaching.

"It's probably just my husband, but hide in here just in case," she said, motioning George into the small pantry just off the kitchen.

John's uncle walked into the kitchen. He looked somewhat startled. "There's a strange dog by our back stoop, Jane. See any strangers about?"

"Yes. John's friend George." Hearing her, George stepped back into the kitchen.

Peter Bleecker was a short, bent man who appeared much smaller than his brother, John's father. He limped across the room and pulled a chair out from the kitchen table for George to sit on.

"John missed the ship. Did he change his mind and decide to stay with you?" George asked.

The Bleeckers exchanged glances. George felt the tension. He asked, "May I see him now?" Their silence made him fear that he may have walked into a trap. He did not fully trust them. Still, he knew he could easily escape from them if they did not use weapons. He saw none about.

John's aunt picked up her poultice in one hand and the candlestick in the other. "Come with us," she said.

George followed. He could hear Mr. Bleecker limping along behind. Then, halfway up the stairs, he heard the clunk of a heavy object like a musket against the railing.

He spun around.

He saw only Uncle Peter's heavy cane supporting him as he climbed the stairs. George hoped they had not noticed his sudden reaction.

At the top of the stairs, George could hear low moaning. Aunt Jane opened the bedroom door and stood back for George to enter. On the bed was a man whom George could not recognize.

He lay on the bedding without clothing, his body covered with goose grease to lift the tar, and poultices where the burns were worst. Between them, George could see swollen, red flesh.

George knelt beside the bed and just managed to say, "John," before he started to cry silently.

George felt a hand reach out and touch his head as he knelt there.

"I'll get through . . . I'm going back," John whispered.

"That's why I came," said George.

"Just . . . a few more days . . . I'll be ready."

"I'll wait," George promised.

Aunt Jane went over to the bed with the fresh poultice for one of the festering wounds. John grimaced silently as she touched his flesh.

Uncle Peter held the bedroom door open and nodded

to George. "We'll be going down now, John," he said. They walked out into the hallway and shut the door. The cool quiet of the hallway was broken as John cried out in pain. George bit his lip and followed Uncle Peter to the stairs.

In a low, husky voice, Uncle Peter mumbled to George, "My neighbours only gave me two weeks for him to stay here. They said that if he wasn't gone by then, they'd be back with more of the same. I went to the local authorities, and they tell me they've got no orders to protect the enemy."

"We'll leave soon," George promised.

"But he's in no shape to travel, and the two weeks are up tomorrow!"

Thirty-two

Geroge's trips to New York City never lasted longer than two days before. He should be back by now," Mother said, wiping her hands on her apron. She and the older children were in the kitchen preserving rhubarb.

Tobias shifted uneasily as Mother spoke directly to him. "I feel you know more about this than I do, and I expect you to tell me now. You aren't saving me any worry by not telling me. I'll imagine the worst."

"He's gone to Wallkill to find John," Mary said.

"He's what?" Mother almost shrieked.

"It will take a while, Mother. George can take care of himself." Tobias tried to sound reassuring.

"You know what Captain Dafoe said. You all know he said George looked exactly like his father." She was still talking in a high-pitched voice.

"George had me cut his hair and he wore the old hat Mrs. Lloyd gave Jacob to play with. It covered his head and shaded his face," Tobias explained.

Mother sank into a rocking chair. Catharine rushed over to the fireplace to make her a cup of tea.

Mary sat cross-legged on the floor at Mother's feet. She tucked her apron neatly around her. "George took Boots," she said, still looking down. "He might even be a help. And he was going on Captain Schoonhoven's sloop. He'll reach Wallkill from the sloop in one night. He'll be fine."

"Are you telling me that George took that dog back on the sloop with him again? As if Captain Schoonhoven would ever forget that incident! The sight of Boots will just trigger his memory!" Mother put her head in her hands and wept.

The children sat in silence, not knowing what to say.

In a few minutes, Mother took her hands from her face. She was still pale but calmer. She got up quietly and walked out of the room.

Catharine turned around, holding the fresh pot of tea. "Where's Mother gone?" she asked.

"To her room," Mary said.

"Well, I'm taking her this tea anyway."

After Catharine had gone, Leonard complained, "I wish he'd let me know. I'd have gone with him. George likes to do everything on his own . . . just because he's the oldest."

***

Sir Guy Carleton looked at the appointment sheet on his desk. Then he sneezed. He still had a heavy cold. His damp trip up the Hudson to meet with Washington a week ago on the 7th of May had only made it worse, even though he had travelled to Tappan on his own ship the *Perseverance*.

Their meeting had been civil enough. Still, he had been vexed by the General's demand to take possession of Westchester County within a week, and he did not intend to lose control of Long Island for the present. He was determined to protect the Loyalist refugees camped there waiting for passage to safety.

Next, Washington had pushed him about the blacks. Britain's promise of freedom had drawn thousands of slaves to run away and fight for them. As far as the British were concerned, those slaves were now free. But General Washington had argued that Carleton had to return slaves to their rightful owners, since according to the peace treaty, all stolen property was to be returned to the Rebels.

This had put Carleton in a dilemma. He offered to reimburse all owners for their losses and suggested that Washington send inspectors to the docks to take down the names of the owners of the blacks as they left. Carleton agreed that he would accept these lists as a guide for payment to the Rebel owners. Washington did not like the plan, but Carleton was determined. When Washington realized that Carleton would not move further on the issue, the hot debate finally ended, and Washington silenced his officers, who had argued fiercely for the return of the slaves.

Washington had then pushed him for a final withdrawal date from New York City. It had been a long day, and Carleton had been a bit abrupt. He'd told Washington that he could not leave New York until he had completed his duties there — whenever that might be.

Carleton sneezed again and came back to the task at hand. He was annoyed that he had to take time from his pressing work to answer another letter from Washington. As he had threatened a week ago, Washington had taken Westchester County and was now pressing for Long Island. If he used force, Carleton knew he couldn't stop him. Still, he had delayed them so far. That was still the best strategy. He took up his fine goose-quill pen.

When he had finished the letters, he called for his secretary to arrange for their delivery. Then he turned to the pile of requests on his desk. He looked at his list of urgent items. He thought again of the danger to Long Island and shook his head.

As he read down his list to the name "Meyers," he mumbled, "I'll attend to this one now," and began to write again.

***

That same afternoon Sir Guy Carleton's military courier arrived at Mrs. Lloyd's door. With alarm, Mary saw her mother take the official-looking sealed envelope.

"What's happened to Father?" Mary thought to herself.

Mother tore the letter open. She read aloud, "You and your children are to report to the New York City refugee centre near my office within twenty-four hours. Bring your personal belongings with you. Be ready to sail for Nova Scotia. I expect to have your passage booked within the week."

Thirty-three

W e can't move John just yet. It would be too painful," Aunt Jane told her husband and George as she came from the pantry with bread and cheese for their breakfast. She placed them on the table beside the fried pork and sliced potatoes.

"Well, he's going to be in more pain if we leave him there," Uncle Peter replied. "When that mob said they'd be back, they meant it."

"I can't think they really did," Aunt Jane said, handing a jar of her wild strawberry jam to George.

"They'll be back. Remember, Jane, their sons died in this war. The ones whose sons aren't coming back right now — they just aren't themselves. If only John had waited a while."

George could see the pain in Aunt Jane's eyes as she nodded.

Uncle Peter continued, "Now I figure we could fix a place for him in that empty shack just beyond our back woods." He turned to George. "We had neighbours there for a short time. They left just before the war. I thought I'd be needing more land for my sons, so I bought it. It would've been right handy for us with a son settled there. Anyhow, I bought the land and after our sons left, I let the property run down some."

"It's no fit place to take John," Aunt Jane interrupted. "Not in the shape he's in."

"We could fix the place up a bit. There's that room that's hidden behind the regular root cellar. I doubt they'd find it. Anyhow it's the best we can do. We've got George now to help us move him."

"Could we make it to the Hudson instead?" George asked.

"Maybe, but you'd have trouble travelling down the Hudson by yourselves. You'd never make it back past West Point. John isn't well enough yet to travel that far. And anyway, I doubt he'd get to the Hudson River without being noticed."

"Captain Schoonhoven is coming in two weeks if we can just wait it out until then. We'll be safe on his boat. He's a friend of my grandparents."

"He could stay in the root cellar till then. Parts of the place have caved in, though. We'll need to work hard to get it ready without leaving any signs that it's been repaired," Uncle Peter told George.

When they completed their breakfast, Uncle Peter motioned George to the door. "Let's go," he said. He was eager to start.

When they came out on the back stoop, Boots had already finished two bowlfuls of breakfast. Feeling quite at home, he trotted along beside the men, wagging his tail.

***

"It's over there, just beyond that clump of cedar trees," Uncle Peter said as they made their way out of the other side of the Bleeckers' back woods. Uncle Peter leaned on his cane.

It was then they heard people shouting.

"I can't believe this," Uncle Peter said. "No one ever comes around here. With the new undergrowth, you can't even get a wagon through the back laneway."

They crouched down behind the cedars and listened. It didn't sound like an angry mob, but they couldn't be too careful. George placed a firm hand on Boots' head. They could not make out what was being said, but the men's voices sounded agitated. Then they heard the piercing wail of a woman.

Before Uncle Peter could stop him, George ran out from his cover towards the sound, and Boots followed.

George saw fewer people than he expected in the yard of the abandoned house. There were only two men and a boy about Leonard's size with the young woman who had screamed.

The woman was still wailing, sitting on the ground, bent over, and rocking back and forth with her apron over her face. George could make out her words now. She was saying, "My baby, my baby."

No one paid any attention to George and Boots.

A few yards from the woman, the men were on their knees looking down a hole about three feet square. Some loose boards had been pulled back from the opening.

"I can't hear a sound," the older man said.

"He didn't answer Margaret." The younger man shook his head. "If he were alive, he would have answered his mother."

The boy moved a few feet back from the opening. "I've changed my mind. I'm not going down that hole," he said. "Even if you do tie a rope around my legs. There's no use now anyway."

After that remark, the young mother's screams started

again and ended with more sobbing. The men ignored her and continued to talk.

"That well may not be as deep as we think. They say the folks there never did reach water. They had to use the Bleeckers' well."

Standing behind the men who were stooped over the opening, George spoke out, "I'll fetch Mr. Bleecker. He'll know."

They looked up then at the stranger who had joined them, but they did not have time to answer before Uncle Peter, who was now standing right behind George, spoke out. "You're right. The man who water-witched for the Smiths was a fake. He took off with his pay while they wasted more time digging for water before they gave up. Finally they threw a lot of the dirt back in there."

"How deep do you figure it is?" the older man asked.

"I don't know. It could be ten feet or thirty."

The younger man stood up and grabbed his cane. He limped a couple of steps towards them. He wore the old blue uniform of a Rebel army officer.

"My son's down that well," he told them.

"How do you know that?"

He held up a piece of cloth. "We found this on the boards over the well — right by the opening. It's from my son's shirt. He wandered off late yesterday afternoon."

"Then he could have been down there all night! How'd you take so long finding him?" Uncle Peter sounded shocked.

"My wife lost him while they were picking flowers. She hunted by herself, never thinking of the well. Finally we found her half-crazed with worry, still hunting in the woods. Then we searched for Thomas."

The youth who had accompanied the men slowly crept away into the woods. Only George noticed him go.

"My son here is agile enough to go down the hole," the older man said. "It's a relief to have the extra help on the rope. Now let's get going." He picked up the rope and turned to his son.

"Eben," he called. There was no answer.

"I'll go down," the young father said without hesitation. "We have more help now to hold the rope. You won't need me."

"No, Ed," the older man said. "Not with that leg. I'll go."

George looked at the agitated young father and the heavy-set older man. In an instant, he realized that neither of them was the man for the job. "Tie those ropes around my waist and feet. I'll go down," George said.

They stared at George for a few seconds. Then the father grabbed the rope and came over to George. The other man helped him.

"You're tall, George. You might just be able to do it." Uncle Peter examined the knot. "Fasten the rope firm," he said to the two men. Then he checked it again.

"Handle the boy careful like," the older man instructed. "He might be hurt badly."

"It'll be narrow at the bottom," Mr. Bleecker added. "No room to turn, George. Bring him up as gentle as you can."

George nodded and threw his hat on the ground. Then he took off his coat and waistcoat, and rolled up his sleeves. Boots followed George right up to the opening.

The woman was quieter now. Her small frame shook only occasionally with a silent sob. Her mob cap had fallen off. Her loosened golden hair had fallen over her shoulders and cascaded down her back. Dirt and tears streaked her pale face. She came closer, and through eyes swollen half-shut, she watched the men.

George leaned over into the well and crawled inside. The men lowered him down, head first. He felt around the sides with his hands. Maybe the child was caught on a side of the well. There just might be a ledge.

He could hear Boots whining up above.

The well became darker as he descended. The sides felt very damp. Maybe the water-witching had been accurate, and the impatient people had not waited long enough. Maybe he'd find water at the bottom. And what if the rope didn't hold?

He kept going down and down, spanning the sides with his big hands. He felt a piece of cloth. He felt further, but there was no body. Then a sharp stone bit into his right arm, just below the elbow. He felt the stinging pain and the blood trickling down his arm across his palm. He couldn't worry about it now.

He figured they must have lowered him over fifteen feet. How much farther did the well go? Then he noticed it was becoming narrower. He must be nearing the bottom.

He stretched out his hands and groped into the pitch darkness. The ends of his fingers touched flesh. He had found the boy!

"I've found him," he shouted, but the words came out all muffled. "Let me down only a little more."

He worked his big hands gently under the small body. Then George lifted the child and drew him close to his own chest.

"Up — pull me up now," he shouted.

At first, he felt no movement from the rope. Then, slowly, it began to move. At the same time he felt the little body tremble in his arms. And he had fresh hope.

The way up seemed much farther. In his cramped position, his arms were aching badly. He had chosen a difficult hold to protect the child better. How long could he continue?

Finally he felt the men grab his feet. With his remaining strength, George tightened his hold on the child. His grip must not slip now.

With great relief, he felt the young father reach down and grab the child's clothing while he and the child were still in the opening.

Then they pulled George up over the edge and reached for the boy. Still clutching the boy, George felt the men's hands loosening his hold.

He stretched out on the ground exhausted while the men examined the child. Boots was licking his face.

They placed the boy on his mother's shawl by the well. The father bent over his child. "I've found a pulse. Thank God, he's alive," he breathed.

The young woman reached out for her boy, but her husband shook his head. "He needs help fast."

He handed the boy to the older man because he could not walk quickly without his cane. "Don't wait for me," he said. "Rush him to our house. I'll follow as fast as I can."

"Bring him to ours," Uncle Peter offered. "It's closer. I can hitch up the team and we can take him to the doctor faster than the doctor can get here."

George was back on his feet now, speaking to Uncle Peter. "I could carry him to the house while you go for the doctor. Maybe we could meet part way."

Without replying, the older man handed the boy to George.

"I'll go for the doctor," he said. "The Huyck farm isn't

far, and they can lend me a horse and wagon. It'll be better not to move my grandchild too much."

George started taking long rapid strides now, and Boots was right in step with him. As he reached the yard only about fifteen minutes later, the little boy roused in his arms and whimpered a little.

Boots ran ahead and barked at the door. Aunt Jane ran out to see what the commotion was — then held the door open and waited for George without asking questions.

"A child fell in the old well," George explained. "His grandfather's gone for the doctor."

Aunt Jane rushed ahead and pulled a blanket over the couch. "Put him here," she said. "I'll find the smelling salts."

George knelt down beside the child and looked at him now for the first time. He was a fair-haired boy of about three. He looked a bit the way Jacob had a couple of years ago. There was blood on the child's torn shirt, but George could not see any open wounds. Then he noticed the blood on his own arm and realized that it could be from his cut.

"Just let him smell this," Aunt Jane said. She held a small bottle to his nose.

The child coughed and opened his eyes. He stared at them with fright. Then his face wrinkled into a cry and he screamed, "Mama."

"I'm here," a woman's voice came from just outside. She came rushing through the doorway and over to the couch.

"I wouldn't move him, Margaret, until the doctor comes to examine him," Aunt Jane advised, "though he doesn't seem to be in pain."

The woman nodded. Aunt Jane pulled up a chair for her so she could sit on it beside the boy.

Uncle Peter and the boy's father came through the door then. The father rushed over to see his son and felt for his pulse. "It's stronger now," he said.

"I can't see any wounds except the big bump on his arm," said Aunt Jane, "but I don't think we should move him too much."

George noticed then how strange the boy's left arm looked. It was bent awkwardly back, and the boy was whimpering now in a steady, low cry.

Aunt Jane brought another blanket for him. "I'll heat some broth so it'll be ready if the doctor says he can have it," she said, then disappeared into the pantry.

The child's crying was becoming louder. George went over to the back door where Boots was waiting, then went outside and started walking down the lane with Boots at his side. He wondered how long the doctor would take to come. He sat down and leaned against a maple tree that was just fully leafed out. Boots sat close beside him, and they both watched down the road.

George thought of John. Would Uncle Peter trust the doctor to look in on John too? He thought not. How he wanted to relieve the pain for his friend! He knew that the trip to the root cellar would not be easy.

Finally, George saw a wagon coming around the bend. It clattered towards him, careered into the lane and came to an abrupt halt at the Bleeckers' door. George stayed at the road. There was no need for him to clutter up the kitchen. There were enough folks around there. He leaned his head against the tree trunk. The sun was hot, and he brushed his hair back from his forehead. His hat was gone. Then he remembered. He'd left it at the well. He'd have to go back for it.

The hat was just where he had dropped it. Beside it, the gaping hole of the well still lay open. He placed the boards across it and then went to the abandoned cabin and found more. He placed these planks securely over the others and then piled stones on top. Boots watched his every move. Together they started back to the house.

George was thinking about the child and John too as he came in sight of the farm buildings. He and Uncle Peter would have to do some work to get that place ready before tomorrow. As he turned into the laneway, George saw the child's grandfather driving away from the house, talking to the doctor beside him. He hoped that was a good sign.

As he approached the house, the child's father stepped out onto the back stoop. George pulled his hat a little lower over his forehead and looked at the man's officer's uniform.

"How is he?" George asked.

"Far better than we expected. His arm's badly bruised, but other than that and a severe chill, he seems to be unhurt. I don't see how he wasn't injured more, but that's the doctor's findings."

"I think his shirt may have caught on the side of the well. There's a piece of it still there. It probably broke his fall. Anyway, the well's not as deep as an ordinary well."

"I want to thank you for saving my son. My name's Edward Foster. Thank you . . ."

"It was nothing," George said. "I've got a brother not much older . . . How is the boy's mother?"

"She's fine now that he's all right. She and Mrs.

Bleecker are busy caring for him. Now I want to know what I can do to repay you."

George hesitated. Now that he was closer to the officer, he realized that Edward Foster was not as young as he had thought. Deep wrinkle lines were set around his eyes and mouth.

The officer was studying George intently now, and suddenly his expression changed. "I knew I'd seen you before, and yet it can't be. You're much younger . . . Could you be his son?" he mumbled in a low voice. He was remembering his guard duty at Ballstown jail when he was still a private. He had been captured that night but freed shortly afterward in a prisoner exchange. He had never forgotten the red-headed leader of that bold rescue team and had listened with reluctant respect to the news of his other bold attacks.

George was busy with his own thoughts and did not hear the officer mumble or notice his preoccupation. George had reached a decision. "Do you really wish to do something for me?" he asked.

Edward Foster did not hesitate to answer, "Yes." But he was still studying George.

"Will you help Mr. Bleecker save his nephew from the mob that's coming tomorrow?"

"You're a friend of John's. It all fits!" the officer mumbled again.

"Will you help?" George repeated.

"I just arrived home a few days ago. Tell me about his nephew. I heard he fought for the Loyalists."

"The war's over now. John came to say goodbye to his uncle and aunt for the last time before he left for Canada. He ran into a mob in town who recognized him. They left him in bad shape on his uncle's doorstep and gave him two weeks to leave. His time is up tomorrow, and he's still in no condition to travel."

"I see," the officer said. George watched the man silently as he looked down and struggled to decide.

Then the officer looked up at George and smiled. "They'd never think to look for him in the home of an American officer, would they?"

***

Towards dusk, a wagon creaked down the laneway of the Bleecker homestead. The Rebel officer drove the team, and his young wife held a whimpering child on her lap. They drove slowly so they would not jar their child's injured arm.

On the back of their wagon sat a farm lad with a three-cornered hat pulled down low over his forehead. Next to him sat a big collie dog. Behind them, a canvas was thrown lightly over a few bags of grain about the size of a man.

Thirty-four

C aptain Schoonhoven scanned the early morning horizon from his sloop. It was the 20th of May, two weeks since he had passed Newburgh on his way up the Hudson. Now on his voyage back, he had dropped anchor there for the night.

"Do I pull anchor now?" a sailor asked.

The Captain hesitated. "Not just yet," he said. "I'm waiting for news from shore."

The sailor came and stood by the rail at the Captain's side. He too stared towards the shore. The town was still. The townsfolk did not waken as early as the crew aboard Captain Schoonhoven's sloop.

"I hear that our troops are occupying Westchester County beside New York now," the sailor said.

"Where'd you hear that?" the Captain asked.

"An American officer who came aboard last night. He's reporting back for duty."

More of the crew came up to the deck to report for work. Again, the Captain looked to the shoreline. He saw a few wagons starting to move along and people coming out of their houses. Now the day was beginning for the town folk, too. Still there was no sign of any passengers approaching the dock. He knew that he must make a decision soon. His men were ready and waiting for his instructions so they could begin the day's work.

Resigned, he turned back to give the order to the sailors to raise the anchor. Then, as he looked across his sloop, he remembered a small, bewildered thirteen-year-old boy and his dog standing on that same deck.

"Don't pull that anchor," Captain Schoonhoven said. "There will be a one-day stopover here. My news has not come. I'll be going into town in half an hour. Have the small boat ready for me."

Surprised but not unhappy at the sudden change of plans, the men watched the Captain head for his cabin. A day in Newburgh wouldn't be so bad.

***

The Meyers family headed for the loading area — without George. It was the 22nd of May, exactly one week and a day after Sir Guy Carleton had ordered them to New York City. True to his promise, he had booked their passage. Mother had protested because George had not returned, but the General had persuaded her that she could not risk the lives of all her children to wait for one.

Finally, she had decided to go. Clutching a pass for George too, she kept watching for her son. Carleton had said he would send George speedily if found. If not, he promised he would remain on the lookout and send him later. They could ask for no more.

With heavy hearts, the family plodded along with their large bags but no bulky household goods. They had been told that the space was needed for people. They passed many auctions along the way. People were selling their belongings for a pittance before they left on the ships. Luckily, they had been able to send word to Mrs. Lloyd, and she had paid them reasonably well for their furniture. They hoped she would arrive in time to see them off at the docks. But most of all, they still hoped that George would make it in time.

"How long is the voyage?" Catharine asked, remembering her seasick trip down the Hudson.

"I don't know," Mother replied.

"I'd say about three weeks," Tobias said. "It depends on the weather. It could be more, but probably less."

"And we won't have reached our destination even then," Catharine complained.

"Yes, but it'll be better," Mary said. "We shouldn't have to stay too long at the barracks in Halifax before Mother can arrange passage down the St. Lawrence to Quebec. Father will be waiting for us there."

"It's three years now . . . ," Mother added quietly. "You've grown so; your father will have a hard time recognizing you. If only George . . ." She could not finish the sentence.

"Especially me," Jacob said loudly as he shifted his heavy load from one shoulder to the other. The family knew six-year-old Jacob would not recognize Father either.

It felt good to set down their bags on the docks. They stayed together, waiting beside them.

"Look, here come Mrs. Lloyd and Sam," Leonard called out over the noise around. Mrs. Lloyd had just reached them when the people with their luggage started to move forward. The Meyers family followed the others. Mrs. Lloyd and Sam, her elderly slave, remained on the shore to watch.

Mother led the way and then hesitated. Tobias stepped up beside her and helped her sort through their passes to have them in order for the inspectors.

Mary, Catharine, and Anna passed by the British officer. Leonard and Jacob followed behind them.

"Where's his pass?" the officer said and laughed loudly. The children turned to see what the problem was. They thought Mother had everything in order.

There stood George and Boots beside Mother! Mother was smiling up at George as she handed over the extra papers to be inspected.

"I mean *his* papers," said the officer. He was pointing at Boots. Although he was panting from running, George laughed at the officer's joke and headed towards the ship with Boots.

The Meyers family were all staring at George with surprised relief. "Where were you?" Mary asked. "And where's John?"

"John's safely recovering at his stepfather's house. It's a long story, Mary. I'll tell you later."

"But Lucy, her mother and Mr. MacKenzie are leaving on the first ship out tomorrow morning," Mary said.

"I know and it's okay, Mary. Mr. MacKenzie got passage for John too."

"But doesn't he have to report back to DeLancey's Corps? He doesn't want to be listed as a deserter."

"Stop worrying, Mary. Mr. MacKenzie is travelling there today with a letter from Sir Guy Carleton to release John so he can travel to Canada with them. He'll be all ready to go by tomorrow."

"I thought his stepfather didn't like John."

George hesitated. "He's a good enough fellow — the war changed all of us at times, I'm afraid. John's starting to think he's okay too. He says Mr. MacKenzie's been awful good to his mother and Lucy."

At last, they were all on their way. With a happy sigh, Mary stepped ahead with George beside her.

"Hey! You can't take that dog," the same officer yelled at George. He looked more serious now.

"Why not?" George shouted back, surprised by the man's abrupt manner. "Other animals have gone."

"That's a useless animal if I ever saw one. The space can be better filled. We're trying to save Loyalists, not dogs," he explained. His voice became less severe, but he still motioned towards Boots and the shore.

By then, the argument had caused a slight stir in the crowd around. Many eyes were staring at them, but at first George did not notice. He was thinking only of Boots.

"Let the children have their dog," yelled a man nearby. "Most Loyalists have been living a dog's life lately anyway."

Another man in the crowd yelled out, "Have you heard Washington's latest remedy for the Loyalists?"

"No, what?" the other asked.

"He said that he could see nothing better for them than to commit suicide," the ragged man replied and slowly added, "Maybe he was right." He staggered on down the street.

George began to shake with anger. Why did this stupid crowd have to notice anyway? Could he believe their remarks? Had General Washington said that? Wasn't it enough that he was winning this war? Wasn't it enough that all their land had gone to the Rebels and they would maybe never see Grandma and Grandpa again? And was he really going to lose Boots?

The officer grabbed Boots roughly by the long hair on his neck.

"No," said George. "I'll take him." The sympathetic crowd parted quickly before him as he raced over to Sam and Mrs. Lloyd.

Breathlessly, he handed Boots over to Sam and raced back through the opening in the crowd. There was no time for goodbyes. Sam held the squirming dog tightly.

"Move along," the British officer said, and the family followed the others onto the ship.

Once on board, they kept together as the ship drifted out. There was not much of a breeze blowing in the harbour yet, and they knew they would not go far until the wind began to blow more briskly.

The Meyers all waved to Mrs. Lloyd and Sam on the shore. Boots was standing nearby watching.

Suddenly the dog sped along the crowded shore and jumped into the water between the ships. He swam steadily towards them. Although the water was fairly calm, an occasional wave passed over him, and only his nose appeared on the surface.

George watched in disbelief for a moment, then yelled, "Come on, Boots." But his words were drowned out in the confusion and noise.

Then reality hit George. They would not stop for a dog, not when people's lives were in danger. More and more people were waiting on shore for the ships to return. The sailors were busy now helping to settle the folks on board. He and his brothers and sisters were the only ones watching Boots.

They watched silently. They knew if their dog followed too far, he'd be too exhausted to make it back to shore.

After his first outburst, George was silent. His breath

catching, he felt the seconds fall away as if they were whole minutes.

A good breeze was blowing now. Their ship's sails were billowing out and the vessel was starting to gain speed.

The distance between the ship and the dog was lengthening. Boots seemed to be growing smaller and smaller.

Then they saw him turn and head back towards the shore. Boots had realized he'd never make it. A few minutes later, they saw Sam pull the wet collie up on the dock.

The children let out a loud cheer, and George said, "Some day I'm going back for him."

Thirty-five

George looked across the cascading waves to the green pastureland and golden wheat fields on the shore. Mountains covered with pine trees loomed in the distance. But George was not really taking in the scenery. He was thinking only of Father. Would he be waiting for them at Machiche, as Captain Dafoe had said?

The family had left New York harbour almost two months before. It had been a long, difficult trip. The seas had been rough, and Mother and Catharine were sick for most of the journey.

Catharine had recovered quickly after they reached land at Halifax, but Mother hadn't. They had stayed in a crowded barracks while they waited for her to improve enough to travel again.

Then they had taken a ship for Quebec. They had hoped to meet Father there. Instead Captain Dafoe had met them and arranged for them to stay two nights in a private home. He told them that Father would meet them at Machiche, a town farther up the St. Lawrence that had been constructed by Loyalist and British soldiers for the refugees.

So now they were going deeper and deeper into this unknown land, with only their clothes, bedding, and a few personal belongings. What if Father was not at

Machiche? Would he be able to clear the land as Grandpa had so many years before at Cooeyman's Landing?

George knew that he would do what was necessary to build a home for the family in this wilderness. He'd be eighteen next week. He was strong and they would make it in this new land just as they had made it through the war.

But how he longed to see his father! He thought of happier times before the war — the first time his father took him into the Adirondack Mountains on a hunting trip and he wandered away from the campsite. He had sat down on a rock and waited just as Father had told him, and in no time at all Father had found him. He also remembered fishing in the Hudson River with Father and his brothers. A great longing and loneliness gripped George again, and he faced into the splashing spray at the side of the boat, straining to see signs of movement and people.

"We're close," Mary said. She stood beside him now, leaning on the railing, and George felt less alone. Mary was sixteen now and, like himself, she was strong and sturdy. She'd taken off her mob cap to let the breeze blow back her thick auburn hair. Her eyes had a childish eagerness as they searched the shoreline.

At last George could see people along the shore, but he could not make out their faces. Beyond them was a settlement that extended nearly right down to the shoreline. In the centre a high wooden palisade surrounded one larger frame building. To the west of it were a half-dozen small frame houses. On the other side were many log cabins. And between these were several canvas tents with smoke coming from open campfires. Thick woods closed in behind the settlement.

Only a few commands in French rang across the deck. Then the Captain spoke out in heavily accented English, "We land now at Machiche."

The village came more clearly into view. People were cooking over campfires and a few wagons sat behind some of these fires. Children were running back and forth in a small grassy space beside the wagons.

George could feel the bateau moving up and down more slowly as the light waves washed against it. Each member of the family picked up a piece of luggage from the pile beside George, then looked expectantly to the shore.

"I'm going to sign up with Father's battalion," said Tobias.

"What's the point in that?" said George. "The war is over."

"I know," Tobias said, "but the army hasn't disbanded yet. I'd get to live with the men in the barracks for a while."

Leonard was next to pick up his canvas duffle bag. "That's not a bad idea, Tobias. I think I'll join too."

"Not at fourteen, Leonard. Be reasonable," George said in a somewhat superior tone.

"Hey, you two aren't leaving me to run all the errands for my sisters," Leonard objected.

"I'll still be here to help," Jacob chipped in, and the others laughed. He was tall for a six-year-old, and he stood proudly holding a large bag over his shoulder.

Catharine and Anna were beside Mother. Catharine's long blonde hair rippled down her back as she studied the shore intently. Anna, with her dimpled smile, looked the most like Mother.

There were only a few other passengers on the small

bateau, and they stood on the other side of the gangway. The four crew members were at their posts.

Standing silently together, the family watched the shoreline get larger as their vessel approached it. Finally George spotted a small group of people waiting on the dock. At the back was father's red head — above all the others, as usual!

Laden with luggage, George let the rest go forward first onto the gangplank. Did he really resemble his father as much as folks said? Would his father notice?

John Walden Meyers, an impressive figure in full military uniform, was waiting by the dock. His breeches and waistcoat of white wool were partially covered by his Ranger's short green coat with red lapels, collar and cuffs. There was a silver epaulette on the right shoulder. At his throat was a ruffle of fine linen lace. The buttons circled with silver lace shone in the July sun. He looked older now and thinner. He had deep wrinkles around his eyes, and his stubble-beard was gone. Under his silver-trimmed cocked hat, his hair seemed a dark auburn. But his eyes sparkled as he saw them all, and a smile lit up his whole face.

Mother stepped off the gangplank. She looked worn and tired, much thinner than she had ever been. Her hands trembled a little as she set down her luggage on the grass beside the dock and looked up into her husband's face.

Father gazed in disbelief at the wife he had not seen for three years. "Thank God we've all made it, Polly!" he said drawing her to him. His eyes seemed to be glistening.

Mary and Catharine were squatting beside a pile of trunks, hugging a big old sheep dog. It was Curly! He was whining and wagging his tail as he rubbed against them.

Father was coming towards George now. In a flash George recalled the last time he had talked with him. Would he remember their differences?

His father slapped a hand on each of George's shoulders and stared straight into the eyes of his oldest son, who was as tall as himself. His eyes were misted over with tears.

George stood there in silence. No words seemed adequate.

Then Father said, "George, I will never be able to thank you for all that you've done. The family is safe, and it's because, with the grace of God, you were able to protect them."

George glanced away, then turned back to his father, who looked so much like a reflection of himself, and with a smile he said, "I did what I had to do."

Epilogue

*I*n spite of constant pressure from Congress and General Washington, Sir Guy Carleton refused to withdraw from New York City until November 25, 1783, when the more than 30,000 Loyalists who had gained sanctuary there were safely removed. He refused to capitulate to General Washington in the matter of the slaves and did not hand over the runaways, but sent them to liberty. In fact, "it was a point of honour with him [Sir Guy Carleton] that no troops should embark until the last person who claimed his protection should be safely on board a British ship." When Washington pressured him, Carleton informed the American General "that the more the uncontrolled violence of their citizens drove refugees to his protection, the longer would evacuation be delayed."

Like John W. Meyers, many disbanded Loyalist soldiers and their families settled in what are now Ontario and Quebec. Eighty to ninety percent of the first settlers in Ontario were disbanded Loyalist soldiers who had served in Canada for a number of years during the Revolutionary War. They were of the following battalions: The First Battalion, Royal Highland Emigrants (84th Regiment), the First and Second Battalions of the King's Royal Yorkers, Butler's Rangers, Jessup's Loyal

Rangers, and Roger's King's Rangers. These soldiers and their wives and children totalled nearly six thousand.

When it was evident that the Americans would make no restitution to the Loyalists, the British Parliament approved the allotment of Crown land to the Loyalists and their families in what is now Canada. Captains were given seven hundred acres. Wives and children were given fifty acres each. These settlers became known as United Empire Loyalists.

John W. Meyers and his family settled and founded the city of Belleville, Ontario, which was known as Meyers Creek for many years. He was one of the first settlers in Upper Canada to free his slaves. According to the stories that have been passed down to descendants of the Meyers family, it was George who chose the site for the family's first home on the Bay of Quinte, where the Canadian Armed Forces base at Trenton is now situated. It was there that John W. Meyers and his sons built one of the first — and family tradition says the very first — brick home in Upper Canada.

George was active in his father's many business operations in Meyers Creek, including the mill and the shipping business, and he later settled on a farm in Sydney township. He married the daughter of a Loyalist family and had three sons and four daughters.

On November 9, 1789, Sir Guy Carleton, who had become Lord Dorchester and was then the Governor-in-Chief of British North America, prepared a resolution that was later approved by George III. He instituted Canada's one hereditary title, which still remains today.

N.B. Those Loyalists who have adhered to the Unity of the Empire, and joined the Royal Standard before the Treaty of Separation in the year 1783, and all their children and their Descendants by either sex, are to be distinguished by the following Capitals affixed to their names:

U.E.
Alluding to their great principle
The Unity of the Empire.

"UT INCEPIT FIDELIS, SIC PERMANET"
("AS SHE BEGAN, LOYAL SHE REMAINS")

Many Loyalists like John Walden Meyers and his son George, shaped by their war experience and farm background, kept their rugged independence and loyalty to family, King, and God, along with a deep sense of duty and a capacity for hard work. These qualities, which were passed down to their descendants, were their gifts to their new country. On these values our nation was built.

Notes

page 13   "Whatever side he was on, it was not on the side of [those] torturers.": Hans Waltermyer recorded in Mary Beacock Fryer, *Loyalist Spy* (Brockville: Beasancourt, 1974), p. 14, and Walter Stewart, *True Blue* (Toronto: Collins Publishers, 1985), p. 2.

pages 53-54   Excerpts from Psalm 121, *The Holy Bible*, King James Version (London: Eyre & Spottiswoode Ltd.).

pages 143-45   Excerpts from "Joy to the World": Isaac Watts, 1719. Excerpts from "O Come, All Ye Faithful": Author unknown for Latin version of eighteenth century; translated into English by S. Oakley, 1841.

page 154   And the angel said . . . good will toward men": Luke 2:10-14, *The Holy Bible*, King James Version (London: Eyre & Spottiswoode Ltd.).

page 165   "God save Great George . . . God save the King." Author unknown, in *Songs, Naval and Military* (New York: J. Riverington, 1779).

page 217   General Schuyler is said to have called

Waltermyer a "troublesome fellow.":
Mary Beacock Fryer, *John Walden Meyers: Loyalist Spy*, rev. ed. (Toronto: Dundurn Press, 1983), p. 117.

page 235   In New York State mothers warned their children that if they were not good, Hans Waltermyer would eat them: *Dictionary of Canadian Biography*, vol. 6 (Toronto: University of Toronto Press, 1966), p. 502.

page 243   "Gentlemen, you are to provide an asylum for . . . your ship is ready and God bless you.": Sir Guy Carleton quoted in Paul R. Reynolds, *Guy Carleton: A Biography* (New York: Wm. Morrow and Co., 1980), p. 139.

page 287   "it was a point of honour . . . a British ship.": Stewart W. Wallace, *The United Empire Loyalists: A Chronicle of the Great Migration* (Toronto: Glasgow, Brook and Co., 1914), p. 60.

page 287   "that the more the uncontrolled violence . . . the longer would evacuation be delayed.": Sir Guy Carleton quoted in Stewart W. Wallace, *The United Empire Loyalists: A Chronicle of the Great Migration* (Toronto: Glasgow, Brook and Co., 1914), p. 60.

pages 287-89 "N.B. Those Loyalists . . . The Unity of the Empire.": Sir Guy Carleton quoted in Lynn A. Morgan, ed., *Loyalist Lineages of Canada 1783-1983* (Toronto: Generation Press, 1984), p. xix.

page 289 "UT INCEPIT FIDELIS, SIC PERMA-
          NET" ("AS SHE BEGAN, LOYAL SHE
          REMAINS"): Ontario's official motto.

Acknowledgements

I would like to thank the Belleville Public Library for allowing me to read their files preserved by the library and the Historical Society; the reference department of Peterborough Public Library for obtaining books and photocopied materials for me through the inter-library loan program; and the reference department of Trent University Bata Library for helping me find historical background material.

Thanks also to Gavin Watt of King City, Ontario, who was military consultant for the film *Divided Loyalties*, for his help in answering my many questions about the military, firearms, equipment, clothing and grooming; Debra Parks of Madoc, Ontario, a member of the costume branch of the United Empire Loyalist Association, whom I consulted about clothing; Peter Johnson of Toronto, Ontario, the president and editor of the Toronto Branch of the United Empire Loyalist Association, for help with the map; Cynthia Rankin, Intermediate Resource Teacher for the Peterborough County Board of Education, for preparing a study guide; Debbie and Dan Floyd, teachers in Oshawa, Ontario, for their helpful suggestions; Kathryn Dean for asking so many questions in editing; and Donald G. Bastian, Managing Editor of Stoddart Publishing, for his support and encouragement.